TE
GOLD

Carolyn Davidson

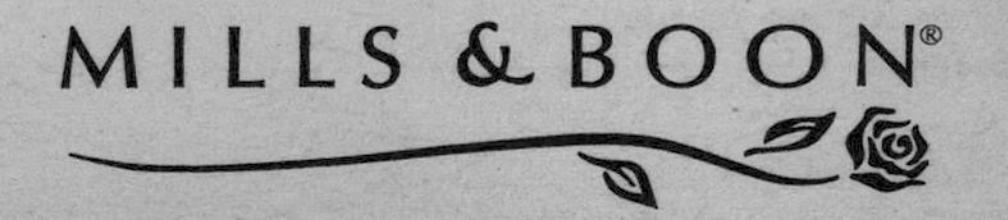

This story was written during a time
when I found, firsthand, just how fragile we are
as human beings. Thankfully, my own private crisis
was resolved and my life partner was restored to
health. To those who shared those months with me,
offering me their strength and hope when my own
faltered, I dedicate this book. As did Faith and Max
in my story, I found, through those long days,
new depths in the relationship of our marriage.

I would be amiss if I did not include Mr. Ed
in these few words, so

To the man whose love I cherish above all else,
I offer my devotion…for all time.

Chapter One

Benning, Texas—1898

Maxwell McDowell. As if the name on the note she held were written in flame, and the ensuing heat had burned her fingers, Faith dropped the crumpled bit of paper to the ground. A lump rose in her throat as she closed her eyes and viewed the promised wreckage of the life she'd managed to put together over the past three years.

"I'd say it's pretty safe to say you recognize the fella's name."

Her lashes rose, and she was silent. Her visitor's gaze was penetrating, his mouth set in a firm line, and for a moment, Faith was tempted to use his broad chest for a resting place.

She shook her head, both at the notion that had possessed her, and in reply to the sheriff's query. "Who did he say he was looking for?" she asked, aware that her voice trembled.

Brace Caulfield touched her arm, and she sensed the respect he offered in the gesture. "Can I do anything, Miss Faith? I don't want anybody coming around here, trying to upset you or give you a hassle.'' And then he sighed as she shot him a look that demanded an answer.

''He said he was huntin' for a woman called Faith McDowell. His wife, if my suspicions run true to form. I told him there wasn't anybody hereabouts by that name, but if he'd write it out for me, along with his own, I'd show it around—see if I could come up with any information for him.''

He bent and snagged the crumpled bit of paper between his thumb and index finger, smoothing the wrinkles until the stark, bold lines of her husband's signature, with her name beneath it, were revealed. ''You know this fella, don't you?'' Brace asked quietly.

Faith shrugged. ''Maybe. Let's just say I don't care to see the gentleman, Sheriff. If you feel obliged to tell him my whereabouts, I suppose I'll understand, but I won't like it one little bit.''

Her mind raced, one idea after another tumbling about, only to be rejected in rapid succession. Running was the first, closely followed by the urge to hide, to bury her identity and find a new place in which to huddle until the danger was past. But, like all her notions, that one depended on a certain amount of financial security.

She had none. Living in a borrowed home, bartering for her very existence and spending her days and nights in a state of anticipation of just this very thing taking place had not given her any degree of serenity.

Now she faced discovery and found she could not, in all honesty, lie to the lawman who had befriended her over the past three years.

''I left my husband back East a long time ago. My reasons are my own and—''

Brace's upright hand halted her words. ''I'm not asking for any explanations, Miss Faith.'' His eyes held more than a bit of disappointment, she thought. Sheriff Caulfield had been subtle, but his interest in her as a woman was obvious. Her feminine instincts were betting he'd been getting up his nerve to come courting.

The knowledge that she was married had put a damper on that idea.

"Are you afraid of him, ma'am?" the sheriff asked quietly. She thought his spine stiffened, and not for the first time, she was thankful for his watchful care.

"Do I think he'll hurt me?" Faith shook her head. "No, Max isn't a harsh man, at least not to women and children. I wouldn't want to cross him in his business dealings, but as a woman, I'm safe enough in his presence."

"How about as his wife?" Brace asked bluntly. "If he's spent a good bit of time hunting you down, he may not have much patience where you're concerned."

She shrugged, dismissing the idea. "His pride's been damaged, that's all. I doubt he's overly concerned with dragging me back home with him. More likely he's wanting me to sign a bill of divorcement so he can get on with his life."

Brace folded his arms across his chest. "Well, what do you want me to tell him? Shall I give him directions, or do you want to go into town and meet him in my office?"

"Send him out," she said, her shoulders slumping in weariness as she thought of what must come to pass. "I'll handle it, Sheriff."

"A wise choice." The dark, deep tones were familiar to her, and Faith had no need to turn around to determine who spoke. Yet she did, knowing she was better off facing him than giving in to cowardice.

Leading a saddled horse, he stepped from around the side of the house, then halted, his gaze intent on the sheriff. "I followed you,'' he said, tilting his hat back in a gesture that revealed his face.

''Thought I'd kept a close eye behind me,'' Brace answered, one hand touching the butt of his revolver. ''Didn't take you for a sneaky man, mister.''

''I wouldn't call it sneaky,'' Max McDowell said quietly. ''I had an idea you knew more than you were willing to admit when we spoke this morning. Didn't think it would hurt to tag along.''

Brace muttered an oath, his face turning crimson as if he recognized his failure to keep Faith's location a secret from the intruder.

''It's all right,'' she said hastily when the lawman would have stepped protectively in front of her. ''I'll talk to Max. I appreciate your concern, but I'll be fine.''

Max nodded, the movement slight. ''I think my wife knows me well enough to be assured of her own safety.''

Brace cut an inquiring look at Faith. ''You're sure?'' Obviously dragging his feet, he lifted the reins he'd dropped to the ground. ''Should I stop by and talk to Garvey?''

Faith shook her head. ''No, there's no point in dragging anyone else in on this.''

Brace Caulfield mounted his gelding and swung the horse in a half circle. ''I won't stand for any shenanigans, McDowell. Miss Faith is under my protection, so long as she's living in this county.''

Max shot him a glittering look from dark eyes that brooked no interference. ''I think I heard my wife tell you I was not a harsh man, Sheriff. Isn't that good enough for you?''

''Max...'' The warning was clear, Faith's use of his name drawing his attention and obliging him to nod agreeably.

"Don't worry about the lady," Max said, his voice chilled with contempt. "I've never hurt Faith before. And I'm certainly not about to change my ways." He led his mount forward, and with a quick movement, released the cinch with an ease of motion that surprised Faith. Max had never been an avid horseman, yet had kept a mare in a livery stable, riding for exercise when the burdens of business became weighty and he sought relief in an hour or two outdoors.

Now he repeated his words, emphasizing each one. "I said, don't worry about my *wife,* Sheriff. She's in no danger."

Brace grudgingly grunted agreement, gave Faith a last, questioning look, and then, at her nod of reassurance, nudged his horse into a trot and headed toward town.

The man she'd married more than six years before had changed a bit, she decided. Max McDowell was beginning to show his age. A scattering of white touched his temples, adding a bit of dignity to his already stalwart appearance. He carried himself well, she thought, as he always had.

For Max the paunch developed by men who ate well and exercised little would never come. His body had always been that of a man who worked hard, and he'd developed a muscular structure, one to be envied by lesser beings. Dark hair, cut short lest it wave overmuch, capped his well-formed head. His features, that arrangement of facial components that made him a prize sought by women wherever he went, had not changed.

Chiseled, or perhaps severe, she decided, was the best description she could come up with for the rigid jawline, the blade of a nose and the deep-set, dark eyes that could slice through her like a bolt of lightning, leaving her trembling, and aware of the effect he'd always had on her.

She trembled now—now that the full force of his attention was directed on her slender frame. Perhaps it had been an error in judgment, sending Brace on his way. Yet she could not imagine holding this postmortem in front of a stranger. And certainly Max would not be leaving until he'd had his pound of flesh.

Perhaps it was only a figure of speech, but given that the flesh in question was ultimately to come from her, she didn't find the vision of the hour or so ahead of her an appetizing prospect.

"Are we going to stand out here all morning?" Max asked. "If you'll allow it, I'll put my horse into the pasture or the barn, whichever suits you."

"I'll take him," Faith said, snatching at the opportunity to walk away from the man who'd pursued her halfway across the country. "Sit down on the porch while I turn him loose out in back."

"I'll help you," Max said smoothly, walking beside her, allowing her not a moment in which to gather her wits before she was faced with the confrontation that was sure to come. His hand brushed against hers as if he commanded her attention, and she drew aside, unwilling to allow him any familiarity.

His chuckle surprised her, and she glanced up, wary of the humor that lit his gaze. "What's so funny?"

"You. Trying to avoid the simple touch of my hand against yours. When we both know you didn't feel so hesitant to have my hands on you once upon a time."

She felt a blush redden her cheeks, knew the haze of anger blurring her vision. "That was a cheap shot, Max. Although it tells me much about your opinion of me. I wasn't aware that you thought so little of my—"

"You haven't the faintest idea what I thought about you," he said harshly, interrupting her before she could muster an adequate defense. "You didn't give me a chance to answer any of your accusations or offer any compromise that might have salvaged something of the wreck we'd managed to make of our marriage.''

''I knew,'' she said quietly, opening the gate to the corral and leading his mount through the dusty area to the pasture gate beyond. She quickly stripped the saddle from the horse's back, and Max took its weight from her, tossing it atop the corral fence.

''You knew?'' he asked, brushing his hands together as he stepped ahead to lift the latch on the narrow entry to the lush grass beyond the fence. Three horses occupied the pasture, two of them the team she used for field work. Her own mare looked up, sent a shrill welcome to the visitor and loped eagerly toward them.

''I'll be damned.'' Max's words were a hushed whisper. ''Where'd you get that mare?'' he asked, his attention taken by the golden creature that approached. Creamy mane flying in the wind, her tail a flag held high, the horse was a vision to behold.

''Bought her,'' Faith said shortly.

''She's breeding,'' he said, his gaze scanning the slender legs and swollen belly. ''When's she due to drop her foal?''

''Anytime now.'' And if he thought he was going to be here to attend the event, he had another think coming, she decided.

''Have you got a buyer lined up?'' Max reached for the mare, spooking her with his touch, and she tossed her head, flirting a bit, as if she were accustomed to attention from visitors.

''The foal will belong to my neighbor, Nicholas Garvey. I used his stud. He'll breed her for me in another month or so, and the next one is mine.''

Max shot her a look of disbelief. ''You're not charging him, just giving him—''

"I made the deal," she said harshly. "I live in this house, free of charge. He owns it, and he keeps an eye on things...sort of looks after me."

The dark eyes grew cold, his jaw tightened, and his mouth was a thin line. "Looks after you? And allows you to live in his house? And where does he spend his nights?"

She felt a chill pebble her flesh at the offending words. "My neighbor's interest in me is none of your business," she retorted.

"I'd say it is. You're my wife. I have a license in my pack that proves it. Any man who's been looking at you—"

His words were stilled by the flat of her hand, the sound resembling a gunshot as she swung her arm in an unexpected motion he stood no chance of halting. "Don't you dare insult me that way," she whispered. "Or Nicholas either, for that matter. He's my neighbor, not my lover. His wife would not stand by and watch that happen, let alone the fact that my own sense of decency—"

Max halted her words by the simple act of holding his hand over her mouth. She felt the calluses on his palm rub against her lips, shivered again as he stepped closer and circled her waist with his other arm.

"I apologize," he said, bridling his temper. His nostrils flared, but he bowed his head just a bit, a conciliatory gesture, she thought. "I had no right to make such a statement."

His grip tightened and she stumbled, losing her balance, her weight held up by his greater strength and the long lines of muscle, sinew and bone that made up his stalwart frame.

She trembled at his touch, the heat of his body radiating through the layers of their clothing. Shrinking from the intimacy of their positions, she felt his hand at the base of her spine flatten, pressing her even closer, and became suddenly aware of the taut, powerful length of his thighs.

And then was taken aback by the unmistakable shape of his masculine arousal against her belly.

"I beg your pardon," he said, his eyes narrowing as if he'd only just recognized the telltale sign of his reaction to her warmth. "It's obviously been a long time since a woman stood this close to me. I didn't mean to be so blatant." A crooked smile curved his lips, and his gaze touched her mouth and softened. "But then, you've always had this effect on me, haven't you, Faith? One touch, one smile, and I was at your beck and call."

"In the bedroom, perhaps," she said quietly. Her hands lifted to press with force against his chest, and he released her. "I never complained, at least not until the last few months we were together, about your attentiveness."

"And that change was at your own request," he reminded her, sliding his fingers into the back pockets of his trousers, as though that were the safest place for them to rest.

Her hands clenched, and she shot him an angry look. "I don't want to hear a discussion of what went on in my bedroom. Please, say whatever you came to say, and then leave." And then anger twisted her features. "In fact, I've changed my mind about even that. Just get on your horse and go, Max."

"It's not that easy," he said sharply. "There are things to be settled, papers to be signed and…" He hesitated, then drew in a deep breath. "Can we just have the day together, Faith?"

"So I can sign papers for your divorce?" she asked.

"Divorce?" He repeated the word slowly. "What makes you think I'm here for a divorce?"

"That would be the logical reason for you to come calling." She tilted her chin, only too aware of the effect he had on her, conscious of her trembling hands, of the rapid beating of her heart, and worst of all, her yearning for the brush of his lips against her own.

"Well, that isn't the reason. Far from it, in fact."

His statement was flat, with certainty underlining each word.

"I'd think you'd want to get on with your life," she said curtly. "Marry again, have a family."

"I'm already married," he reminded her. "And my wife has shown herself capable of giving me a family."

The pain was sharp, quick and urgent, and she clutched at her waist as if wrapping her arms around the aching emptiness would alleviate the knife thrust he'd dealt. "I gave you a child, and then proved incapable of being a good mother." Her stomach ached as if a giant fist clutched at it, threatening to empty its contents. "Our baby died, Max. And it was my fault."

"I never said that," he said quietly.

"Didn't you?" Her laugh was forced and harsh, and held no semblance of humor. "Perhaps not." She gave him the benefit of the doubt. "But others did."

"My mother?" he asked, watching her closely. "If it came from her, I can only say she's difficult to please, and she was hurt by the loss of her first grandchild."

"Is that supposed to fix everything? Your mother was *hurt?*"

"Let's not get into this right now," he suggested mildly. "There are other things we need to decide. I know this is painful for you, sweetheart."

"Sweetheart? I think not," she said sharply. "You lost the right to call me that a long time ago."

Her eyes were like daggers, he thought, stabbing in an attempt to draw blood. In fact, this woman bore little resemblance to the wife he'd last seen almost three years ago. Never had Faith aimed such venom in his direction. Seldom had she even shown a sign of anger, and rarely had she disputed his word or challenged his opinions.

A new light shone from her blue eyes, a sharp, knowing glance aimed in his direction, as if she judged him and found him wanting. Her hair was loose around her face, soft tendrils clinging to her forehead and temples. The ends were caught up in a braid that failed to subdue the curls and waves of gold.

A golden hue almost matching the color of her horse, he noted, glancing from woman to mare. The woman who had been his, the woman he'd called his sweetheart.

''Pain is what I feel when you deny my touch, Faith. When you glare at me with distrust and hatred in your eyes.''

''You call *that* painful?'' she asked, a subtle undertone suggesting wry humor. ''You don't know what painful is, my friend. And neither does your doting mother.''

''And you, Faith?'' he asked, aware that her eyes held not a trace of softness. ''Have you suffered? Or has leaving our home alleviated your pain? Were you able to leave the past behind and *get on with your life?*'' He hadn't meant the sarcasm to be so biting, and he sighed, wishing those final words unsaid.

And so he apologized once again. ''That was uncalled for. I recognize that you've carried scars.''

''Really?'' Her own sharp retort revealed her doubt about his sincerity. ''What would you know about my scars, Max? Your main interest in life is your business and the money you're capable of adding to your bank account.''

''Is it? Was I so bad a husband, then?''

Her brow furrowed, and he recognized the signs. Faith was cogitating, developing an answer. And, he feared, the longer she considered her words, the worse the picture she would paint of him.

"Look," he said quickly. "Can we put this whole rehash of things on the back burner? At least long enough for me to have a cup of coffee. Maybe even a bit of breakfast?"

She swung her gaze from the horses, which had run in tandem to the far side of the pasture, to meet his again. "You haven't eaten this morning?"

He shrugged. "I saw the sheriff as soon as I got up. The man at the hotel pointed him out to me as he was leaving the dining room there. By the time we spoke, and he had me put my signature on his ridiculous piece of paper, I knew he was pulling my leg. There was no doubt in my mind he knew exactly who you were, once I described you in detail.

"I decided to follow him, but it took me a few minutes to get a horse from the livery stable on the other end of town. Then it was a chancy thing, staying far enough behind him so he wouldn't look around and see me dodging among the trees and taking shortcuts through the brush."

Max lifted his hands in a gesture of defeat. "I'm not at my best when I'm hungry, Faith. Will you take pity?"

Her look was scornful, and her sigh told of patience at its end as she led the way to the house. "A piece of toast and a couple of eggs wouldn't be beyond me, I suppose," she said, climbing the steps before him.

Her slender form was garbed in heavy cotton, and yet she was as appealing as she'd ever been when dressed in silk and lace, he thought. Possibly even more so. There was a maturity about her that held his interest, a beauty gained by the years, perhaps even abetted by the struggle she'd undergone in this place. He'd admired her three years ago, and been smitten by her lovely face and figure before their marriage began. How could he help but be even more intrigued by the woman she had become since he'd last seen her?

She'd been young, twenty-two years old, with the promise of acceptance from Boston society and a husband who held her in highest esteem. And yet she'd still been not much more than a girl, hurt by circumstances that fate dealt out in a cruel fashion, and unsure of herself and her place in the world in which they lived.

She'd changed, he decided. Faith was a woman, full grown. The promise of beauty she'd worn like a shimmering shawl of elegance had become a deep-seated, golden radiance that illuminated her as if sunshine itself dwelled within. Her eyes were intelligent, the small lines at the corners adding a certain maturity to their depth.

Her hair had lightened considerably, probably from hours spent in the sun, he thought. And she was lean, her youthful curves shaped by whatever work she'd been doing into sleek, feminine contours that drew his eye to the length of her slender form.

And then she was gone from sight, entering the dim kitchen, and he hastened to follow. He blinked, his eyes adjusting to the shadowed interior, and watched as she walked unerringly to the stove against the far wall. A coffeepot sat on the back burner and she pulled it forward, then lifted a skillet from where it hung amid a collection of pots and pans, all neatly arrayed against the wall.

"Two eggs?" she asked, turning to him as one hand reached for a bowl of brown eggs on the kitchen counter. A heavy cupboard adorned one wall, glass doors above displaying dishes, solid doors beneath apparently concealing foodstuffs.

"Yes, two is fine. Three would be better, but I'll settle for what I can get."

She lifted her shoulders in a delicate shrug. "I can afford to feed you." Her hands were deft, unwrapping and slicing a loaf of bread and placing two pieces on the oven rack.

The eggs were cracked and dropped with care into the skillet, to which she had added a scoop of butter from a dish on the table.

"Do you bake your own bread?" he asked, settling in a chair, stretching his legs full length and crossing his boots at the ankle before he placed his hat on the edge of the table.

"The nearest store is close to an hour's ride away," she said, "and they don't carry a selection of bread. The ladies hereabouts bake their own."

"And the butter?" he asked. "You know how to make that, too?"

"Any fool can learn how to lift a dasher and let it fall into a churn," she told him. "The difficult part was finding a neighbor with a cow."

"Why didn't you buy one of your own?" he asked idly, his gaze fixed on the neat economy of her movements as she set the table before him, turned the eggs in the pan and rescued the toasted bread from the oven.

"A little matter of money," she said. "Mine is in short supply."

"Where do you get your milk, then?" he asked, intrigued by her methods of survival. She'd never been so complicated a woman during their marriage.

"I told you," she said impatiently, serving his eggs and placing the toast neatly on the edge of his plate. "I barter for what I need. There are a couple of neighbors close enough to swap milk for eggs, or garden produce. Right now, I get my milk from Lin's cow." She looked up quickly to meet his gaze.

"Lin is Nicholas Garvey's wife. I taught her how to milk her cow, and since I have chickens, and she hasn't had time to develop much of a flock yet, I provide eggs for their table."

Max nodded, picking up his fork. The woman was downright resourceful. "And how about your staples? You know, the everyday things you need in order to put food on the table."

"I have a big flock of laying hens," she said. "I carry eggs to town once a week, and I do sewing and mending for folks. Then there's my garden."

"You raise your own food?" The eggs were good—fresh, with bright golden yolks. And the bread was finely textured and browned with a delicate touch. He spread butter on the piece he'd torn off, and tasted it. "Someone taught you well," he announced.

"Trial and error, for the most part. Though I had a neighbor, while I was still a squatter, who shared her yeast with me."

"A squatter?" His face froze, as if he was stunned by the term.

"Yes, a squatter. Not a pretty word, is it, but it applied to me. I lived in a cabin in the woods on property not my own."

"I know what a squatter is, Faith. But I hate it that you were reduced to that. Why didn't you take money with you when you left? You knew the combination to my safe."

"I had money," she said stubbornly. "And I sold my mother's jewelry."

"I know. I bought it back," he said quietly. "I traced you that far during the first week. And then you vanished from the face of the earth." His fork touched the plate with a clatter, and he looked down at it in surprise, then lifted it to place it carefully beside his knife on the table.

"I thought you were dead, murdered perhaps, or killed in an accident, and someone had hidden your body. I was only too aware that the city was not a safe place for a woman alone."

She sighed, and her voice held a note of regret. "I'm sorry. Truly I am, Max. I fear I wasn't thinking rationally when I left. But there *was* the note." Her pause was long as she awaited his reply, as if he might admit to the accusations her note had held, listing his sins, one by one.

She prodded him. "You did read my note, didn't you?"

"Of course I read it. As a matter of fact, I've read it since, several times, and it still doesn't make much sense. At any rate, I was never able to fully understand your reasons for walking away from me."

"I'm a bit surprised that you even knew I was gone," she said casually.

He glanced up, aching as he recognized the truth. "You had become like a shadow, Faith, barely causing a ripple in the household. I thought it best to leave you to grieve as you saw fit, I suppose. I certainly hadn't helped the process by trying to comfort you with my presence."

Her laughter was broken by a sound that he thought resembled a sob, and he felt a familiar sense of helplessness wash over him as she turned aside. "I don't recall you even speaking of our son's death, Max. Let alone offering me any comfort."

Then she spun to face him, and her face was contorted by pain, her eyes awash with tears she could not hide. "Please. Just eat your breakfast and be on your way. We have nothing else to discuss as far as I'm concerned."

"We haven't even begun," he said quietly. "I'm not going anywhere."

"What about your business?" Her words were a taunt. "Surely it will fall into ruins without you there at least sixteen hours a day to keep it on the straight and narrow."

The sound of her voice was shrill now, and if ever he'd seen Faith lose control of her emotions, it was at this moment. Even the tears she'd shed at their son's funeral had not torn at his heart as her helpless sobs did now.

"I've left it in competent hands," he said. "I'm on hiatus for a while."

"Well, coming here wasn't a smart move, Max. I don't want you in my home," she said harshly, backing toward an interior doorway. It led into a hallway behind her, and she seemed unaware of all else but the urgency to rid herself of his presence. "Go away," she said, her voice rising. "Leave me alone."

From the yard beyond the porch, a call rang out. "Faith! What's wrong?"

Max turned to look out the screened door, his attention taken by the man who stalked up the steps onto the porch and then into the house. Tall and bronzed by the sun, he was dark-haired, with brilliant blue eyes and a demeanor that might have stricken a lesser man speechless.

Max had faced down wrongdoers in his life, but he was aware that in this case he might be considered to be at fault, and as such, didn't have the proverbial leg to stand on. But there was always the truth, he decided.

"Faith is my wife," he said quietly, halting the intruder's headlong approach.

The man looked to where Faith leaned for support against the wooden framework of the door. "Faith?" he asked again, the query implicit in his voice. Hands clenched at either side, he was a formidable opponent, Max decided, one he'd just as soon not be forced to do battle with.

"Yes." Her response was a bare whisper. "Max is my husband."

"Has he threatened you?" the man asked quietly, alert to every nuance of expression, each breath that Max took.

Faith shook her head. "No, not the way you're thinking, Nicholas."

"Ah—so you're the neighbor who has provided my wife with shelter," Max said, allowing no inflection of sarcasm to enter his voice. He ached with the urge to oust the stranger from the kitchen, though it was a moot question whether or not his attempt would meet with success.

"Faith is living in a house that I own…so I suppose you could say that I've provided her with shelter."

"I should probably thank you, then," Max said nicely, rising in slow motion, lest the visitor take it in his head to consider him a threat.

"You should probably vacate the premises, is my guess." Harsh and unyielding, the man stood aside and waved a hand toward the door. "I think you've gotten the message that my tenant doesn't want your company."

"Please, Max," Faith said quietly. "Just leave. There's nothing for you here."

He hesitated, his eyes taking in the tearstained face, the slumping shoulders, and her arms wrapped in mute agony around her waist, as if she were attempting to soothe an ache that threatened to tear her asunder.

"I'll leave, Faith. But I'm coming back. I have the right to speak with you. Hell, I have the legal right to haul you back to Boston with me, if I want to push it that far."

The man she'd called Nicholas spoke up, his words icy, his demeanor threatening. "I wouldn't try that if I were you, Mr. Hudson. Faith is among friends here."

"Hudson?" Max felt the stab of pain at her denial of his name. "Her name is Faith McDowell. Mrs. Maxwell McDowell, to be precise. The day she married me, she lost any need for her maiden name."

"Well, maybe she needs to see a lawyer about having it changed back legally."

"No, Nicholas." Faith stepped from the doorway.

''Don't make a fuss over it. It isn't worth your while. I'm all right. I just want to be left alone.''

Max bowed his head for a moment, bitter disappointment washing through him. He'd never thought to effect such a confrontation with her. He'd hoped to speak about their problems, maybe solve some of the issues she'd apparently thought were important. And now he'd managed to lose even that small opportunity.

Staying would solve nothing.

''There's a hotel in town,'' Faith said quietly.

''I know. My baggage is there. I took a room yesterday.''

''There will be a train heading east tomorrow,'' Faith told him. ''If you want me to, I'll come to town and see a lawyer with you, have him draw up paperwork to dissolve our marriage.''

Max shook his head. ''No, I'll go to the hotel and decide what has to be done. If you'll call off your watchdog, that is.''

''Speaking of dogs, where's Wolf?'' Nicholas asked, a frown creasing his brow.

''There's a female over on Clay Thomas's place. Wolf has gone calling, I think.''

''Wolf? Your dog…'' Max paused, envisioning a massive guard dog, and was suddenly thankful the absent creature had been stricken by the sudden desire for a mate.

''Yes, my dog is called Wolf.'' Faith lifted her chin. ''I wouldn't return in a big hurry, Max. He doesn't like strangers.''

Chapter Two

Morning brought an end to the restless night she'd endured, and her usual sunny nature was lacking as she stepped onto the back porch. Some critter had threatened her henhouse in the early morning hours, causing the dog to sound an alarm, and then had vanished when she'd peered from the window. Just in case, she decided, she'd be prepared for its reappearance, and she caught up her rifle as she opened the back door, hoping for a shot at the varmint.

And then stopped dead still. Max had returned, and was in the process of gaining Wolf's loyalty. Her "watchdog" lay on his back, wiggling joyously as long, agile fingers scrubbed at his belly.

"Wolf!" She called his name harshly, aggravated beyond belief at the creature's fickle behavior.

"He doesn't seem endowed with any savage tendencies," Max said, smiling up at her, coaxing the dog's friendship with his knowing touch. And then he rose, and she lifted her free hand, forced to shade her eyes from the sun as she met his gaze once more. Her other hand held her rifle, its barrel pointed at the ground, its presence patently ignored by the man before her.

Wolf scrambled to all fours and then sat down with a flourish of his tail, as close to Max's left boot as he could get. His tongue lolled out of his mouth, his eyes shone with mischief and he watched these two humans, as if seeking instructions for the next bit of fun on the agenda.

"I'd say he needs some training in order to qualify as a bona fide watchdog," Max said dryly. "I didn't even have to coax him with the bits of bacon I brought with me." He slid his hand into his jacket pocket and removed his handkerchief, where remnants of what had probably been his breakfast lay wrapped.

Wolf transferred his attention to the bacon, one ear lifting, the other at half-mast, and Max laughed—an exuberant sound, Faith thought, as though he had not a care in the world. And maybe he didn't, after all.

He'd ridden into the yard unchallenged, had dismounted and tied his horse to the hitching rail, and then made an instant ally of her much-touted watchdog. His glance was accusing. "You tried to make me believe your defender would eat me alive."

"Obviously, I failed in his training," she said quietly. "But—"

Her attention caught by a movement behind him, she shifted the rifle swiftly, her finger squeezing the trigger with a practiced movement, her aim on target.

At the sound of the blast the dog yelped and scampered to one side, but Max was immobile, his eyes narrowing as they remained trained on her face. "Was that a warning of sorts?" he asked.

She shrugged, as though the matter was of little importance. "I didn't want my dog bit by a rattler." And then she motioned with the rifle barrel toward the ground to Max's left. The snake's body twitched in its death throes, and she thought Max's jaw tensed as he surveyed the remains.

"I suppose I should thank you," he murmured, and then looked up at her. "Or was it only your dog you were concerned about?"

"I think you can figure that out for yourself," she said, rather pleased by the effectiveness of her shooting skill.

"Well, at least your watchdog likes me," he added, and then smiled slightly. "I remember—"

"I know," she said quickly. Even the small pooch he'd brought home to her after their honeymoon had much preferred Max's attention, given a choice.

He rose now and faced her, his eyes narrowing as he assessed her, skimming her clothing, lingering a bit as he examined her face, paying particular attention to her eyes. "You didn't sleep well," he said finally.

"I never sleep well when I'm in the midst of a problem."

"Have you solved it with your tossing and turning?" he asked. He stepped across the expanse of ground between them and reached up to brush the lavender shadows beneath her eyes. She jerked away from the gentle touch. It was a less than subtle reminder of his effect on her.

"I don't think you made any headway, did you?" he asked quietly.

"If you were a more agreeable man, it might be a simple matter," she said, already aware that he was neither agreeable nor given to simple solutions. Not when it came to having his own way. Max was stubborn and possessive, and in this dispute she doubted he would give up easily.

"I consider myself a decent fellow," he told her, his smile an obvious attempt to charm her into good humor. "The lawyer in town was very helpful. I suppose I should tell you that I stopped by to see him this morning."

"Really? And what did he say that put you in such a good mood?"

"Oh, that I had the law behind me, should I decide to make demands on you."

"Demands?" She felt her heart stutter a bit and then begin beating again, albeit at a more rapid pace than was its habit. "Are you thinking of taking me to bed, Max?"

He lifted an eyebrow. "Did I say that?" And then he smiled, a grin that reminded her of Wolf at his friskiest. "Does the idea appeal to you?"

"You know better. I left you and my responsibilities as your wife a long time ago. So far as I'm concerned, our marriage is over. If you force the issue, you'll have a fight on your hands."

His grin evaporated, and his hands snagged her waist, drawing her toward him. "I don't think you stand a chance of winning that sort of battle, sweetheart, even if I were to offer the challenge. You forget, I'm close to a hundred pounds heavier than you, almost a foot taller, and even though you've toughened up considerably over the past three years, I'm relatively certain I could have you in your bed in less than five minutes."

His voice lowered as he held her captive and leaned to touch her lips with a fleeting kiss. A kiss she felt her hungry mouth return, lingering against his for a heart-shuddering moment before he eased away, looked down at her and smiled. "Not that I'm going to do such a thing."

She thought his dark eyes grew shadowed then. "Mind you, I didn't say I wouldn't like to," he amended. "In fact, I can't think of anything that would give me more pleasure than to spend the whole day in your bedroom."

"Really?" she asked, her voice splintered by a loss of breath, her lungs finding it difficult to draw in a full measure of air as she recovered from the brief meeting of lips that had managed to rock her equilibrium.

Her knees felt weak, her breath caught in her throat with a shudder, and she stepped past him without awaiting a reply and walked toward the chicken coop, where her hens awaited their morning meal. Doing the ordinary, simple tasks that were her daily routine seemed the route to follow right now. She'd given Max the response he wanted, had fallen on him like a woman deprived, and had managed to embarrass herself in the process.

Now she would feed the hens and gather the eggs and ignore his presence. Hopefully, the man would give up and be on his way. The thought of being involved in another confrontation with her neighbor made her cringe. She was a woman more than capable of tending her own affairs, and getting her benefactor and his wife involved in this mess was not to be considered.

"Can I help?" Max asked, following at her heels as she opened the gate to the chicken yard.

Leaning the rifle against the fence, she looked up at him. "If you don't mind chicken poop on your shiny boots," she said dryly. "There's a pan just inside the door, hanging on the wall. You can be in charge of gathering eggs. Your best bet is to get the job done while I'm feeding the hens. You'll save yourself getting all bloody that way. My hens don't take to strangers."

"That's what you said about the dog," he reminded her, glancing back to where Wolf lay in the shade, watching the ritual of tending the chickens take place.

"Wolf's a traitor," she said, dismissing the pooch with a wave of her hand.

"Don't write him off too readily," Max told her, opening the door to the coop. "Given the right circumstances, he'd be a loyal defender. He just sensed that I wasn't a threat to you."

She turned to look over her shoulder at him. "Aren't you?" And then she dipped her pan into the barrel of feed and scattered it across the chicken yard, shaking the pan to call her flock.

"While you're looking for something to do, you might dispose of that rattler," she said, delighting in his look of distaste.

He'd done as she asked and then headed for the barn, where he put his energy into cleaning stalls, a chore Faith had been certain he would try to avoid, given the resultant boot cleaning involved once the work was complete. Her memories of Max involved knife-edged creases in his trousers and gleaming leather shoes and boots, plus a tendency to always appear well-groomed, even when he rose from her bed.

She, on the other hand, had usually felt like a well-used dishcloth, limp and still warm from his kisses and the profusion of caresses he was wont to include in their sessions in the darkest hours of the night. Quiet in his retreat, he'd left her yearning for his arms on those nights when he slept in his own room, and she'd never been able to bring herself to join him there.

Max called the shots. And she'd allowed it. Prim and uneasy with the marriage relationship, unwilling to approach him with any degree of eagerness, she'd been what her mother-in-law had been prone to speak of as "an ideal wife, who knows her place in her husband's life and in society."

And wasn't that the saddest excuse for marriage she'd ever heard. Yet it had been, for a while, an experience she'd cherished.

She shivered, forking hay from the loft, where the temperature hovered above sizzling and pretty close to sweltering. The man was a piece of work, trying to fit himself into her life, as if he had a right.

But after all, hadn't the lawyer in town told him as much? Faith leaned on the pitchfork for a moment, wondering what else the lawyer had had to say during that early morning chat. Surely Max had not mentioned his inclination to claim his marital rights. If he had, and if she were to ever face Mr. Handle in town, it would be a most humiliating experience. Probably the discussion had concerned Max's right to drag her back to Boston with him.

It could be done, of that she was certain. Women were at the bottom of the heap when it came to surviving conflict in the relationship between husband and wife.

"You going to stay up there all day?" Max called from the bottom of the ladder.

She jerked, almost dropping the pitchfork on top of him, and then lost her balance. Tossing the sharp-tined weapon aside, she fell back, lying flat, looking upward toward the barn ceiling. Truly not one of her better moments, she decided, rolling to her knees and rising to stand on the uneven bed of hay.

"Are you all right?" Max's head appeared through the hole in the floor, followed by his shoulders as he lifted himself from the ladder to stand before her. "Here, let me give you a hand." He reached to steady her, and laughed outright.

"Your hair is a mess," he said, plucking wisps of hay from her braid and brushing bits and pieces from her sweaty brow. The movement of his hand slowed, then ceased altogether, and in a hushed moment, he touched her lips with his index finger.

"Faith." It was a whisper of sound, and she glared up

at him, unwilling to be so readily coaxed by his gentle approach.

"I'm fine. Go on down. I'll toss enough hay down for the next couple of weeks and then pile it in the corner. It saves me climbing into the loft more than twice a month."

"It's nice up here," he said, looking off into the shadows, where a bird had built a nest and was busily fluttering on the edge, feeding her young. "If it wasn't so blasted hot, I'd enjoy lying back in the hay and talking for a while."

"You'd be talking to yourself," Faith said, lifting her pitchfork from the hay and stabbing it into the pile she'd so recently occupied. Hay fell through the opening, scattering on the barn floor beneath, and she lifted another layer, sending it after the first.

A large, lean hand took the fork from her, ignoring her tightened grip on the handle. "Let me do that," Max said. "How much do you want below?"

She stepped back, giving him the necessary room, and drew in a deep breath. He was pushing her, and she didn't like it. Edging ever closer in a game she had no intention of joining. "Enough to fill the far corner of the aisle, next to the last stall," she said.

"All right." Obligingly, he tossed hay through the opening and then halted, stepping back to allow her passage to the ladder. "After you," he said cheerfully.

She climbed down swiftly, pleased that he hadn't preceded her, aware that her legs were exposed as she held her skirt high enough to keep it from tangling around her feet on the ladder rungs. Gaining the floor, she looked up and reached for the pitchfork.

"Let me," she said. "I'll move it out of the aisle."

"I'll take care of it." His voice was gruff, as if he was scolding her for her spark of independence, she decided.

"You work too hard, Faith." He made his way down and then stood beside her. "This isn't a job for a woman, tending livestock and grubbing in the dirt for a living."

"And what's wrong with it?" she asked. "It's honest work, and I'm not going to apologize for earning my own way. I'm happier here than I ever was in the city, Max. I know you have a hard time believing that, but it's true."

He hung the pitchfork on the wall and turned to her, grasping her hands and holding them up to the light. "Look at the calluses," he muttered. "Your hands should be soft and smooth. Instead, you work at one thing or another from morning till night. I hate it that you've been forced to live this way."

"Aren't you listening to me?" she asked, snatching her fingers from his. "I love it here. I enjoy what I do, and I'm happy to *grub in the dirt.* I raise my food, and then I cook it and eat it. Whatever is surplus is set aside for the winter months. It's called making a living, Max."

He had the grace to look shamefaced. "I didn't mean to make it sound...the way I did," he said quietly. "There's no shame in working hard. It's just that I hate to see you so tired. You've lost weight, Faith."

"I was too plump, anyway," she said quickly. "I'm strong and healthy, and you might as well forget whatever you're trying to accomplish here. I'm not going back with you, Max. No matter what, I'm staying here."

"The sheriff would like that, wouldn't he?"

"And what is that supposed to mean?" She felt a flush climb her cheeks, only too aware of his gibe being more the truth than she would like to admit.

"You know exactly what I'm referring to," Max shot back. "He's sweet on you."

"Well, I'm not sweet on him. I'm not sweet on anybody." She stalked out the barn door and headed for the house, then turned to face Max, walking backward several paces until she reached the porch steps. "I wish you'd just leave me alone. Go back to Boston and find yourself someone who wants you for a husband. I'll sign anything you like. You'll be free as a bird."

He halted halfway across the yard, and his expression was unreadable. "I told you there were papers for you to sign, Faith. In all the fussing we've done, I haven't told you what they are. I brought them with me in my pouch today, and I think we need to go inside so you can look them over."

She felt a dull ache begin in her breast. If he had indeed given in on the idea of getting a bill of divorcement, this would perhaps be the final time she was forced to see him. Surely a judge could handle the whole thing, so long as she signed her rights away.

Climbing the porch steps, she opened the kitchen door and waited for Max to enter. He hesitated, his manners dictating that he let her precede him, but she cast him an impatient look and he did as she wished.

In a few minutes she'd washed her hands, smoothed her hair back and settled across the table from him. His pouch open, he sorted through it for the documents he'd mentioned, then placed them on the table before her.

"Your father left you his estate when he died fourteen years ago," he began. "It was held by the court until you reached the age of twenty-five. I don't know why he thought you'd be all grown up by then, but for some reason, that was the milestone he chose."

She looked down at the papers Max had brought to her, and focused on the names and the collection of "therefores" and "whereases" covering the first page. They were a hodgepodge of legality, she decided, and pushed the papers across the table toward him. "Read them for me, and tell me what all these fancy phrases have to do with me,'' she told him. ''I'm not at all sure what it signifies.''

''You're a woman of means,'' he said simply. ''The estate is yours.''

''And being mine automatically makes it yours, if I recall your mother's tutoring session correctly.''

''Tutoring?'' His eyes narrowed as he repeated the word she had chosen to use. ''My mother *tutored* you?''

''Lectured might be a better way to put it,'' Faith said bluntly. ''Never failing to remind me how fortunate I was to have been chosen by the great Maxwell McDowell.''

His mouth tightened. ''I can't imagine my mother used that term to describe me.''

''Believe what you like,'' Faith said. ''Suffice to say, I never measured up to what she felt you needed as a wife. I was too young, too boring, too—''

''Stop it,'' he ordered, cutting short her list of failures, a catalog of flaws that had come to light during her years as his wife. ''My mother means well, but she gets carried away on occasion.''

''Ah...I should have known you were still her champion.''

His jaw tensed, and a profusion of blood colored his cheekbones brick-red as he made an obvious attempt to be silent.

Faith waved a dismissive hand. ''Explain what all this means, the paperwork I'm supposed to sign, and the money my father left for my use.''

''By signing your name where the lawyer has designated, you are accepting the money into your care.''

''I can put it in a bank here and use it as I like?'' she asked, doubt coating each word with disdain. ''But that's not going to happen, is it?''

''The money will go into the bank in Boston, under my

supervision,'' Max said bluntly. ''You have access to it as my wife. Your father felt secure in the knowledge that I would take care of you, supply all your needs.''

''Fine,'' she murmured, snatching the sheaf of paperwork and arranging it before her again. ''Where's the pen, and where do I write my name?''

''No more questions?'' he asked, drawing a fountain pen from his pocket and removing the cap. He offered it to her, and she accepted, examining its length.

''Is this the one I gave you?'' She thought she glimpsed a flash of sorrow in his gaze as he nodded. ''It was the only gift I ever bought you with my own money,'' she recalled. ''From then on, I used the allowance you gave me. I often thought it was like carrying coals to Newcastle, buying you paltry gifts when you were capable of ordering up anything you wanted with the snap of your fingers.''

''You gave me much more than a pen or hemmed handkerchiefs, or even the small watercolor I hung beside my bed, Faith.''

''Oh? Really?''

''I appreciated every gift I received from you, cherished each gesture of affection you offered.'' His pause was long, and she felt the breath leave her lungs, knowing what he would speak of next.

''Most of all I treasure the memories of the times I held you in my arms. You gave me the pleasure of loving you.''

''Loving?'' she asked. ''You're telling me now that you loved me?''

''You know I loved you,'' he said, his jaw taut, his mouth narrowing as if he recognized the doubt in her query.

''On the contrary, Max. You never told me you loved me. You said I was lovely, that I pleased you, that I wore the elegant clothing you bought for me with a degree of grace…but not once did you tell me—''

"You knew," he muttered, his voice an accusing growl. "Don't try to pretend otherwise, Faith."

"Then where were you when I needed you the most?" And as soon as the words were spoken aloud, she rose from the table and turned her back to him. "No, don't bother answering. Please. I don't want to hear excuses about your work, or the trips you were forced to take to expand the business. I heard all of that from your mother, and it wasn't any more palatable coming from her than it would have been from you."

"You wouldn't even allow me into your bedroom," he said, exasperation lacing his accusation. "I wasn't allowed to touch you."

"And who told you that?" she asked, bowing her head.

"It was implicit in your behavior."

She spun to face him, stalked back to the table and snatched up the pen she had cast aside. Her signature was a scrawl as she shuffled through the pages, leaning over the table and scattering documents hither and yon as she searched out the places marked for her name to be signed.

"There. It's done," she said sharply. "Now just leave, and take the promise of a few more dollars for your bank account with you."

Max leaned back in his chair, oblivious to the hash she'd managed to make of the papers. The table and floor bore mute testimony to her anger, and yet he ignored it, his attention focused on the woman who had wreaked havoc in these few moments.

"I don't want your money," he said finally. "And I'm not leaving. In fact, I've made arrangements to have my things brought here from the hotel. I'm moving in with you, Faith. The only way you can stop me is by calling your neighbor and telling him to shoot me down or evict us both from his property."

"Why?" she asked. "Why do you want to hound me this way, Max? Surely you don't want to breathe life to the ashes. And trust me, that's all there is left of our marriage. I don't want you."

He was silent a moment, as if digesting that claim, and then a twitch at the corner of his mouth revealed his doubt. "Don't you? When I kissed you, I felt something between us, sweetheart."

"You're wrong," she said sharply. "I might respond to anyone who knew how to kiss as well as you do. In fact—"

"Don't lie to me," he said flatly. "We both know you're grasping at straws, and threatening to seek out another man is impertinent. It doesn't become you."

"I've never known anyone so arrogant as you," she said, her teeth clenched against the anger that roiled within her. "Impertinent, am I? That goes right along with your mother's assessment of me when she called me an *upstart,* a month after our wedding."

His brow lifted, and for a moment he looked distinctly uncomfortable. "Apparently, my mother said several things she should be taken to task for." His frown drew his brows together as he thought for a moment. "*Upstart?* She really used that word?" And then he grinned.

"Damn you, Max. It wasn't funny. She made me feel lower than dirt, that I had dared to marry the great Maxwell McDowell."

"Dared? I begged for your hand. I groveled at your feet." His grin widened, and Faith was tempted to match it with one of her own. Max on a roll was something to behold. But better sense prevailed.

"You've never groveled in your life."

"I think I may have to before this is finished," he said, his look pensive as he watched her cross the kitchen to the stove. He sat up straight then, watching as she lifted a long spoon and stirred the contents of a kettle. "Is that dinner?"

"Yes. I killed a chicken and cleaned it before breakfast. I'm making stew."

"Am I invited, or do I have to be an interloper?"

"I'm not capable of tossing you out on your ear."

"I'd call that a backhanded invitation," he said, rising from the table and pushing his chair back in place. He bent, picking up the sheets of paper she had scattered, sorting through them to place them in order, and then tapped them on the table to neaten the pile.

"This can go in the mail to my lawyer, I think," he said. "I'll take it into town the next time I make the trip. Perhaps we can arrange for the money to be sent here to the bank for your use."

"With your supervision, I suppose," she said quietly, laying aside the spoon and seeking out a lid for the kettle.

"It's your money, Faith. As to the rest, I intend to supervise everything you do for the next little while," he said. "For as long as it takes."

He'd known it wouldn't be difficult to find the neighboring ranch house. Yet once it came in sight, Max revised his estimate of Nicholas Garvey. The man had a considerable amount of financial clout, it would seem, if the size and design of his home was anything to go by. It stood in the shade of tall trees, as if it had been there for many years, yet the newness showed. Like a jewel in a particularly lovely setting, it drew his eye, and Max, ever a man to appreciate beauty, felt a twinge of envy for the man who lived there. Not that he couldn't have duplicated the home, given the urge, but such a site, with such perfection of surroundings as Nicholas had chosen, might never again be available.

A woman stepped out onto the back porch as Max rounded the corner of the house, a small female with russet hair and a creamy complexion. She wore a smile of welcome, tinged with curiosity, her brown eyes taking his measure as he rode closer.

"Welcome," she said quietly. "I'm Lin Garvey. Are you looking for my husband? Nicholas is out riding in the pasture with our daughter."

"Do you welcome all visitors so graciously?" Max asked, smiling because there was no other choice. She'd taken his defenses and shattered them with her warmth.

Her own smile became touched with mischief. "I know who you are, Mr. McDowell. I've almost been expecting you, once Nicholas told me you were visiting with Faith."

"I'm surprised you haven't come by to chase me away," he said.

"Nicholas told me to mind my own business," she admitted, "even though I threatened to ride over and give you fair warning."

"And now?" he asked.

She bit her lip, obviously deliberating. "I thought to give you a chance, once I laid eyes on you myself. I'm a good judge of character, Mr. McDowell, and I don't see any danger in you where Faith is concerned. She needs some happiness in her life, and if you're the man to bring it to her, I'll be grateful."

She stepped closer to the edge of the porch, and her hands slid into the deep pockets of her apron. "However, be warned. If I find that you've caused her pain, you need to know that I'm very good with a shotgun."

"I'd say you and my wife make a good pair, then." He bowed his head, admiration for the woman causing him to hide his grin, lest she think he mocked her. "I'll consider myself on guard, ma'am,'' he said politely. ''And now I'll see if I can round up your husband for a short visit.''

She gazed past him and her expression assumed a degree of tenderness. ''You won't have to look far, sir. He's riding this way right now.''

The transfer of a small girl into Lin Garvey's care took but a moment, and then Nicholas dismounted and indicated that Max should do the same. They walked toward the shade of a cottonwood tree, and Nicholas tugged his gloves off and tucked them into his back pocket.

''You wanted to see me, I assume?'' he asked, his gaze darting toward the house as if he were checking out the whereabouts of his wife and child.

''I felt it only right to let you know that I'm going to be staying with Faith for a while. In fact, I came to offer you a fair price to rent the house while I'm in residence.''

''Faith is my tenant. If she chooses to have you live there, I have no say in the matter,'' Nicholas said bluntly. ''Not that I approve, you understand. But it's Faith's choice.''

''Actually, it isn't,'' Max admitted. ''I told her I was having my things sent out from town. She's not real happy about it.''

''But she's your wife, and you're taking advantage of that fact.''

''That's about it,'' Max agreed. ''I'm not a sneaky man, Garvey. I'm here on a mission, and I won't allow anyone to stand in my way.''

''Is this a warning?'' Glittering blue eyes met his as Nicholas glared a response to Max's challenge.

''You can call it that if you like. I'm also a peaceable man. I have no intention of fighting with you.'' He glanced back at the house and smiled. ''Although I've already been cautioned by your wife that my days are numbered if I hurt Faith. I understand Mrs. Garvey is handy with a shotgun."

He thought the blue eyes softened at the mention of Lin's threat, and then Max watched in amazement as Nicholas smiled.

"You don't want my wife to be on your trail," he said. "She's a formidable opponent. I'd watch myself if I were you."

"That's fair enough," Max said with a nod. "I'll be on my way. I've taken up a sufficient amount of your time."

"You'll see me again," Nicholas told him.

"I expected I would."

Chapter Three

The rain was heavy, running from the roof in sheets that blurred the image of the barn, yet presented a clear picture in Faith's mind of how totally drenched she would become should she brave the elements to feed her flock of chickens. The garden needed the rain, though, and she rejoiced in the thought of her thirsty plants soaking up the life-giving moisture.

The chickens were another matter. Though some of them, more brave than the others, would squawk and flutter about the puddles in the chicken yard, many of them would probably refuse to leave the dry interior of the coop.

Debating in silence, she looked through the screened door.

"You're not planning on going out in that mess, are you?" Max stood behind her, his presence warming her back as she shivered in a gust of wind and the smattering of raindrops that accompanied it across the width of the porch.

"I was thinking about it," she confessed. "The hens will be hungry."

"They'll live another couple of hours," he said dryly.

"And from the looks of that sky, it'll be at least that long before this lets up."

She nodded. "I know. I figured that out already." Stepping back, she shut the inside door, dodging him as he moved from her path. "I might as well fix breakfast, I guess."

"Where's the dog?" He went to the window and bent to peer through the glass. "I didn't hear him last night at all."

"He doesn't bark unless someone comes around or varmints show up near the chicken coop. Right now, he's no doubt warm and dry under the porch. I stuck a wooden box under there, facing away from the wind, and he has an old blanket he sleeps on."

"All the comforts of home," Max said, straightening and stretching a bit. Faith wondered if the bed she'd offered him was too short. Certainly it was not akin to the mattress he'd paid a pretty penny for back in Boston.

"How long have you had the pooch?" Max asked. "He doesn't look very old."

"He's not. Nicholas and Lin gave him to me last year when they built their new place and let me move in here. They decided I needed him worse than they did."

"Probably a good move on their part. It never hurts to have a dog around."

Faith was silent, thinking of the pet she'd left behind in Boston.

"He's fine," Max said, as if he discerned her thoughts. "He missed you terribly after you left. After he'd howled for a couple of nights, I let him sleep on the rug beside my bed to make up for your absence."

"I wanted to take him with me, but I couldn't see any way to do it."

"Maybe he'll make coming back with me more appealing."

And wasn't that a cunning way to coax her into his way of thinking? "I don't think that ploy is going to work, Max," she said, hoping to dash his hopes before he could make a full-fledged assault on her defenses.

He picked up the coffeepot from the stove and filled two cups with the dark brew. "Give me points for trying, anyway."

"I've already given you more of an advantage than I should have," she said, breaking eggs into a bowl. "Your moving into my home was certainly not a part of my plan. If I weren't unwilling to bring the wrath of the sheriff and Nicholas down on your head, it never would have happened."

"Well, I suppose I must be thankful for small favors," he murmured dryly. Opening the bread box, Max lifted a wrapped loaf and placed it on the table. "Do you want this sliced?" At her nod, he picked up her cutting knife and neatly severed four thick slices, then opened the oven door to place them on the rack.

"You know, the sheriff has no power to keep me from you—not legally, anyway," he said quietly. "And your neighbor is wisely keeping hands off."

Faith quickly glanced up at him and then turned her attention to the work at hand, pouring the eggs into a hot skillet. "You told the Garveys to stay away?" she asked. And then she looked at him more fully. "I'm surprised that Nicholas didn't run you off."

"His wife is the one who warned me that my hide would be at stake if I harmed you in any way. She's a formidable woman." A grin softened his description of her friend. "She told me she was very good with a shotgun. And her husband let me know I was here on sufferance."

"They've been wonderful friends to me, and I fear they may be a bit protective," Faith told him. "Lin and I hit it off the first time we met, and I was on hand to help deliver their little boy a while back."

Max looked surprised, she thought. "I saw the girl, but no one mentioned a baby."

"He was probably asleep. Lin has help—a woman called Katie, who runs the house with an iron hand."

"It's a big place. Looks more like it belongs in Boston than out in the middle of nowhere," Max said. "The man must be successful at ranching."

"He's a banker by trade," Faith said. "Still owns a bank in a town south of here. He and Lin have quite a background."

"I'm more interested in what you've been doing the past few years," Max said. "I want to know how you ended up here."

She thought for a moment, remembering the day she'd walked away from the big house in Boston. Actually, she'd only walked to the end of the front walk, then loaded her sparse amount of baggage into a passing conveyance for the trip to the train station. "I was interested in finding a place where I wouldn't need a great deal of winter clothing," she said. "And Texas was in the south, so I headed in this general direction."

She smiled, recalling her naive mind-set. "I had no idea that winter in Texas could be brutal at times. Anyway, I traveled as far as I could afford to by train, and then walked as far as my legs would carry me," she said simply. "I was told by a farmer's wife closer to town of a cabin in the woods, and I decided it would serve the purpose."

"A cabin? Was it weather-tight and furnished?" he asked, his frown dark with concern.

Faith pursed her lips, remembering. "A little of each.

Barely leaked at all, and it had a bed of sorts and a small stove for heat. Thanks to the friendship of folks who lived here before Nicholas and Lin arrived on the scene, it became my home. When my cash supply reached rock bottom, I asked around and found folks who needed mending and sewing done. Even the sheriff sought me out, asking me to take care of his financial matters, writing letters for him and such.''

''I think he sought you out for another reason, too,'' Max said in an undertone.

''Whatever you might think, Brace has been a good friend, and I've appreciated his help. Then one day, he came to pick up his mending and told me he'd heard of a horse for sale. The owner was moving on and needed money in a hurry and couldn't take the horse. Brace paid him up-front and I earned it back.''

Max's mouth thinned as if he held back words better left unsaid, and Faith shot him a dour look as she spooned his eggs onto his plate, reserving a helping for herself. She pulled the bread from the oven and joined him at the table.

''When the original owners sold this place a couple of years ago, it sat empty for a long time, and I was given permission to take anything I needed from it in order to improve the cabin. What I took were the books from the parlor.''

''Books? I don't recall you being that much of a reader,'' he said, buttering all four slices of toast, and then offering the plate to her. ''What were they? Classics?''

''Actually,'' she said, breaking apart a slice of toast, ''a couple of them were textbooks on herbal healing, along with a medical book that had to do with anatomy and the setting of bones. I read everything I could that winter. It seemed like spring would never come.'' Her voice sounded pensive, and she cleared her throat, unwilling to let Max think she was asking for his pity.

"You were lonely?" He was truly interested, she decided. Not feeling sorry for her, but wanting to know how she had survived.

"A little. But I learned so much. I fed the birds and the small animals that gathered in front of the cabin for handouts. I'd collected corn from the fields after the harvest was over, and gleaned wheat from the farm to the east, when the threshers were through. It gave me something to feed the wild things, and they were company for me."

She looked up into his gaze, aware that he'd watched her closely. "You'll think I'm foolish to be so bound up in the little things of life, Max, but I learned a lot about myself that first year or two. I found I could plant a garden and harvest it, and live from the land if I had to. A neighbor gave me a setting hen and a dozen eggs and I began my flock. Within a year I had a lean-to built to hold my hens and nests for their eggs."

"You built a lean-to?" he asked. "By yourself?"

"Brace helped," she said. "I found a barn that had fallen to bits on a deserted farm the other side of town, and dragged home enough wood to nail together. All it cost me was the price of the nails, and Brace lent me a hammer until I could buy one of my own."

Max looked stricken. "I had no idea. I wanted to follow you when you left, Faith, but..."

She hesitated, then spoke the thought that had been itching to be expressed since his arrival. "Why didn't you? I suppose I wondered why you let me go so easily, Max. And when you made no apparent attempt to find me, I decided you'd figured you were well rid of me."

"Not true," he said harshly. "Things happened after you left. My brother had an accident the next day and was laid up with severe injuries for several months. I was torn between abandoning the family business or setting out on your trail.''

''And the business won, hands down.''

''We employ a great number of people, and Howard's wife was distraught. We thought at first he wouldn't live, and my time was divided between the hospital and the business for longer than I like to remember. I couldn't just walk away from all that, no matter how much I wanted to chase after you.''

She shrugged. ''I suppose you're right. I doubt you'd have found me, anyway.''

His mouth set in a grim line as he eyed her narrowly. ''Trust me, I'd have found you. As it was, by the time I set detectives on your trail, it was stone cold, and I had to offer rewards all across the country before I heard word of a woman of your description here in Benning.''

Her brow lifted. ''You paid a reward for me?''

''Just for the information that led me here,'' he said.

''And how did you manage to get away from your work once you located me?''

''Howard owed me. I'd covered for him for almost a year, and I told him he could handle my end for however long it took to find you and bring you home.''

''You really expect me to come back with you?'' Her voice rose as she spoke the query. ''After all I've said, you still think—''

He lifted a hand to halt her words. ''I warned you I was going to try my best to win you back, Faith. I haven't given up. I keep thinking of you out here in a cabin while I sat in Boston in a warm house, with food enough for a small army in the pantry, while you scrabbled for your very existence.''

''I never starved,'' she told him. ''And eventually, I earned enough money to get along well.''

''And then Garvey let you move in here.''

''Yes,'' she said. ''And after I helped deliver his son, he told me I had a home here as long as I wanted it. And when they moved back to Collins Creek for a short while, they left the wagon and team with me.''

Max ate silently for a few moments, digesting more than the food. And then he laughed softly, as if mocking himself. ''And here I thought I was riding to your rescue, sweetheart. Like a champion coming to carry you off.''

''I don't need rescuing, Max. I'm very comfortable, and satisfied with my lot in life.'' She cleaned the last of the eggs from her plate and rose to head for the pantry. ''Would you like some jam on your toast?''

''Please. That sounds good.'' He watched as she opened the jar, and stuck a spoon into its contents. ''Did you make that?''

''Of course. If you expect sweets on your bread, you start by combing the woods for berries. These are from a patch not too far from the house.''

''You're a woman of many talents,'' he murmured, spooning jam onto his remaining piece of toast. None of which he'd been aware of, he reminded himself. He'd thought Faith to be a lovely addition to his home, a luxury he'd paid well to acquire. Her presence in an adjoining bedroom had guaranteed him satisfaction when the need arose, and he'd considered himself a good husband.

''You get along just fine without a man in your life, don't you?'' It came as a surprise to him when the words erupted from his lips. And Max was not given to speaking without forethought. He offered her the jam and she accepted it, looking up with surprise lighting her eyes.

''Most of the time, yes,'' she agreed. ''I decided I'd

rather live alone and depend on myself than be any man's trophy. I didn't like myself much, Max."

"You felt like my *trophy?* Did I do that to you?"

Her shrug excused him from his self-assigned guilt. "I let you do it. I married you and then sat on a shelf, carted along to social events, gracing your table when you entertained business associates and their wives. And once in a while, you visited me in my bedroom and found me pleasing. At least you said you enjoyed my company there."

"I was proud to have you in my home, Faith. And what I found in your bed was beyond enjoyment. You filled a very important need in my life."

"Well, that's good to know," she said lightly. "I'd thought the feelings were all one-sided on that level."

He was surprised at the anger rising in protest as he considered her remark. "You knew how I felt about you," he said, his voice rigid with control. "I was pleased when you told me you were going to have our child."

She stood and gathered the plates and silverware, holding them in both hands as she met his gaze. "I've always thought the best way to make certain someone knows how you feel is to express it in words." Her face was pale, and he caught a glimpse of pain shadowing her expression. "I couldn't tell you then, but I can tell you now how I felt, Max. Then, because I was too shy, too unsure of myself to admit aloud that I loved you beyond all measure—now, because I've gotten over the need to love you."

"You loved me? But now you don't?" He pushed his chair back and circled the table, taking the plates from her hands and settling them with a clatter on the oilcloth-covered surface. Gripping her waist, he pulled her to himself.

"What do you feel for me then? Simple desire? Lust? There's something there, Faith. I can feel it, and the way you returned my kiss gave it away.'' He bent and she turned her face aside, as if unwilling to allow his lips access to hers.

''That won't work,'' he muttered, his hands rising to clasp her head, turning it toward him. ''I've been wanting to do this again ever since I tasted you the other day. And since you consider me such an unfeeling brute, you shouldn't be too surprised at my lack of finesse, should you?''

He kissed her, his mouth firm against hers, allowing no retreat, and for a fleeting second, he rued his clumsy approach, remembering the long moments he'd wooed her in the past, easing past her timidity and coaxing her into a heated response.

But that was then, and this was now, and she was no longer the same. It wasn't just the self-sufficiency of the woman, her skill with the rifle, her nonchalant ability to cook and work with her animals. She had become a different woman entirely.

Now he held a trim, vibrant creature whose sleek curves melded in a perfect fit against his body, whose breasts, more firm than in another time, pressed against his chest, their inviting contours bringing him to instant arousal. But some things never change, he thought, even as a craving he refused to deny drove him to complete the kiss she'd tried to withhold from him.

For her mouth was as soft and perfect as it had ever been, and she carried the same scent, one he'd longed for during dark nights when he'd entered her empty room and slept in the bed they'd once shared. That aroma of femininity that rose even now from her body to invade his nostrils with the perfume of desire.

She lifted her hands, clasping his wrists, her fingers wrapping around them as if she must cling for balance, even as her body pressed more closely to his, with a warmth that fanned the flame of passion into a bonfire he stood no chance of escaping.

Her mouth, that wide, appealing arrangement of lips and teeth and tongue that had ever been available for his delight, opened for him now, and a sigh escaped her throat. She was accepting his kiss, returning the pressure of lips and welcoming of his invasion, sparring in a leisurely fashion, then sliding her tongue in a seductive movement the length of his, as if she offered her own for his pleasure.

His lips closed around hers and he tasted the jam she'd eaten, shared the sweetness of her breath and savored the flavor of the woman he'd once had at his beck and call.

And not appreciated as he should have.

"Faith?" He lifted his head and watched as her eyes opened, a slow process, one she seemed loathe to complete, as if she prefered to capture the moment and hold it inviolate. "Will you let me—"

She stepped back, breaking his hold, shaking her head, and he silently cursed his foolishness in posing the question. He should have picked her up and carried her to a bedroom, any bedroom. Anywhere there was a flat surface on which to—

"No." Her simple response was spoken flatly and loudly, a denial of her own desire and a rejection of his plea. She swayed before him and his hands held her waist, steadying her lest she lose her balance. "Don't expect that of me, Max," she said, her voice trembling.

"All right." There was no point in arguing that she'd entered into the kiss with a passion that was unmistakable. She was well aware of her own vulnerability, and he had to give her credit for her ability to back away from him, keeping her dignity intact.

"You're here because...maybe because I'm allowing my

curiosity some satisfaction. Because I want to see just what it was about you that had me so in thrall to you when we were first married.'' She looked up at him. ''Maybe that sounds foolish to you, but I need to know...''

''What?'' he asked sharply. ''Tell me what you need to know, and I'll do my best to provide it. I'll try to be what you want me to be, Faith.'' And wasn't that a new idea, he thought. *He* wasn't the one who needed to make sweeping changes—not from where he stood, anyway. ''I thought I was a good husband in the past. Obviously, you decided I wasn't.''

She nodded and turned aside, and his hands fell to his sides. ''Well, you've got that right,'' she said flatly.

The anger he'd controlled rose again, and he walked to the kitchen doorway, opening the screened door and stepping out onto the porch. He allowed the wooden framework to close gently behind him, catching it before the taut spring could snatch it from his hand. And then he strode across the yard to the barn, the rain pelting him, soaking his clothing and penetrating the layers. By the time he reached the barn he was drenched, his boots sinking an inch into the mud with every step.

And even the chill of sodden clothing and the force of the wind that required him to use a considerable amount of strength to open, then close, the barn door behind him, was not enough to cool the anger that roiled within him. Faith had never had the capability to turn him upside down this way during those early years of their marriage. Now her words of scorn brought his temper to a boil, and he recognized the fact that it was because he *cared.*

Maybe cared too much. She'd scorned him, mocked him and told him she didn't love him, and still he was here, asking for more punishment. He shook his head. The woman had him running in circles.

His horse turned his head, the length of rope that tied him in his stall limiting his movement. And for a long moment, Max was tempted. His pride was taking a beating.

It would be an easy matter to saddle the animal, although any sane creature, man or beast, would be reluctant to ride out into the downpour that pounded unceasingly against the barn roof. Yet Max could probably make the horse obey him, force him to carry him to town, and to the hotel. A train would be heading east within the next twenty-four hours. That was almost guaranteed.

If he had any sense at all, he'd be on it, making arrangements for Faith's inheritance to be deposited for her use, once the papers were delivered to the lawyers in Boston.

The papers. They were even now in his pouch, beside the bed where he'd slept. And wasn't that handy? The deciding vote had been cast, he thought, leaning his head against the wide doorjamb. Leaving right now was not an option. And unless he left while he was still angry enough to walk away, he feared his stubborn need for Faith would keep him here until he could breach her defenses and…and what?

Make love to her? His manhood's urgent plea for attention had subsided during the trek through the rain, but now it made itself known again at the thought of Faith in his bed. Or him in her bed. Either way would do, he decided with a rusty laugh. And *neither* way seemed to be in his immediate future.

He spent a long moment contemplating a vision of Faith awaiting his attentions, and somehow could not visualize the body that hid beneath coarse cotton and sturdy underclothing. For he'd almost guarantee that the lace and fine fabrics she'd worn beneath her dresses in Boston no longer had a place in her wardrobe.

"And who cares?" he said aloud, then looked around at

the dim interior of the barn, as if some listener might have heard his words. His horse, and Faith's in the stalls beyond, were patently uninterested in his presence, standing patiently in their beds of straw.

He cared, he admitted. For a moment he desperately desired the chance to view her slender form again, to take special note of the formation of breasts and hips, the narrowing of her waist, the changes time had wrought in the body he'd once been privileged to own as her husband.

Now, he stood little chance of ever owning more than he'd already snatched from her. She'd refused his suit, denied him in no uncertain terms. And he was hiding in her barn like a callow youth, pouting over his inability to seduce the love of his life.

The love of his life. He was taken aback at the idea. He'd thought, long ago, that he could set her in a compartment labeled Wife and keep her there, taking her out now and then for his pleasure or to grace his arm, or sit at the head of his table as his hostess. And he'd never really known the woman inside the shell of elegant beauty she possessed.

Now she was set free, had escaped the mold he'd formed for her, and in freeing herself, had filled him, heart and mind and soul, with her presence.

The love of his life? Was she? Could he find another woman who appealed to him as Faith did? Did he even want to try? The answer was clear, as clear as if he looked in a mirror and faced the dour countenance he knew he wore at this moment.

"I beg your pardon," Max said. He stood outside the screened door, looking as bedraggled as any man she'd ever seen. The rain had long since ceased, and Faith had fed the hens and gathered the eggs, one eye on the closed barn door, behind which her husband was taking his ease.

The sun shone brightly, and a nice wind blew from the west, drying up the puddles that dotted the yard. He'd trudged through them on his way to the house, his hair dry, but totally disordered, his clothing clinging to him, even as it dried against his body. He'd shed his shirt halfway across the yard, hanging it over the clothesline, then continued on his way.

Sitting on the edge of the porch, he'd tugged his boots off, then wrung out his stockings before he hung them on the short line between two posts, where she made it a practice to pin her dish towels to dry. Now he stood before her, his dark eyes shadowed, his beard causing him to look unlike the male creature she had known in Boston, who took immense pride in his immaculate, elegant facade.

He resembled nothing more than a man with an apology to offer, and she hesitated as she decided if she was willing to hear it. "You beg my pardon?" she asked, facing him through the screen.

"Yes. I need to ask your forgiveness for my behavior earlier." *Humble* was not a word she would have chosen to portray the Max she remembered from her earlier life. Yet it seemed an appropriate description for his appearance at her door. *Hat in hand* would be a more accurate depiction, she thought, except that his hat was even now hanging on a hook inside her kitchen.

"My forgiveness?" she repeated, attempting to digest his meaning. "For the kiss you took? Or the assumption you made that I would toss back the sheets and invite you into my bed?"

He looked taken aback at her words. "You've changed, Faith," he said finally.

"Have I? Because I speak my mind?"

His nod was slow, his eyes lighting with amusement. "Not only that," he said, "but you're so damned independent.'' He chuckled and opened the door, walking past her to stand near the stove, rubbing his hands together. ''Your barn doesn't provide much in the way of creature comforts. It's cold out there.''

She shrugged. ''You're the one who chose to tramp through the rain and spend half the morning with the horses. I hope you put them out to pasture, by the way.''

He seemed ready to make amends as he nodded in reply, and then reinforced it with a quiet plea. ''If I ask nicely, will you let me have a cup of coffee?''

She considered for a moment, enjoying his penitent mood, although he had almost ruined it with his smile and smart remarks. ''There's enough in the pot, I think. Probably too strong, but still fit to drink if you're desperate.''

''I am,'' he said solemnly. And the glance he shot in her direction appeared to hold more than one message in its dark depths.

It was something she decided not to examine too closely, and instead, lifted a cup from the shelf and poured it full of the strong coffee she'd kept warm for just this moment. ''Did you clean the stalls?'' she asked casually.

''Yes. I used the wheelbarrow and lugged the whole mess out to the manure pile. Managed to ruin my boots. I'll probably end up buying another pair.''

Her shrug was uncaring. ''You'll learn how to clean them if you stick around long enough. I manage to get by with one pair.''

''You wear house shoes,'' he reminded her. ''Your boots stay on the porch for the most part.''

''I'd say it was a good place for yours, too.'' She turned from him, lifting her dish towel to wipe at a spotless pane of glass in her kitchen cabinet, then concentrated on watching her fingers as they traced the wooden framework.

''By the way, I'm sticking around,'' he said, catching

her attention. ''I haven't given up on changing your mind.'' His hesitation was long and then he spoke again. ''Will you go to town with me, Faith?'' he asked quietly. ''I think we need to send off the papers you signed, and I'd like to buy you some things at the general store.''

Her breath snagged in her throat at the thought of appearing in Benning with Max at her side. ''What sort of things?'' she asked.

''Turn around and look at me.''

She did as he commanded, leaning back on the cabinet. ''All right. I'm looking.''

''Do you need to make everything so difficult?'' he asked quietly. ''Can we just be...pleasant to each other for one day?''

''Does being pleasant involve you spending money on me? For things I can do very nicely without?''

''I want to buy you new dresses. Nothing fancy,'' he amended quickly as she opened her mouth to deny her need for such things. ''Just simple cotton. Bright colors, maybe, and I'll almost guarantee any undergarments you brought with you have long since worn out. You can choose new ones, and maybe a nightgown. Or whatever you might need,'' he added quickly.

''Why?'' she asked, shoving her trembling fingers into her apron pockets. ''What's the purpose of spending money on me? To put me in your debt? Maybe make me look at you differently?''

''Maybe,'' he said slowly, ''because I want to. Because it would give me pleasure to buy you something to show off your pretty face and form a bit more than that dress you're wearing is capable of doing. And because I feel more than a little guilty that you haven't had anything new, while I have a closetful of suits in Boston.''

''You want to show off my—'' She halted, pressing her

lips together. "I don't need fancy things here," she said. He'd never been so forthright in his assessment of her charms before, and the thought of how much more delicate and fragile she'd been in those early years made her smile.

"I'm not nearly as attractive as I once was," she told him. "Or else your vision has deteriorated in your old age."

At that he winced, then grinned. "Ah, you've no idea how lovely you are, Faith. You're a mature woman now, whereas you were only a girl when I married you. I find myself leaning toward maturity, I think."

"Well, that's nice," she said, at a loss for words. She sought his dark eyes, trying without success to fathom their depths. And then she shrugged. "I expect you can spend your money on me if you like. My wardrobe is sparse enough that it could use a few additions."

His smile was immediate, and she thought he looked more than a little triumphant as he swallowed a good bit of his coffee. "Would you like to go today?" he asked.

"Why not?" she replied. "I need to carry a load of eggs to the general store, anyway. Yesterday was my usual day to deliver them and pick up my mail."

"Half an hour?" he asked, rising and heading for the room he'd slept in. "I just need to wash up and change my clothes." His fingers scrubbed at his jaw. "And shave, too, I suspect."

"Half an hour," she agreed.

The eggs were secured in a burlap sack, each wrapped in a bit of newspaper and layered between inches of straw. It was a good method of transporting them, she'd found through trial and error. The same way she'd discovered other ways of surviving.

Faith saved all her newspapers for this purpose, after

reading and rereading the printed pages. It was her one luxury, the mailing of a weekly edition from the nearest large city. As she fetched them and began wrapping her precious eggs, Max watched for a moment, then started to tear the newsprint into pieces appropriate for her use. "One sack full?" he asked as she tied the first burlap bag in a loose knot.

"No, I only fill the bags halfway, so the eggs on the bottom don't break from the weight," she said, reaching for a second bag from the pantry shelf. "One on each side of my saddle, behind me. I could use the wagon and team, I suppose. In fact, I do, when I'm in need of bulkier supplies."

She looked up at him. "The truth is, I enjoy riding my mare. I don't usually have much of a schedule to keep. I've learned to appreciate the view, Max."

"As I'm doing, even now," he said, sliding a quick glance her way.

She laughed, deciding to appreciate his humor and the dry wit she'd almost forgotten he was capable of. "You were fun to be with," she said, her thoughts making themselves known before her better sense prevailed.

"Thank you," he replied. "I enjoyed your company, too. In fact, I was probably one of the proudest men in Boston when I escorted you from home."

"Were you?" She heard the note of surprise she could not conceal.

"You didn't realize how much of an asset you were to me?"

She thought about that for a moment, her hands slowing in the methodical task of egg wrapping and securing. A layer of straw came next, and she lifted it from the supply she'd sent him for, a washtub filled with the yellow, rough, scratchy residue from thrashing the wheat, donated for her use by the neighbor to the east.

"I don't suppose I ever considered myself an asset to you, just a decoration for your arm, and a partner when you chose to dance with me." And then she thought of the nights when their return from an evening in company usually ended with him visiting her bedroom. "Did I seem more appealing to you when I was dressed in my finest?"

"You've never been more appealing to me than you are at this very moment," he said, his hands touching hers as they spread straw in the confined depths of the burlap sack. The straw fell to the bottom, covering the layer of eggs, and their fingers entwined, his gripping hers with a gentle strength she did not attempt to escape.

She was speechless, feeling pursued by a man intent on seduction, and yet willing to allow it. There was an inner sense of satisfaction that permitted him this moment of intimacy, as small as it might be.

For just this moment, she felt exceedingly feminine, wonderfully desirable and just a bit breathless as she knew the warmth of a man's hands clasping hers, and recognized the desire gleaming in his eyes.

Chapter Four

"Didn't know Miss Faith had a husband," Mr. Metcalf said, lifting an eyebrow as Max introduced himself upon arrival at the general store.

"I've been back East," Max told him. "Business has made it impossible for me to be a part of my wife's life for the past little while," he added casually, slanting a glance in Faith's direction as he answered the storekeeper's pointed remark.

Mr. Metcalf nodded, apparently swallowing the ambiguous theory for Max's sudden appearance at Faith's side this morning. She'd liked to have kicked Max in the shins for his arrogance, and then smacked Mr. Metcalf a good one for his gullible acceptance of the explanation.

Instead, she bit her tongue and decided to hustle Max from the place before he caused any more speculation among the townsfolk. It would be hard enough to explain away his disappearance once he gave up on her and headed back to Boston. There was no point in folks thinking he was going to be a permanent fixture in her life.

Tucking her precious newspaper beneath her arm, she approached the counter where Max waited. Her mail was generally pretty scanty, and today was no different, only the delivery of the Sunday issue of the Dallas paper. Subscribing was a luxury she could barely afford, but the news it offered fed her need to keep up with the world outside of Benning, Texas.

Max looked impatient now, and well he might, since Mr. Metcalf, apparently accepting his presence, was bending his ear with a tale about a customer who had refused to pay his long-standing bill. "Yessir, that fella just about fried my gizzard," the storekeeper cackled. "I told him, in no uncertain terms, what he could do with—"

Max cut him off with an uplifted hand and an apologetic smile. "Here's my wife now, sir. I'm sure she's in a hurry to get back home, aren't you, dear?"

Faith glanced at him, his term of endearment causing her to grit her teeth. She vacillated between rescuing him from the storekeeper and leaving him to stew. Rescue won, hands down, as she recalled other days when she'd been the victim of Mr. Metcalf's droning monotone.

"Here's my list," she said quickly. "I left eight dozen eggs on the counter, Mr. Metcalf, in the crock where I usually put them."

He glanced up at her and nodded, then took her list with a resigned sigh, turning to the shelves to search for the items she needed.

Max shot her a grin and leaned against the counter. "How do we go about choosing clothes for you?" he asked in an undertone.

"I look for Mrs. Metcalf," Faith said quietly. "I think she must be in the back." And as she spoke, that lady appeared through the curtain that divided the store from the stockroom.

"Good morning," she said brightly, spotting Faith and heading in their direction.

"We need some things for my wife," Max told the

woman, and Faith watched as the plump lady who had the misfortune to be wed to Mr. Metcalf figuratively fell at Max's feet.

"Why, land's sakes," she said brightly. "I surely didn't know our Miss Faith had a good-looking husband like you. She's been keeping secrets."

Her smile was wide, her eyes sparkling as Max nodded agreeably, charming her almost effortlessly, it seemed. At his request, she sorted through bins of clothing that lined the shelves and within moments had placed several dresses on the counter for Faith's approval. Two were set aside quickly, as being too dark and plain, according to Max. A blue-checked cotton with lace edging the collar was chosen, along with a leafy-green frock Faith privately thought was too dressy for her style of living.

She drew the line at two, and then watched as Max pointed a finger at one bit of lace and batiste after another, choosing undergarments for her from the assortment provided by the wide-eyed shopkeeper's wife. A finely woven lawn nightgown was added to the growing stack, and Faith almost blushed as she considered wearing such a garment to bed in the old farmhouse where feed sacks had been sewn together for her last nightgown.

"That's enough," she said finally, and as Max looked at her, he shrugged, acknowledging defeat at her hands.

"Maybe next time we'll—" he began, but was cut off midsentence by Faith's hand on his arm, hauling him toward another counter where boots were displayed.

"You'd better buy either new boots or a pair of shoes to wear indoors," she said firmly. "You've bought me all you're going to. I don't even need that much, and if you don't quit now, I'll give back that whole pile of things."

Yet her heart nudged her as he finally nodded acceptance of her terms. "I don't mean to sound ungrateful," she said quietly. ''I appreciate that you want to help me, Max. I just don't need any more than that.''

''This may come as a surprise to you, but I needed to do this for you,'' he said finally. ''We're not going to discuss it right now, but I'm fighting with a load of guilt, and this has only *begun* to alleviate a bit of my burden.''

He tried on boots, walking back and forth across the floor under the surveillance of Mr. Metcalf and his wife. They both looked pleased by the prospect of Max and his money dropping by their establishment today, and Faith settled down on a seat near the cold, potbellied stove while she waited for him to make the decision.

Max, it seemed, was the center of attention, as several ladies came into the store and stood about in a group, speaking softly and darting glances his way. Ignoring them all, he focused on Faith, asking her opinion, and then choosing several candy sticks, obviously with her in mind.

''You like peppermint, as I recall,'' he said, bowing as he offered her a red-and-white-striped specimen. Root beer was his favorite, she remembered, and she watched as he sucked on a bit of candy, recalling another day when they'd walked in the park, early in their courtship, and he'd broken off a piece for her.

I like peppermint better. She'd smiled up at him and thought him the most gloriously handsome man she'd ever seen. And then she'd laughed aloud as he drew another candy from his pocket and unwrapped it solemnly before he offered it.

Whatever the lady wants. And she'd accepted it, yearning for the taste of root beer from his lips, knowing he would kiss her before he left her in the front hallway of her aunt's home.

''I said, are you ready?'' Max asked, and Faith was

aware that he'd repeated the question while her mind had wandered to the park in Boston.

She rose quickly. "Yes. We need to be on our way."

The clothing he'd purchased was folded neatly, wrapped in brown paper and placed in the egg sacks. The bits and pieces of dry goods, salt and coffee, and a slab of bacon Max had determined they needed, were gathered together, wrapped and placed in another burlap bag, then tied behind Max's saddle. The bags hung on either side and Max was forced to lead his horse to a mounting block in order to gain the height necessary to fit himself in the saddle without dislodging his purchases.

Faith laughed aloud as he rode beside her. "You look like Louie the peddler," she said, chuckling as they headed out of town.

"And who the dickens is he?" Max asked, returning her smile with a look of satisfaction. "And by the way, I like hearing you laugh, ma'am."

"He's a little old man who rides up to my back door about three times a year, with a packful of odds and ends. I always ask him in for coffee, and he shakes his head and tells me he prefers tea. Which I already know, of course."

She smiled apologetically. "You have to be a part of his ritual to understand. I put the kettle on to heat as soon as I see him heading toward the house, and he digs around in his pack and finds a special blend of tea, and we share whatever I have in the pantry. Usually a slice of bread and jam or cookies, or sometimes...." Her words trailed off and she shrugged, thinking Max must surely consider her small pleasures to be foolish.

And then he surprised her, his voice almost wistful as he said, "You make it sound like fun. I never thought about you entertaining a peddler man, Faith. I would have worried that he might not be safe, that you'd be in danger from him."

Max looked at the serenity of trees and meadows surrounding them, and then up at the sky overhead, where fleecy clouds decorated the brilliant blue like an overturned, China-blue teacup with dabs of whipping cream on the surface. The sun was leaning toward the west, and by the time they reached the farmhouse, it would be past time for supper and the evening chores.

For now, though, he intended to savor the moments they spent together. "It's different here," he said. "Peaceful and quiet. Perhaps I've worried for nothing."

"You should talk to Nicholas and Lin," she said, "if you think it's always so tranquil in these parts. We've had our share of trouble, and there've been occasions of cattle rustlers or men on the run who can pose a threat to our well-being."

She touched the rifle she carried with her, firmly sheathed behind her saddle. "That's why I take this with me when I leave the house. I learned early on to watch my back." And then she sent an apologetic look in his direction. "I don't mean to spoil your image of this part of the country, Max. For the most part, it's safe and I feel secure."

Lines marred the width of his forehead as he listened, and then he shrugged, as if setting aside his concern. "I suppose there's danger no matter where you live, Faith. Boston has a beautiful, orderly facade it offers to visitors, but there are pockets in the city where no one in his right mind would walk alone at night."

"Well, for the most part, I feel at home here. I can roam the woods at night if I please. And with the dog beside me, I doubt anyone would bother me. We have a good sheriff," Faith said. "Brace has a reputation for upholding the law, and there are few men in the area who would want to face him in a gun battle.''

''And with him to look after you, you've felt pretty—''

She halted him with an uplifted hand. ''I look after myself, Max. Make no mistake, I can use this gun, and I'm not afraid to fire it.''

His grin was a teasing reminder of the session with the rattlesnake. ''As I well know,'' he said, bowing his head in a parody of respect. ''My wife, the gunslinger.''

She shrugged, sending him a fleeting smile. ''I've been called worse.''

''I don't think I want to know about it, if you have,'' he said. ''I'd probably be ready to go to your defense, and end up getting shot for my trouble.''

''Haven't you ever fired a rifle?'' she asked. At his silent denial, a subtle, seemingly reluctant shake of his head, she posed another question. ''Would you like me to teach you?''

''I suppose I could get the hang of it in a hurry,'' he said. ''I've carried a small pistol for years. I'd think shooting a rifle or shotgun wouldn't be beyond my intelligence to figure out.''

''We'll do it tomorrow,'' Faith said. ''I have a supply of shells, and I can get more when I go to town next.'' And then she closed her eyes, thinking of what she had just said. Assuming he would be here, she was already planning for another trip to Benning, and making out a list.

''Don't worry, sweet,'' Max said quietly. ''I'll be sure you're stocked up with whatever you need to run the place, no matter how many trips to town we have to take.''

''You probably won't be here that long, anyway,'' she said stiffly. ''I doubt your business will tolerate your absence more than a week or so.''

''My brother is in charge while I'm gone,'' Max said.

"I told you he owes me some time off. He can consider this our honeymoon. The one I never gave you, due to pressing business." His voice ground out the words—words she'd considered one small part of her litany of complaints during the years of their marriage.

"Pressing business" had been one, "family responsibilities" another. And Faith had dangled at the end of the list of his priorities, a wife who demanded little and expected less. Perhaps, she thought, as recognition of her own faults brought pain to her heart, she might have been better at this marriage business had she made more noise, gotten his attention more frequently.

"I'm trying to make amends, Faith," he said quietly. "I'm not sure if I'm making any progress or not, but if there's any chance to mend our marriage and have you back in my life, I'm willing to spend all the time it takes to bring that about."

"I won't deny you that right," she said, "but don't count on anything where I'm concerned, Max. My memories leave a lot to be desired, and to be honest with you, I'm not sure you're capable of the sort of marriage I might demand."

"I'm asking for time," he told her. "And a chance to prove to you that I mean business. I want you back."

"I'll never be the woman I was," she warned him. "Don't try to make me into that docile little wife you once knew." He gave no reply, but his jaw firmed as he nodded. They rode in silence, and then as they approached the back of the house, she slid from her mare.

Turning to him, she reached up to loosen the sacks from behind his saddle. "I'll lift these to the ground first, so you can dismount easier."

He snagged the burlap bags from behind his saddle and helped her, lowering them into her hands. Then he slid from the saddle himself and took them up to carry them into the house. ''If you'll wait a minute, I'll help you tend the horses,'' he told her.

But she was already on her way to the barn, leading their mounts. ''I'll start,'' she said. ''You can finish up.'' Besides, she wanted a minute to herself, needed a few long moments of reflection as she thought of what would come next. Max was creeping into her life as he'd once crept into her heart. And she could not allow that to happen again, no matter how empty her days would be once he was gone from here.

''I think I'll use the wagon and my team from now on when I go to town,'' Faith said, setting aside her grooming tools and shaking out the saddle blankets before she spread them on the rail where they were stored. She'd groomed her mare, paying special attention to the rounded belly, then sighed, as if she recognized a sign Max was not aware of.

''Because the mare is ready to deliver?'' he asked. ''How can you tell?''

''It's her time. I should have stopped riding her a month ago, I think,'' Faith said. ''But I'm not very heavy and I didn't push her.'' She looked up at him. ''I'm selfish, I suspect.''

He shook his head. ''I doubt anyone could apply that word to you. At least I can't. You were always generous with me.'' He thought back, remembering. ''Even now,'' he said, ''you've made me feel welcome, even though I know you didn't want me here. You've shared your food with me, given me a bed.''

And then he smiled, his mouth twitching at one corner, and she felt her heart thud in response. ''Even though it wasn't the bed I'd have chosen, I appreciate the fact you didn't toss me out on my ear.''

"And I appreciate the fact you've not tried to invade my bedroom," she said quietly. "Not that it would have done you any good."

"No, probably not," he agreed. "I value my hide too much to expose it to your rifle."

"I keep a revolver in the drawer beside my bed," she told him. "Nicholas lent it to me a while back."

"I'll buy you one, if you like," Max said sharply. "You can give Nicholas's back to him. I'd rather you owe me."

She smiled; and he thought he caught a glimpse of satisfaction in her eyes. "I do believe you're a jealous man, Max. And all for naught. Nicholas has no designs on me. I would have thought you'd figured that out by now."

"I'm aware of that." His words sounded stiff and awkward in his own ears. "I'm also more than aware of my shortcomings. The fact that I've done a poor job of being a husband only makes me more determined to plug the leaks.

"Are you willing to allow me some time to prove my intentions?" he asked as they climbed the steps to the back porch. "I didn't want this whole thing to come to a matter of legalities, Faith. I know I can stay here, whether you like it or not. But that isn't my intention. In order for me to have a shot at mending my fences, you'll have to accept me in your life for a while."

She shrugged, opening the back door. "Suit yourself. I think you will anyway."

Her nonchalance galled him, and he was tempted to bite his tongue, lest he offer a retort that would put her back up. "Shall I help with supper?" he asked instead.

"If you like." She opened the stove lid and peered inside, then bent to pick up wood from the box. Placing it carefully on the coals, she checked the damper, then went to the sink. Folding her sleeves to her elbows, she performed the small ritual he'd watched several times over the past days—bending to scoop soap from the jar beneath the sink, then scrubbing at her hands and rinsing them in the shallow basin.

A quick movement of the pump handle allowed fresh water to pour from the spout, and she caught it, then lifted her cupped hands to her face, splashing it. When she reached for the towel he was there, holding the bit of linen, and she glanced up quickly, surprise alive in those blue eyes.

"Thank you...I think," she said slowly, as if seeking to determine the reason for his approach.

"Let me," he said quietly, dabbing the towel against her cheeks and forehead, soaking up the droplets of water before he pressed the cloth into her waiting hands.

"I haven't needed a ladies' maid for years, Max," she said quietly. And had he not caught a glimpse of the pulse at the side of her throat, he would have thought her unmoved by his touch. As it was, he found pleasure in the leap of her heartbeat, knew a moment of joy as she tried to hide her reaction to him.

"I enjoy touching you, Faith, even if it is a trumped-up excuse."

"Do you?" He thought she looked a bit cynical, and he laughed aloud.

"If you only knew how badly I want to touch you, lady, you'd have that revolver in your hand, and I'd probably be on my way out the door."

"Don't you think you're foolish to give me fair warning?" she asked, her lips twitching as if she joined his game.

"No. I've tried to play fair with you," he said. "Even now, I'm telling you what my next move will be."

''And?'' She prodded him a bit, laying the towel aside and turning from the sink to head for the pantry.

He followed her, aware that she occupied a dead-end space, an effective trap for the unwary. Faith did not qualify as such. She knew exactly what she was doing, and he felt a surge of triumph that her mood had changed, that she'd relaxed her guard.

He blocked the narrow doorway and she glanced up at him, her hands readying several jars for transport to the kitchen cupboard. ''Are you offering to help?'' she asked.

''In a moment.''

Her smile faded, as if she thought better of her ploy, and recognized the inherent danger of her position. ''What are you doing, Max?''

''I'm going to kiss you,'' he said quietly. ''I want you, Faith, very badly. But I'm not about to make a mess of things by pushing for what I can't have. I'll settle for a simple kiss.''

''Kisses are never simple where you're concerned,'' she said bluntly. ''You make a production out of them, once you set your mind to it.''

''Do I, now?'' He felt a thrill of delight at her words. The woman was admitting more than she knew, and she'd given him an edge. One he was more than willing to take advantage of.

Settling his hands on her shoulders, he turned her to face him, recognizing her reluctance and ready to release her should she deny his suit. He bent his head, and she lifted her face, exposing the clean, long line of her throat and offering him a glimpse of vulnerability, of soft skin drawn tautly over the fine bones of her face, of eyes shielded with lashes that fanned her cheeks.

''You're a beautiful woman,'' he said quietly, his palm settling at the nape of her neck, holding her before him as he looked his fill. The pantry was shadowed, his body blocking the light from the kitchen, and he wished for a moment that he might see her more fully, might examine each lovely part of her face at his leisure.

As it was, there was no guarantee that she would be so acquiescent for more than a moment, and he bent his head lower, knowing that this instant in time was a gift of her choosing, that he must accept it quickly or suffer her refusal should she change her mind.

Their lips met and he felt a soft sigh escape her mouth. He inhaled it, tasting the sweetness of her breath, then pressed more firmly against the plush, wide mouth that offered no resistance. She stood erect, and he'd have preferred she lean against him. Her hands hung by her sides, and he wished for their weight around his neck.

But her mouth—that generous, warm mouth he'd once known was his to conquer when he chose—offered heat and hummed with a hint of passion he could not mistake.

His lips opened, his tongue touched hers, teased and tangled within the opening she allowed, and then she sighed again, as if she could no longer remain aloof, but must seek pleasure of her own. Her hands rose to creep up his chest, meeting finally behind his head, her fingers clasping him.

She eased her breasts against him then, and he felt the firm roundness of womanly curves, and knew a moment of desire so intense it all but washed aside his control.

''Faith.'' It was a whisper, a warning, a plea. And she responded by opening her eyes, her lashes lifting slowly as if she sought to awake from a dream. ''I want you, Faith,'' he murmured. And she nodded, a slight movement of her head.

He slid one hand between them and leaned back, allowing his fingers to spread wide over the fullness of her breast. It felt familiar, yet different, more firm than he remembered. The sign of her arousal was there in the forming of that small bit of flesh that pushed for attention against his index finger, and he inhaled sharply.

His mouth sought hers again, his tongue taking ownership with a deep, thrusting movement that she responded to, possessing him even as he sought to stake a claim. It was a draw, he decided, allowing her to suckle the invader as she would. He shifted against her, his body responding in accord with her coaxing, and heard the soft sounds of desire she made no attempt to conceal.

Her dress was unbuttoned rapidly, his fingers trembling but agile, and then he met the resistance of a chemise and hesitated. It was his undoing, that moment when he contemplated tearing the thin fabric that kept her skin from his. He felt her stiffen, knew the exact instant she recognized her danger, and silently cursed his hesitation.

"No, Max." Her voice trembled and her hands slid from him. She whispered the words again, and he thought he saw a tear hover on her eyelashes as she looked up at him. "I'm so sorry," she said. "This is my fault. I only…"

No matter her reason, she'd changed her mind, and he was duty bound to recognize her right to do so. That he'd managed to coax her so far along the road to seduction was somewhat of a miracle, he decided, and he'd do well to accept defeat rather than press his luck. Another time he might have been angry that she called the shots. Now, he only backed away and allowed her to escape.

She buttoned her dress, turning aside as she forced her shaking fingers to complete the task. Her head was bent, as if she would hide her face from him, and he wondered if she was embarrassed by her behavior. It would not do. He didn't want her to feel shamed by the moments of desire and passion they had shared.

And so he halted as she tried to escape, and spoke her name again. "Faith? Look at me, please."

She hesitated, then lifted her chin in a brave movement that cost her, if he was any judge of the woman. Her cheeks were pale, but a blush rose to color them in moments. "You'll think I'm—"

He touched her lips with his index finger, silencing her. "You have no idea what I think," he said quietly. "But I'm about to tell you."

Her lips moved beneath his touch, as if she would speak. And he smiled, shaking his head. "I cherish each moment we spend together. You allowed me to kiss you and gave me leave to..." He looked down at her breasts, noting the still-turgid crests that pressed against worn fabric, enticing his touch.

"You're a generous woman, sweetheart. I appreciate it, and I won't press for more, no matter that my...my body is rebelling against your refusal. You needn't be embarrassed because you accepted my kiss."

"It was more than a kiss," she said quietly, her hand clasping the finger that would have stilled her words. "I led you on, Max, and that was wrong of me."

He attempted a smile. "I think I'm a better judge of your guilt than you are, and I decree that you are innocent of all but the crime of feeling desire for your husband."

"I haven't considered you my husband for a long time," she admitted.

"No matter," he said bluntly. "I'm your husband, and I'm likely to remain in that position, given the fact that I'm not going to divorce you."

Her gaze dropped from his and she pushed at his chest, sliding past him as he stepped aside. "Even more reason why I had no right to lead you on," she said, escaping to the kitchen.

"I'm not sure you can call it that," he said, shifting his trousers before he turned to face her. He was more than uncomfortable, and probably faced a sleepless night. Yet it had been worth it, to know that he had the ability to arouse Faith beyond her own set limits. That he had given and received pleasure for those few moments, and perhaps started her rethinking her adamant denial of their future.

He watched her face as she remembered her failure to carry the jars from the pantry, knew the instant she realized she must pass by him again to retrieve them in order to begin cooking supper. And took pity on her.

His hands full of her bounty, he offered the jars to her, one of green beans, another of what appeared to be applesauce and the third filled with chunks of meat. "Is that beef?" he asked.

She nodded, as if relieved to have the subject matter changed. "I canned up a good supply last fall when Nicholas butchered a steer and I bartered for a quarter of it."

"What did you give him?" Max asked, his curiosity aroused by her methods of survival. "Surely it was worth more than a few dozen eggs."

She cast him a long-suffering look. "Of course it was. I helped Lin and Katie butcher the meat, and showed them how to preserve it. In return, they gave me a share."

"Your independence makes you more attractive, you know," he said, settling at the table and watching her as she moved back and forth between the kitchen dresser and the stove. She'd opened the jars with ease and then spilled the contents into two pans for heating and a bowl in which to serve the applesauce.

Now she looked up quickly, her expression uneasy. "Do you think so?"

He nodded. "I know so. I find you more attractive than any other woman I've ever known in my life. You are the very essence of femininity, all wrapped up in a neat package.'' He allowed a grin to escape. ''I bow to your excellence.''

Faith's lips tightened. ''Now I think you're teasing me.'' Her chin lifted a bit and she narrowed her eyes. ''You're just playing a game with me, Max, trying to coax me into your web.''

''My web?'' He laughed aloud. ''You'd think I was a spider, sitting here spinning a trap for you.''

''Aren't you?'' She placed the applesauce on the table and the pans on the stove.

''No. I'm not that devious, love. You know exactly what I want from you. I've never made any bones about it. If I can coax you into reestablishing our marriage, I'll do it. In any way I can manage the deed.''

Faith turned back to the pantry, emerging with a bowl in her hands. She placed it on the table and he leaned forward to watch as she mixed flour and lard together. ''Biscuits?'' he asked, guessing her plan. ''Can I get the milk for you?''

She nodded and he rose, returning to the pantry, where she kept a jar of milk beneath the bottom shelf, in a small safe that sat beneath floor level. The space was several degrees cooler than the temperature in the pantry, and he'd watched her other times as she stored items there for safekeeping.

''This is a smart idea,'' he said, returning with the bottle and tilting it to pour a small amount of milk into the flour mixture. ''I hadn't thought about how you kept your food fresh until I watched you open that trapdoor.''

''It's cooler in the cellar,'' she said. ''Even more so in the dugout.''

''Dugout?'' he asked, puzzled by the word.

''In the back of the cellar, there's a room for storage. It

doesn't freeze in the winter, but food stays fresh there for a good long while."

"I never noticed it."

"It's a part of the wall," she told him. "You have to know it's there before you can tell where the door is."

"I suppose an icebox is out of the question," he said. "I'm spoiled by such things."

"You learn quickly what works best," Faith said. "I've appreciated the cellar since I moved in here. I didn't have the ability to keep food in the cabin for longer than a day."

"How did you do it?" he asked.

"I just kept enough perishables on hand in the warm weather to last a day or so. We all do what we have to, Max. And I had no choice. It was get used to it and survive, or call it quits. I chose to survive."

They ate in silence. The biscuits she'd formed and baked while the food heated atop the stove were tender and fluffy, and he broke one apart and spooned gravy over it. "You're a good cook," he said, after he'd finished his second helping.

She bowed her head, a small smile of satisfaction lighting her features. "Thank you. I do my best."

He pushed away from the table and carried his plate to the sink. It was wiped clean, the last of the gravy having been soaked up by his biscuit, and he placed it in the empty dishpan. "I'll wash these if you like," he offered.

"No," she said quickly, nudging him aside. "I'll wash and you can dry."

"All right," he agreed, and took up a towel from the stack in the pantry to do as she bade him. It was a job quickly accomplished and she took the towel from him when they were finished, carrying it to the porch and pinning it to the line.

The sun was below the horizon, and the clouds hovering

there were rosy, the sky above them darkening with twilight. A stray star or two glittered overhead, and Max stood beside her, enjoying the silence and the rare beauty of the night.

His gaze swept over her, touching upon her profile and the uplifted thrust of her breasts as she inhaled the scent of summer blossoms newly opened. This moment, this instant of time, was one he intended to cherish, as long as his life should last.

And hoping against hope that she would accept his touch, he placed his hand on her waist. She glanced up quickly, her eyes questioning his motives, he thought, and he offered a smile.

"I've enjoyed today," he told her. "Thank you."

"No, I think I'm the one who owes you those words," she countered. "You're a generous man, Max. I doubt you're going to use my inheritance to pay for the things you bought me, right?"

He shook his head. "I'm not sure generosity has anything to do with our shopping trip," he said. "I'd say that word applies more to you. In fact, I think it's how I described you a little earlier this evening," he murmured, and watched as she recalled the moment he referred to.

"No, don't draw away," he said, his fingers curving to hold her next to him. "I want you to know that I don't expect any more from you than you're willing to give me."

She bowed her head again, and her whisper was almost too low to be discerned. He bent his head and his heart beat more rapidly as she spoke his name. Simply his name, and then sighed, leaning for an instant against him, her head resting on his shoulder.

Chapter Five

The mare moved more slowly over the next several days, and Faith kept a close eye on her, grooming her daily, feeding her well and standing at the corral fence to watch as the four horses stood in the grass and grazed in the summer sun. The animal was sleek and golden, a sight for sore eyes, Max had said, admiring her beauty.

Although his gaze had turned to Faith herself as he whispered the words. She smiled, remembering his admiring glances, his small gestures that were aimed at cementing their relationship. Even the word painted a picture of marriage, she thought. And they were far from being committed to that grand and glorious estate.

She'd gone that route once, had given herself fully to the sort of marriage expected of her, and what had it gotten her? A sigh escaped as her thoughts traveled back through time, recalling the years she'd spent in Boston as Max's wife. As daughter-in-law to the elder Mrs. McDowell. Bending her head, Faith touched her forehead to the top rail of the corral fence, where it adjoined the pasture.

"You looked happier a few minutes ago," Max said from beside her. "Now, the life has leached out of you, as if someone blew out your candle and left you in the dark."

She looked up at him, pasting a smile on her face. "You have a silver tongue, Max. Good morning."

"I don't know about the silver tongue bit," he said, "but I know you're thinking dark thoughts right now, and when I walked out of the barn you were glowing. Something changed your mood."

"I just felt a goose walk over my grave," she said quietly. And then laughed. "We can't all be bright and chipper in the morning."

"I was, until I got out to the kitchen and found you gone," he told her. "I smelled the coffee and thought I'd snatch a cup and then help you with breakfast." He looked up at the clear sky, where the sun had already burned off the haze and was well on its way to working on the dew.

"Another nice day," he said, inhaling and grinning widely, for no obvious reason that she could see. And then he looked at her and she found a tenderness in his gaze that surprised her. Max was not given to a soft touch, not in the years of their marriage, at least. For some reason, he'd assumed a different set of rules for his life during the past week or so, and she felt the old familiar wariness take hold.

"I don't know you sometimes," she told him. "You're not the man I left behind three years ago. And…" she gathered herself for the words she would say, knowing he might take offense "…I wonder if I can trust the man you've presented to me as the real Max McDowell."

"Well, that's what I'd call laying it on the line," he said quietly, once he'd caught his breath and considered her comment. Faith had never been cruel, had seldom disputed his word or asked for anything he didn't offer. She'd been docile and easy to please during their marriage.

Or else she'd been a fake. Perhaps this was the real woman, and he'd never known her at all for those three years they'd shared a house with his mother, and the privacy of their own quarters.

"You think I'm playing games with you?" he asked. "You doubt my sincerity?"

She shook her head and then he caught the hesitation as she rethought the gesture. "No, I don't doubt that you want me back," she said finally. "But I don't think I know you, Max."

And wasn't that ironic. That she should think of him in the same light he'd considered her only a moment since.

"Perhaps we don't know each other, Faith." He turned his back to the fence and looked at the corral and the barn, and beyond them, the house. "This..." He waved his hand at the buildings and fields he faced. "This is what you've become, and I'm trying hard to fit you in place here. And I've about decided it's easier to do that than try to recall whether or not you were what you seemed to be, back in Boston."

"What I seemed to be?" Her query was quiet, and he turned his head to meet her gaze. She looked puzzled, as if she were truly unaware of the difference. "I was exactly what you wanted me to be, Max," she said firmly. "I was the nice, obedient wife who directed the cook and housekeeper, when your mother allowed it—"

His hand rose, halting her words. "Hold on for just a minute, Faith. You've said several things about my mother that make her sound harsh and cruel. I don't recall that she ever treated you so badly."

"In front of you?" She shook her head, then looked directly at him from angry eyes. "Of course not. She's no fool. But behind your back, or when you told her to give me pointers, to help me..." Her lips pressed together in a grim imitation of a smile. "Max, your mother has cruelty down to a science."

He felt a jolt of anger at her cutting statement, and his words were defensive. "I'm not sure you're being fair." He tried to recall the dignified, immaculately attired woman who had dwelled in another wing of their home, and had difficulty placing her in the role Faith described.

"My mother has always been rather..." His pause was longer than he'd have liked, but he was having a problem coming up with a word that was all-encompassing. "...aloof," he said finally. "She's not easy to get close to, I suppose. But I assure you, Faith, she really means well."

"Well, I'll try to remember that, Max. Not that I'll ever have direct contact with her again. Trust me, that isn't going to happen."

He digested her words and felt bile rise in his throat. "You mean, when you come back to Boston and we're together again, my mother will have to live somewhere else?" His hesitation was brief as Faith remained silent, and then shrugged, accepting that circumstance as being inevitable. "I'm sure that can be arranged."

"No, I wouldn't want to put her to the trouble," Faith said flatly. "I'll just stay here and *you* can go back home and live with her."

He felt a sudden urge to stamp his foot, a stunt he'd pulled once as a child, before his mother had convinced him that gentlemen don't have temper tantrums. Since that outlet wasn't an option, he folded his arms across his chest and leaned back again on the corral fence. It was time to take a definite stand, since Faith seemed to be ignoring his every concession.

"You'll have to face it, Faith. No matter what you say, I'm not planning to go back to Boston alone," he said, aware that his words sounded more like that same little boy of almost thirty years ago than a man of thirty-three. And yet he continued. "I want you in my home and in my life, Faith, and that's all there is to it."

He heard his words as if someone else had spoken them, recognized his stilted, dogmatic message and groaned inwardly. All he needed to do now was stick out his chin and pout a bit to make the picture complete.

And unless he missed his guess, Faith was imagining him in just that pose, her hand over her mouth, her eyes wide as she fought to curtail the laughter that bubbled in her throat. "Oh, Max," she said, gurgling with delight. "You sound like my little brother, Timmy, when he wasn't getting his way and gathered up his marbles. I can still see him dropping them into the leather bag and tugging at the strings, his face like a thundercloud and his mouth all pooched out."

"Your brother, Timmy." Max repeated her words and glared at her, his anger taking a back seat to the desire that skittered through his veins as he watched her eyes light up and her face turn rosy, her laughter setting loose a noisy case of the hiccups.

She touched his arm lightly with her fingertips. "I'm sorry," she said between the soft hics that shook her. "I just never once saw you lose your temper so quickly, and with such little reason."

He dropped his arms and swung around, then changed his mind and turned again to face her, his long fingers clasping her shoulders and drawing her into his embrace. "Such little reason," he repeated, feeling like a parrot with no vocabulary of his own. "You don't think that you announcing your intention to remain here while you pack me off to Boston is reason enough for me to be angry?"

"Well, so far I haven't seen you running down the lane toward town, Max," she said, "so apparently my *intentions* don't have much influence on your behavior." She tilted her head, managing to look totally in control of the situation—a difficult task, given the fact that she was clutched against his body and his arousal felt like a fence post in his trousers against her belly.

And then she frowned and attempted to draw away from him, apparently recognizing that his state of mind had done a switch from anger to awareness of her as a woman. Moving her feet a bit, but failing to make any headway due to his iron grip and the fact that he was enjoying her soft curves right where they were, she shot him an accusing look that was aimed to insure her release.

"I don't think you're playing fair."

"It's my game," he retorted. "And if you think I'm going to run away so easily, you're wrong, lady. I've got a proposal to make, and I want you to listen to me."

"All right." She stood still before him, her hands splayed wide on his shoulders, as if she might push hard, given the opportunity. Her mouth was open a bit, and as he watched, her tongue touched her upper lip, then retreated. "I'm listening," she said.

Her eyes were shiny, and a blush was staining her cheeks, but she'd ceased wiggling against him, and he could only be thankful for that small miracle. It was hard enough to concentrate on his words when his attention was almost totally wrapped up in the distraction of his male member making itself known on such a grand scale.

"Look," he said, snatching at a straw. "Can we go sit down somewhere and discuss this?" So long as he had her plastered against him, he couldn't think straight. Especially when his body was begging for an hour alone with her, preferably on a bed.

"If you'll let me go, I'll head for the kitchen and make breakfast," she said agreeably. "I think you need to cool off a bit."

He turned her loose and she backed away, stumbling, her legs seeming to wobble. His hands held her upright and he looked down into eyes that threatened to overflow. "What?" he asked, his voice rising. "What have I done to make you cry?"

"Nothing," she said. "I'm just wishing you hadn't taken so long to finally step down off your pedestal and speak your mind to me. You've spouted off nicely, instead of coming across as a pompous, arrogant businessman. It's too bad it's just about four years too late."

"I spouted off?"

"Not a delicate way of putting it, I suppose, but it fits. You always managed to be solemn and stern when you laid down rules for me in Boston, Max. You read the riot act like a champion, never raising your voice, never showing any emotion, just straightening me out and putting me in my place."

"I did *that?*" he asked, searching his mind for one single instance that would match her description. And then he thought of the night of their last society event, a party given to entertain business associates, just a week before she'd left the big house.

"You need to wear something a bit more dignified, Faith." He'd held out his mother's diamond necklace and then retrieved it at Faith's look of abject horror. *"Put on your black taffeta dress and I'll fasten this around your neck."*

"I thought this looked more like a party. I needed something to cheer me up." And she'd stood before him in a flowered gown, a spring blossom ready to face a roomful of society's finest crop of women, all of them garbed, no doubt, in dark, dignified black or navy.

"My mother asked that you look the part tonight."

Faith had tilted her chin and nodded, then returned to

the wardrobe where dresses his mother had chosen for her were arrayed. She'd changed into an ornate, ruffled black gown that had enveloped her like a shroud and made her look like a corpse without a coffin.

He closed his eyes now, remembering the starkly pale look of her, the stricken eyes that refused to meet his and felt again the shudder that had enveloped her as he'd placed the heavy diamond necklace around her throat and then bent to place a soft kiss against her temple.

"There's a good girl."

Max opened his eyes, guilt washing over him in a tide that threatened to drown him. "My God." The words were a whisper, a prayer, he supposed. Perhaps even a plea for forgiveness as he recalled in stark detail the events of that last evening they'd spent in company.

"What is it?" she asked, anxious now, leaning toward him as he felt a chill take possession of his body. "Max? You look so strange."

"No," he said quickly. "I'm fine. Just thinking about something."

"It must have been a very bad memory," she said quietly. "You looked absolutely ill for a moment there."

"It was," he said tightly. And then he took her hand. "Can we drop this whole thing for a little while, Faith. Let's go fix breakfast and sit together and talk about something we can agree on for a half hour or so."

She looked up at him, her smile dubious as if she wondered at his sanity. "Are you sure you're all right? I didn't mean to make you sound so sour and dignified when I said that about..." Her words trailed off as he shook his head and attempted a grin.

"It's all right. You rang a bell, sweetheart, and I didn't like hearing it. But I need to think about it a bit, and then we'll talk."

"You don't have to worry," she said quickly as he set off for the house, pacing through the barn, towing her at his side. "I wasn't going to throw you out."

She was smiling at him. The woman he'd trampled into a shell of her former, glowing self that night three years ago was smiling up at him. She should be aiming her rifle in his direction and sending him out of her life, but for some unknown reason, he was being given a second chance.

"Thank you," he said. "I really didn't want to leave today. I have plans for helping you with the garden this afternoon. I thought you could show me the difference between the weeds and vegetables, and I'd help you sort things out."

It was the best he could come up with at the moment, and from the puzzled look on her face, he guessed it was distracting her from the fuss they'd managed to create.

"You're being too obliging, Max." She trotted at his side now, and he slowed his pace. "I'm not sure I know you when you're acting like this."

"Well, you already said something along that line, didn't you? Maybe we'd better begin at the beginning and make a fresh start, Faith."

"A fresh start?" She climbed the steps to the porch, and whirled to face him. He'd managed to get to the second step, and they were almost at eye level.

He couldn't resist. His body was still craving hers and with this vision of golden hair shining in the sunlight, blue eyes that glittered and a face that beamed a smile in his direction, he stood no chance of turning temptation aside.

His mouth sought hers, even as his hands touched her waist, not grasping, but holding her erect. The kiss was warm, damp and perfect, as were the full, wide lips that spoke his name with a gasp of surprise.

"Max! What was that for?"

He thought she was a bit stunned, certainly surprised at the sudden change in his demeanor. "I felt like it," he said, lifting her to one side as he opened the screened door. He bowed his head, waving one hand to usher her inside.

Faith awoke well after midnight, sitting up in bed with a start. What had wakened her was not readily apparent, but she rose quickly, trusting her instincts. Outside her window Wolf was whining, the pleading sounds interspersed by sharp yaps. From beyond her bedroom door, she heard footsteps—boots if she was any judge—and then a quick, hard rapping on the wooden panel that announced Max's presence.

He opened it, calling her name as he did so, his voice low and husky, as if he'd just awakened and hadn't yet used his vocal cords. "Faith? Something's going on outside. The dog's having a fit."

"I'm up," she said, quickly stripping off her nightgown and pulling her discarded dress over her head. She drew up a pair of drawers beneath it and shoved her feet into her house shoes. Max was in the doorway, his eyes intent on her and she snatched at her brush, pulling it through her hair and then tying it with a kerchief so that it hung down her back in a tail reminiscent of her mare's in color and length.

"Get a shawl or sweater," Max said. "It's chilly out there."

"It won't be cold in the barn," she told him, but nodded in agreement, reaching for her shawl as she ran through the kitchen.

"Did you think she was ready before we went to bed last night?" Max asked, gripping Faith's elbow as they raced across the yard.

She shook her head, unable to speak. The dog ran beside them, silent now that his humans were awake and aware of the disturbance in the barn. ''What woke you?'' she asked Max.

''I don't know. I thought at first you had called me. Then I realized it was a noise from outside. The dog was whining.'' He pushed the barn doors open and plunged into the darkness. ''I'll get the lantern,'' he told her.

Faith stepped carefully, aware of the rustle of straw and the sounds of her mare straining and whuffling in the confines of the standing stall. ''I need to get her out of there,'' she said. ''But first, I want the other horses out in the pasture.''

''All right,'' Max said. The lantern was lit, the globe replaced, and he hung it high over the aisle behind the stalls. ''She's down,'' he told Faith. ''Damn. There isn't enough room in that stall for the mare, let alone either one of us to help her.''

He released the other three horses from their stalls and led them to the back door, then outside and through the corral. The glow from the barn lit a path for him to travel and within minutes he'd turned the animals loose in the pasture and returned to Faith.

''She's trying to get up,'' Faith told him. ''Help me get her on her feet.''

''Not as easy as it sounds,'' Max muttered, climbing over the side wall of the stall to join Faith at the animal's head. She'd fastened a second rope to the mare's halter, and Max grasped it, then tossed it over the wall and climbed back to the adjoining stall.

''Don't let her get on top of you,'' he told Faith, worry lacing his words with a harsh note.

''Just pull,'' she told him, lifting the mare's head from

the barn floor and then standing atop the manger as the animal struggled to get to her feet.

With a loud whinny, the golden creature got her front feet beneath her, struggled to find purchase on the straw-covered floor with her hind legs, then backed from the narrow enclosure to the wider aisle.

''That's got it,'' Max called out, scrambling to stand beside the mare as she swayed on her feet. He grabbed a pitchfork and tossed a small mountain of straw about the area and within moments the mare was down again, but this time in a space large enough for both Max and Faith to work in.

''What can we do?'' he asked, kneeling beside the horse, one hand rubbing the mare's side in a distracted movement.

''Nothing, for now,'' Faith said. ''Just watch her and see if things are going to happen the way they should.''

''What do we look for?'' he asked, and she heard the note of helplessness he made no attempt to conceal. ''I haven't the faintest idea what I'm doing here, sweetheart. But if you'll tell me what to do, I'll help you.''

As he spoke, a gush of fluid flooded the floor behind the mare's body, and Faith smiled at him. ''You might want to toss a little more straw over that for starters. This is a messy business, Max. Are you sure you want to be involved?''

''Do you think for one minute I'd leave you here alone with her?'' he asked. ''Not on your life, lady.'' He eased down behind the mare and placed his hands on her heaving side. ''Have you ever done this before?'' he asked.

''I watched a colt be born a couple of years ago in this barn, before Lin and Nicholas moved here. It went like clockwork. But then that mare had had several foals, and *she* at least knew what was happening.'' Faith rubbed her mare between her ears, and her voice softened. ''This one is new at the job.''

''What's her name?'' Max asked. ''It seems as if we should be calling her something. Or haven't you named her?''

Faith glared at him. ''Of course I have. I call her Goldie.''

He grinned. ''Makes sense to me. I couldn't have come up with a more appropriate name myself.'' He looked down at the straining horse, and his mouth pressed into a thin line. ''I've always wondered how animals in the wild survive this sort of thing. If something goes wrong and they're all alone...''

''Sometimes they don't survive,'' Faith said. ''Even cattle ranches lose a number of cows and calves every year.''

''What goes wrong?'' he asked.

''The baby is supposed to emerge front legs first, with the head between them,'' Faith told him. ''If things don't go right, it might be butt first, or upside down.''

''Well, I'm counting on this lady making this easy for us,'' he said quietly. ''What does the stud look like?'' he added. ''Are you pretty much guaranteed to have a colt with the coloring you want?''

''That's the odd part about this whole thing,'' she said. ''In order to get another golden or cream-colored foal from the mare, you have to use a sorrel for breeding. If you use a stud of the same color as my mare, you could very well end up with an albino.''

Max shook his head. ''Did you find out all this yourself, or did your neighbor do the digging? Where did he find a suitable horse to breed?''

''Nicholas found a sorrel stallion in Oklahoma,'' she answered. ''He had him shipped on the train.'' Her smile widened. ''The railroad car may never be the same. That stud didn't like being confined that way, and had a fit. By the time Nicholas got him out into daylight, there was hell to pay. The man assigned to travel with the horse was banged up and the stall was torn to smithereens.''

''Weren't you worried about your mare when you introduced the two of them?'' The thought of Faith working with a wild stallion in a confined breeding area was enough to make Max's heart stall.

''Nicholas handled most of it,'' she said. ''Brace helped him and they were careful to see that the mare was safe.''

''You weren't there?'' The thought of Faith participating in such a deed was beyond his imagination. It was something any well-bred young woman would shrink from. But then, Faith had managed to overcome most of the restrictions her former life had imposed, it seemed. Probably helping to breed her mare wouldn't faze her.

She shook her head. ''I stayed in the house with Lin. Nicholas didn't want any interference, and Lin tends to be vocal at times. And he wanted to be certain that their little girl, Amanda, was nowhere around.''

''But Lin did as he asked?''

''I suppose the idea of Brace being there put us both off a bit,'' Faith admitted. ''There's something about the process that seems more suited to the male temperament.''

Silently, he agreed. He'd heard that stallions were lusty creatures, certainly not averse to violent behavior, should they be thwarted in their pursuit of a mare.

''I think we're in for a long wait,'' Faith said quietly. ''She doesn't seem to be making much progress, does she?'' Her hands were moving against the mare's head and neck, petting and stroking as she spoke, her words soft and coaxing, aimed at keeping the animal calm. ''We'll give her a while before we do anything else.''

Yet it seemed the mare was not about to cooperate, her

body convulsing in one long contraction after another with no progress evident. When an hour had passed and Faith had been as patient as her concern would allow, she moved to the rear of her horse and grasped the tail, braiding it quickly and tying it so that it no longer hung in the way.

"I'm going to have to go in and see what's happening," she said. "Will you return to the house and get the bucket of lard from the pantry?"

"Lard?" Max asked, rising slowly. "What are you going to do?"

"Grease down my arm and hand and see if I can figure out what's wrong."

"Inside the mare?" he asked, his voice incredulous.

"Can you think of a better method of helping her?" Faith looked up at him, and he grimaced. Her forehead was lined with concern and her brow was damp with perspiration, yet her hands were gentle on the mare, her voice soothing as the animal struggled to rid herself of the burden she carried.

"All right." Max hurried out the barn door, leaving the door open behind him. Faith watched as he trotted across the yard, heard the screened door slam behind him as he entered the kitchen, and in less than a minute watched his return.

She knelt beside her horse, rolled her sleeves above her elbows and then dipped her hand into the pail of lard, spreading the white grease thickly over her right arm. "I'll reach inside and see if I can find the problem," she said quietly. "Can you hold her still? I don't want to take a chance on my arm being broken if she tries to get away from me."

Max felt his heart stutter and then resume its normal pace. She said it so calmly, seemed so matter-of-fact, as if this were an everyday event, this aiding in the delivery of a foal. He tried for a fleeting moment to equate this slender, wiry woman with the soft, elegant female he'd married six years before, and saw no resemblance between them.

Faith was a product of the life she'd lived over the past three years, a sturdy, capable creature who feared nothing so much as losing her mare. Not even the threat of a broken arm caused her to hesitate in the job she faced.

Max nodded in agreement, then offered her a choice. "If you think it would work better, I can try it," he said. "My arm is longer than yours and I'm stronger."

"Let me give it a shot," she said, "and if I can't reach the foal, you can try."

She watched closely as the mare whinnied quietly, then lying on her side, her face a mask of concentration, she pushed her hand deep into the mare's body.

Her eyes widened and she bit at her lip, then her gaze swept up to meet Max's. "There's one leg coming down, Max. I don't think I can reach far enough to push it back and grab both of them together."

"I'll do it," he said, hesitating not at all, relieved, in fact, if the truth were known, to see Faith's arm appear, her hand intact.

He rolled up his sleeve, and greased his arm, Faith helping as he coated his skin liberally with the lard. Blood and mucus stained her dress, and she had never looked so far from the pristine woman he'd lived with in Boston. She moved from her place behind the mare to crawl forward until she cradled the great, golden head against herself, her whispers and cajoling murmurs catching the horse's attention.

Again the mare strained and Max reached inside, locating a tiny hoof and spindly leg. He pushed gently against the extended limb, felt it withdraw farther up the birth canal, and followed it, groaning as the mare's muscles clamped down on his arm. She strained harder, and he groped with fingers extended for the slender, fragile legs that must emerge first, lest the mare die without giving birth.

There. He closed his eyes, both hooves in his hand, drawing them forward, easing his arm back from the mare's body. He pulled with a steady, hard grip on the tiny, fragile bones, and the mare whinnied, a shrill sound that rang among the rafters of the barn.

"Max?" Faith called his name, and he grunted a reply.

"Got him," he said, the words a guttural sound of triumph as he delivered the miniature creature onto the soiled straw. "He's out, Faith."

And indeed the baby was born. A replica of the mare, it drew breath, trembled with the effort and struggled to stand.

"It's not a he," Faith said quickly. "We've got a filly, Max. A girl." She knelt, leaning back on her heels. "And the color is good."

"Isn't she a little dark?" he asked. "Or is that just because she's wet?" He leaned closer. "What do we do about the cord that's attached?"

"I think Goldie will tend to it," Faith said quietly. "We'll give her a chance anyway before we do anything about it." And then they watched as the mare nuzzled her newborn and nosed over the entire length of the foal until she found the pale cord that had been its lifeline during the long months past. Her teeth nipped sharply at the limp, ropy length and it fell to the floor.

"Amazing." The single word was all Max could speak aloud as he watched the natural instinct of the mare respond to the birth of her foal. Goldie snorted and whinnied again, and with a stiffening of her whole body, expelled the sodden afterbirth upon the straw. She ignored it then and returned to the inspection of her offspring.

Faith snatched up a towel from a stack she kept close at

hand. "I'll dry her off so she doesn't take a chill. And I think her color will lighten up in a few weeks or months."

"Well, she's a beauty, I'd say," Max breathed quietly. "Not that I know a whole lot about the breed, but I'd say you managed to produce a winner for Nicholas. He should be happy with her." He looked up at Faith as she rubbed vigorously at the wobbly filly. "Was he hoping for a colt?"

She shook her head. "No, he'd like to establish his own breeding program. This should make him happy. Now he'll have to locate another stud, though. I doubt he'll want to breed back to the same stallion."

"How about you? Are you interested in a breeding program?"

She shook her head. "No, I'd like to have a colt from Goldie, but raising horses is too big a job for a woman alone. I have my hands full just keeping ends together here."

"Well, at least you recognize your limitations," he said. "I'd probably be filled with grand ideas about having a whole pasture full of these beautiful creatures."

Goldie staggered to her feet, her flanks shuddering with effort. Faith stood quickly, touched the mare's quivering side and whispered soft words of encouragement, and then watched as the new mother turned to her foal.

"Well, there's no guarantee that I'd get a perfect colt each time," Faith said after a moment. "It's a gamble, but the chances are good that the next breeding will work out the same way this one did," she told him, stepping back as the mare nuzzled her daughter. "Nonetheless, Goldie going through this twice is all I'm planning on. I'll be content with that." And then her attention was caught as the mare nickered softly as the gangly filly got her legs beneath her.

"Does she know enough to nurse?" Max asked, enjoying the picture that played out before them. He'd never been privy to such a thrilling event, and recognizing his own contribution somehow made it even more exciting.

"Just watch her," Faith said. And sure enough, the newborn's nostrils widened as if she scented the life-giving milk that was even now leaking from the mare's bag. Her long neck bent in an ungainly pose as the filly twisted to investigate the source of the aroma she sought, and within moments she was suckling noisily. All four legs spraddled wide, giving her a fairly firm foundation, and she set to nursing with a will.

Faith laughed softly. "I feel like we've been in the presence of a miracle, Max."

She had squatted beside the filly, watching closely as the baby discovered her mother's milk, and now Faith looked up at him. Her hair was tangled and had a fair amount of straw caught in its length. Her clothing was stained by birth fluids and her arms were coated with the residue of lard and blood.

She was altogether a mess, Max thought, and yet she was blessed with a glow of accomplishment that overshadowed her disarray, lending her a patina of beauty that superceded the dirt and grime of the past hours.

Within him, he felt the rise of an emotion he did not recognize. Not desire or passion, for those were familiar to him. But instead, a warmer, more alluring excitement that had to do with the whole woman. It was not her beauty alone that attracted him, he decided, although there was a certain amount of appeal in that.

Rather, he was taken by the strength and wisdom she had attained over the past years, by the purpose in her every action. Faith was a woman to be admired. And beyond that, a woman to be won, no matter the cost.

And if it took every bit of stamina he owned, every dollar

he had managed to stockpile in his accounts, every iota of intelligence he possessed, he would assail the fort of her stubborn willfulness and storm the walls of her defenses until he prevailed.

The woman didn't stand a chance.

Chapter Six

Nicholas sat atop the sorrel stallion, his hat pulled low over his forehead. From all signs, he'd just arrived, and Faith looked up at him, weariness gripping her with talons that caused her to wince in the sunlight. Her neighbor frowned, and then in less time than it would have taken to greet her with a wave of his hand, he stood before her. One gloved hand rose and he touched her face with his index finger.

In a quick movement, he doffed the leather coverings and tucked them in his belt, then looked beyond her to the open barn door. "What does the other guy look like?" he asked, not a trace of humor lacing his words. He bent to peer into Faith's face. "Is that blood?" he asked, his words rasping.

She nodded. "Probably. But then, along with everything else I'm covered in, a little blood doesn't seem to matter, does it?" She yawned widely and Nicholas looked confused. That same index finger touched her arm, and withdrew to rub off the grease against the side of his denim trousers.

"What the hell is going on here?" he asked bluntly. "Are you hurt, Faith? And where's Max?"

"Right behind you," Max answered.

Nicholas spun to face the other man, and his back stiffened. "Hell, you don't look much better than she does. What did the two of you do? Have a war?"

Max grinned, nodding. "You might say that. And we won, too."

"We?" Nicholas turned back to Faith, his eyes registering his confusion. One finger tipped back his hat and Faith took pity on him.

"You have a filly, Nicholas. We've been busy delivering the prettiest little golden foal you've ever seen."

"We?" Nicholas repeated the word again, his attention veering from Faith to the man who had stepped around him to hand her a bucket of water.

"It's not hot, but warm enough, I think," he said. "I'll go in and get you some clothes out of the wicker basket. All right?"

She nodded and placed the bucket on a stump just outside the barn door and then lifted her skirt a bit to rub at her arms, removing the layer of lard covering her skin.

Nicholas folded his arms over his chest and eyed her grimly. "When do I get to hear this story?" he asked, and then his expression lightened a bit. "And just when do I get to see my filly?"

Faith grinned up at him, then peered into the bucket, then fished out a small bar of soap. "Go on in if you like," she said, "but you might want to know that Max is the hero of the day. He pulled your filly after I had to admit defeat. My arm wasn't long enough to do the job."

"The mare had problems?" Nicholas asked, watching as Faith soaped her hands and arms generously. She lifted suds to her face and scrubbed, then rinsed in the bucket. Another sudsing followed and finally she looked up, blinking water droplets from her eyelashes.

"I'll say. One foot was presenting and Max was able to return it, then grasp both hooves and deliver the filly."

"First time I've ever played the midwife," Max said cheerfully from behind Nicholas, and once more the neighbor was forced to turn to acknowledge the man.

"You have my thanks," he said, albeit a bit grudgingly. "Something told me to ride over here this morning. Guess my instincts were on target."

"Go on in and meet your girl," Faith said, inspecting her arms and frowning. And then she looked up at Max and grinned. "I may never get all this lard off, you know."

"Give it one more scrub," he recommended easily. "I brought out more warm water for you." A wrinkled dress was tossed over his shoulder and she nodded her thanks.

The bar of soap was pressed into use once more, and she managed to produce a thick layer of suds that gave promise of removing the rest of the lard. "Here, I'll rinse for you," Max offered, pouring the clean water over her outstretched hands and arms. It splashed on her dress, and his gaze narrowed as the outline of her body beneath became apparent.

Nicholas opened the barn door after one short glance in her direction, and Faith subdued a grin. Her neighbor was a gentleman to the core. Given the fact that her state of grubbiness was fast giving way to the danger of her more feminine parts being on display, he was wisely disappearing within the shadows of the barn.

Max seemed to have no problem with the clinging dress she wore, surveying her openly. "When Nicholas comes out, you can change your dress in one of the stalls," he suggested. "That old one isn't worth washing. I'll toss it on the burn pile."

She looked down at herself and grimaced. "You're right." And then looked up as Nicholas reappeared from the barn. "What do you think?"

He looked directly at Max and held out his hand, not seeming to be concerned by the collection of stains that wide palm had gathered throughout the early morning hours. "I owe you, McDowell. She's a beauty."

Faith slipped behind him into the barn, carrying the dress Max had snatched from her wash basket. It was a simple matter to strip off her soiled garment and slip into the wrinkled dress that had been awaiting the ironing board. She was far from clean, but at least decent enough to go in the house and cook breakfast while Max tended to his own washing up.

"See if there's enough warm water left in the reservoir, would you?" he asked as she dumped the dirty water with a splash to one side of the barn. "I'll wait on the porch."

"All right," she agreed, then headed for the house, calling over her shoulder as an afterthought. "Would you like to join us for breakfast, Nicholas?"

"Nicholas said he needed to head for home," Max said, finally rid of the layers of lard and the messy residue of the filly's delivery. He stood at the back door, shirtless and obviously unwilling to enter the kitchen.

"Could you find me a pair of trousers, Faith?" he asked. "I don't want to sit on the chair like this."

She nodded and set aside the skillet she held. "The eggs are about ready. I'll pull the bread from the oven and be right with you." A folded dish towel in her hand, she nudged the sliced bread from the oven rack onto a plate and set it in the warming oven, then turned to the hallway and hurried to the room where Max spent his nights.

His clothing was neatly arrayed in the dresser drawer, and she chose a pair of trousers and a clean shirt for his use, then carried them back to where he waited. "I'll turn around if you want to change here," she offered.

Busying herself at the stove, she heard the rustle of his clothing, then the distinct clunk of boots being dropped out the door onto the back porch. Giving him a few more moments of privacy, she filled two plates with the eggs, added two pieces of toasted bread to each and lifted bacon from the second skillet on the back of the stove.

"Ready for this?" she asked, her gaze averted as she turned to the table.

"Well, I may not be clean clear through, but I'm a sight better looking than I was fifteen minutes ago," Max said, sliding into his chair and reaching for the plate she held.

"I'll get the coffee," she offered, reaching for cups from the kitchen cabinet, and she felt his gaze touch her as she lowered her arms, a cup in each hand. He was leaning back in his chair, his eyes narrowed assessingly, and she felt a distinct measure of discomfort. "You're watching me," she said.

"I watch you frequently," he answered, lifting his fork with a casual gesture. "You're well worth my attention, Faith." He accepted the cup of coffee she brought him and sipped at it briefly before placing it by his plate. "I'm constantly amazed at your beauty." And then he shook his head.

"No, *beauty* isn't the right word." His gaze touched her again and she was warmed by the admiration in his eyes. "I don't know the words to describe what I see when I look at you. You're lovelier than any other female I've ever known."

She laughed and took a bite of her scrambled eggs. "Well," she said after chewing slowly, "that's either a compliment designed to get on my good side, or you're going blind."

"Neither." His movements matched hers as he quietly and steadily ate the pile of eggs she'd cooked for him.

''You're right, though, in one sense. A compliment is usually issued for the purpose of flattery, but I'm aware you don't have the need for that. It was the truth, and my vision is top-notch, sweetheart.''

He looked up, catching her gaze, and his own radiated a sincerity she could not doubt. ''Even in that wrinkled dress, and with shadows under your eyes from lack of sleep, you radiate an inner beauty that leaves me stunned sometimes.''

She shot him a quick look and tilted her head, as if assessing his words. ''You've never looked stunned, so far as I can remember.''

''Believe it or not, sweetheart, you take my breath away sometimes.'' He tore his toast in half and glanced toward the cabinet, a smile touching his lips as he changed the subject. ''Is the jam over there or in the pantry?''

''The pantry,'' she said, and began to rise from her chair. His outstretched hand halted her and he was on his feet.

''I'll get it.''

She felt his gaze on her as he walked behind her chair, knew the moment he returned. And then his hand touched her shoulder and he leaned past her to place the jam jar on the table before her. His scent was in her nostrils, the smell of soap and just a hint of hay and straw, and the muted aroma of male flesh.

Her breath caught in her throat and she grew still beneath his touch. He bent, and his mouth pressed against her temple, then slid to her cheek, his lips warm and damp, yet at the same time cool against her skin. And how that could be was a question she was not up to solving.

''This is the truth, Faith. You stun me sometimes, just looking at you, watching your eyes shine, your hair gleam in the sunlight.'' He sighed and chuckled softly. ''But that wasn't what I meant to say just now. I'd thought to thank you,'' he said, his words a quiet murmur.

''For what?'' she asked, unable to move, lest he step away and leave her wanting more.

''For allowing me to be with you in the barn, for sharing the birth of your foal with me. For giving me the credit in front of Nicholas. You didn't have to do that, and it offered me a little more stature in his eyes, something I need right now.''

She turned her head and his mouth touched hers, a soft kiss without passion, a brush of lips that spoke only of this moment between them, asking nothing more than her compliance. ''You saved the filly's life and possibly—no, probably—that of my mare,'' she said as he lifted his hand from her shoulder and paced around the table to sit again across from her. ''I owe you, Max.''

''No.'' He lifted his fork and shook his head.

It was a simple refusal of her debt to him, and she considered him for a moment, pulling her toast into small bits. ''You won't accept my thanks?''

''I accept your thanks, but not your obligation to me. You owe me nothing, Faith. What you give me has to be of your free will and because you find in me something worth your affection and friendship.''

''Affection and friendship.'' She repeated the two words and considered them. ''I didn't know you wanted my friendship,'' she said finally.

''More than you know.'' He ate the final bits of eggs and spread jam with a lavish hand on his remaining piece of toast. ''I feel like I've started over in my courtship of you during the past days. And the one part I left out of our original relationship was that of being your friend.''

''I never felt smart enough or experienced enough to meet you at that level,'' she said. ''You were an intelligent man of business, with people surrounding you who flocked to your side and listened to every word you spoke.''

He had the grace to look uncomfortable with that analysis, and shook his head.

"It's true, Max. I looked on like an orphan at a family picnic sometimes. I couldn't begin to know what you spoke about, and I was too awed to ask the questions I should have in order to learn." Her shrug expressed the sadness she felt as she recalled those moments in the past.

"And then when we were together, you were more interested in my..." Unable to speak the words, she chose rather to shrug again.

"Your body? Making love to you?" His eyes were filled with another message, as if he, too, recalled those moments. "I always wanted you, Faith, but it was sometimes almost a desperate need for you after one of our evenings in company. You were so lovely, looking almost untouched, and the men watched you with looks that made me jealous. Yet at the same time, I knew I was going to take you to bed, and I felt the luckiest of all the males that surrounded me."

"The men watched me?" She felt sudden surprise at the thought. "I was probably the least experienced, least appealing woman of our social circle," she said flatly. "I doubt I inspired much lust in anyone." Her glance touched him then and she smiled faintly. "Except you, perhaps."

"Your youth and naive behavior made you attractive to those men who had seen and tasted women with experience, women who knew the rules in society and flitted from one man to another."

"Most of them were married," she said. "How..."

He smiled, but it was a poignant one, and failed to reach his expressive eyes. "Marriage is a commodity in society, Faith. Men marry for reasons other than love, as do women."

She stood and reached for his plate, then turned to the sink and the dishpan that held a residue of water. The plates were rinsed quickly and the water sloshed into the sink, which drained out the side of the house into the soil. And then she turned back to him, her hands clutching the sink on either side of her.

"Why did you marry me, Max?" Suddenly the reason was important, and she waited, holding her breath as he considered her query.

"If you're asking me whether or not I loved you, I have to plead no contest, Faith. I wanted you badly. I knew the only way I'd get you in my bed was by way of a wedding ring, and so I asked you to marry me. I was too selfish to think about love." His jaw firmed as he leaned back in his chair.

"I never even considered whether or not you loved me," he continued. "And that was my first mistake. Looking back, I should have known you couldn't have given yourself to me so generously had you not felt a deep emotion for me."

"I loved you," she admitted. "I've already told you that."

"And now?" he asked, his mouth flattening into a thin line as if he awaited news that would not be pleasing.

She shrugged and turned away. "Now I don't know how I feel about you. I like you better than I did three years ago, but that's not too difficult to admit. I didn't like you at all the night I left."

The teakettle was full of hot water at the back of the stove and she lifted it with both hands, protected by a dish towel, lest she be burned by the metal handle. The steaming water poured over the dishes she'd placed in the dishpan, and the dollop of soap she'd added bubbled up into suds. With deft movements, she returned the teakettle to the stove, and then pumped twice to release a flow of cold water into the pan.

Max sat at the table, his countenance dark, as if he were digesting her words. And she felt a nudge of guilt as she considered her statement. It was not complete, and fairness decreed she must speak the truth with this man.

"You're a different man these days than you were then, Max," she conceded. "I like you better because you're more willing to talk to me, because you treat me almost as an equal. And that's something you never did during our marriage."

"Almost?" He snagged onto the one word she'd used to qualify her statement. "I didn't generally treat you as my equal?"

"I wasn't your equal," she stated smoothly. "You were smarter, more suave and sophisticated, more knowledgeable than I about almost everything in our lives. I was a dummy. I did what you told me, tried to get along with your mother and rarely succeeded at either task."

His eyes darkened as he spoke, his words harsh. "My mother. I think we might as well get her out of the way, Faith. If what you say about her is the truth, as you perceive it, then she was a real problem in our marriage."

"It isn't *as I perceive it,* Max. The day you come to realize that your mother felt I was unworthy of you and your attentions is the day we may be able to come to an understanding." She scrubbed at a plate that was already clean, and set it aside for rinsing. Her heart was thumping unmercifully in her chest as she remembered the days of submission to the woman who had found it necessary, on a daily basis, to put her son's wife on probation.

"Can we talk about something else?" Faith finally asked, setting aside the second plate and picking up the silverware.

Max was beside her, teakettle in hand, pouring the water with care over the plates, rinsing off the residue of suds.

He returned the kettle to the stove and picked up the dishes and dried them, a meticulous performance that caught her attention.

"You don't need to help me with these," she said.

"Yes, I think I do," he answered, taking the pieces of silverware from her and rinsing them as he had the plates. They were dried and replaced in the drawer where she kept them, and then he waited while she cleaned and wiped out the skillets. Soap did not touch the cast-iron surfaces, and when she was finished, she placed them upside down on the stove to dry.

"You can hang the towel on the line," she said, turning to wash the oilcloth on the table. Then she watched as he walked out onto the porch, her gaze caught by the long line of his back, the muscles that flexed as he lifted his arms to pin the dish towel to the rope stretched between two posts.

His hips were lean, his legs muscular. Even with the fabric covering his body, she remembered only too well the masculine form of the man beneath his clothing. His hair hung a bit long over his collar, and she thought of the nights she had threaded her fingers through those dark locks, remembered the thrilling touch of his long fingers that had brought pleasure to her with unstinting generosity.

He turned from the rope line and opened the screened door, crossing the threshold and blinking in the relatively dim light of the kitchen. "Anything else I need to do?" he asked. "If not, I'll check on the other horses and give the mare some hay and a bit of feed from the barrel. Do we need to pen up the filly?"

Faith walked toward him and lifted her hands to his shoulders, and he became as a statue before her, his eyes narrowing as he bent his head to look deeply into her gaze.

"What's wrong?" he asked quietly.

"Nothing. I just wanted to touch you. May I?"

His nod was slow, his breath hitching as if he found it difficult to inhale properly. ''Feel free to put your hands on me anytime you like,'' he said roughly, and then waited, watching her as if his very breath depended on her next move.

She touched his hair, ruffling it a bit and smiling. ''I need to trim this a little,'' she murmured, her fingers easing through the dark strands and clasping his head. She lifted herself on tiptoes and pressed her mouth against his, a brief touch of lips that spread warmth throughout her body.

''I was remembering,'' she said, as if an explanation was due. And perhaps it was. Fairness decreed that she not take advantage of his good nature, and yet she was enjoying these brief moments of control, as his hands clenched at his sides and he stood before her, a ruddy line across his cheekbones revealing the effect she had on him.

''I always liked it when you kissed me,'' she said. ''I'd almost forgotten how it felt to have you that close to me, to inhale your scent and know that you wanted me.''

''Like now?'' he asked, and his voice was harsh. His jaw firmed and she thought his teeth clenched. ''You're pushing it, Faith,'' he said after a moment. ''I'm not sure how long I can keep my hands from you.''

''Right now, I don't want to be just your friend,'' she told him. ''Yet I think, on the other hand, maybe I need to know that you like more about me than my…'' She looked down to where her breasts formed soft peaks beneath the fabric of her dress. Before her eyes, the crests became taut and hard, and she felt the sharp inhalation of breath he could not conceal.

''You're handing me a puzzle to unravel, you know. I'm not sure what you want of me,'' he said, and lifted his hands to circle her waist. ''I know what I'd like to give you, but I don't think you'll allow that yet.''

"You've given me much today," she said, rising again on her tiptoes to press her mouth against his, this time opening her lips to lend her breath to his. "I just want you to know that what we shared in the barn was important to me. Not only what you did for my mare and the filly," she said, "but that you were willing to crawl amid the dirt and blood and subject yourself to the pain of having your arm clamped by Goldie's straining. Because you saw a need and jumped in without hesitation."

He returned her kiss, his lips parting to deepen the caress, yet his hands only clutched at her waist, and she felt his restraint. She closed her eyes as he nibbled at her mouth, as his tongue tasted the soft tissue beyond her lips, and then she leaned against him, turning her face upward.

"Faith." It was a single word of warning, and she jolted in his grasp, standing upright as he removed his mouth from hers, his hands from her waist. "I'm going outside," he told her. "If I stay here, I fear you'll be angry at my next move."

She hesitated, then nodded, acknowledging his choice. Sharing a bed with Max would solve nothing today, only confuse her more. And she'd had about all the dithering she could handle for one morning. She'd been unfair, approaching him and expecting him to accept her kiss and not reciprocate. Yet he'd obliged her, only calling a halt when he deemed it necessary.

Stepping back from him, she watched as he turned away, heard the screened door slam as he released it from his grasp, and then her gaze followed him as he strode across the yard to fling the barn door open with a sharp movement.

The man was strung higher than a kite, she decided, and she'd done it to him. Yet he'd walked away, something the old Max, back in Boston, would never have done. He'd have felt the need to conquer, the necessity to stake his claim had she ever approached him in such a manner.

There was no doubt about it. Max had changed.

The mare and filly were in the corral and Max was hard at work, opening two single stalls to form a larger pen in the barn. Faith watched from the doorway, her eyes on his every movement as he ripped off the boards and piled them to one side.

"I thought it would be better if they had a larger stall," he said. "Maybe you'll want to fence off a smaller part of the pasture for them."

"No." She shook her head and walked closer to where he worked. "After a day or so, we can put them with the other horses. I just want to keep a close eye on Goldie, till tomorrow at least."

"She looked all right to me," Max said. His grin was quick. "Of course, I didn't really know what I was looking for, but there wasn't much blood or anything to be seen, and she seems to have plenty of milk for the filly."

"Too bad humans don't recuperate as quickly as animals when they give birth," Faith said dryly. "It takes a few days to recover when a woman—" She broke off as his gaze intensified on her, and she laughed a bit, embarrassed as she considered the topic of conversation. "I don't suppose you want to hear a discourse on reproduction, do you?"

"That didn't bother me," he told her. "I was just remembering the day you gave birth to our son." He tossed the broken board he held to one side, and straightened. "I don't think I appreciated what you'd gone through. As I recall, you were all cleaned up and the baby was wrapped in a blanket when I finally made my appearance in the bedroom. You must have thought me uncaring, not to have been with you."

"Your mother said it wasn't seemly for a husband to see his wife that way." For just a moment Faith regretted the clipped sound of her words, and then her chin lifted in defiance of the absent woman's edict. "I wanted you beside me, but I didn't have enough gumption to ask the doctor to get you."

"My mother..." Max spoke the words quietly, then shook his head. "She told me it would be best to leave you alone with the doctor and his nurse. Said I would embarrass you with my presence." He looked beyond Faith, out the open barn door to where the sun shone on the trees and bushes around the house. "I listened to her, more's the pity. And never knew what I missed out on."

"Don't hit yourself over the head, Max," Faith told him quietly. "Most men wouldn't have been caught within fifty feet of a room where a woman was giving birth."

"I had no such compunction about being with you when I got you in that condition," he told her bluntly. "I owed it to you to be with you when the baby was born. Just one more time I missed the boat."

Faith felt a jolt of compassion for the man. He was hurting. Even as he saw things in a different light, he was having to reevaluate his mother and her place in their existence, and the pain of his discovery was there to be seen on the stern, fixed features set in a grim mask.

"I've long since forgiven you for that," Faith said.

His gaze lifted to hers. "As I said before, you're a generous woman. And for that, I'll be eternally grateful."

She walked to his side and eyed the mess he was making of her stalls. "Well, let's forget it for now," she told him. "I'll give you a hand and we'll have this ready for the mare in no time flat."

He nodded, pulling another board off and she took it, then carried it to the stack he'd accumulated. One by one, she toted them out the door of the barn to toss them on the burn pile, a safe fifty feet or so from the structure. In half an hour, he'd accomplished his purpose and had sorted through the straw to collect any forgotten nails. The edges of the boards were sanded off with a stray bit of sandpaper he'd found in her toolbox, and together they viewed the results.

"I'll put together a gate for it," he said. "In the meantime, I think a rope will be enough of a deterrent to keep Goldie in, don't you?"

Faith nodded and tucked her hand through his arm. "We make a good team, Mr. McDowell."

He looked down at her and smiled. "Thank you, ma'am. I aim to please."

And you do, very much. The words were silent, but her heart was aware of the message as she returned his look. It thumped in her chest, and she was forced to look away, lest he see the emotion that spilled through.

She was in danger. And instead of fleeing from it, she was well on her way to embracing it openly.

They stood to the west of the pasture, where Max had decreed he should practice using Faith's rifle. The straw stack was almost down to rock bottom, but he'd decided it still would provide a backdrop for his shells to reside, without worry about them traveling into the woods and being deflected by the abundant trees.

Faith loaded the rifle and he watched, taken by the smooth gestures she employed, aware of her confidence as she handled the long gun. "Who taught you to shoot?" he asked.

"Brace," she answered, and Max was not surprised. It

seemed the man had been on hand more times than not as Faith adjusted to her life in this place. And yet Max saw no trace of any more than a deep, abiding affection for the lawman in Faith's demeanor. She'd welcomed him as a friend, and not allowed him to cross the line she'd drawn.

And the sheriff, gentleman that he obviously was, had accepted her limits and continued to bask in the warmth of her smile and her presence.

"You're very good at this," Max told her as she handed him the loaded gun.

"Thank you," she said, and smiled up into his face. "I've had to use it a few times."

"Have you?" He considered her a moment. "Ever shoot a man?" And then he waited for her denial.

Instead, he was more than a little surprised as her smile faded and she nodded in reply. "Yes, I shot and wounded a man over a year ago, when Lin and I were on our own for a bit and a couple of gunmen came here looking for her and Amanda."

"Amanda?" Max asked, wrinkling his forehead as he tried to place the name.

"She's actually Nicholas's niece, but she belongs to them legally now. Back then they were fighting for custody and Lin and I ended up in a gun battle with a couple of low-life ruffians from New York."

"You were lucky to come out of it alive," Max growled, aware that his heart thumped in a heavy rhythm and his chest was tight, as if a band were wrapped around him, not allowing him to draw a deep breath.

"Yes, we were, and I was thankful I'd been taught well how to fire this thing."

"Lin wasn't just trying to josh with me then, when she claimed to be right handy with a shotgun, was she?"

Faith shook her head. "No, she wasn't. She shot the

second gunman and took a bullet herself. I thought Nicholas would throttle the men with his bare hands. Probably would have if they hadn't already been bleeding like stuck pigs."

Max felt a cold chill creep up his spine. "I suppose I didn't think about you facing that kind of peril here," he said slowly. He lifted the gun to his shoulder and sighted down the long barrel.

"Squeeze gently," Faith said from beside him. "That thing has quite a kick, so don't give it a chance to bounce off your shoulder."

He aimed carefully, then squeezed the trigger, narrowing his gaze as the target he'd set up in front of the straw was torn asunder. "Well, I guess I'm not a total washout," he said with a feeling of satisfaction.

"Try it again," she told him. "Get used to it."

"It's really easier to hit a target with this than with a handgun," he told her after several more shots had effectively shredded the target.

"You have a better range," she said. "A handgun is only good close up. I feel better with my rifle in the house. I can pick off a bird on a limb halfway across the pasture if I want to."

"Sharpshooter." He looked down at her and felt a thrill of pride at her accomplishments. He'd married a young woman of society, albeit an orphan with but a single, younger brother living, plus the aunt and uncle they'd both lived with. At the time, Max had thought himself a Sir Galahad of sorts. Now he viewed her with different eyes and recognized she'd become a woman to be respected.

"Thank you for the lesson," he said, bending his head a bit, as if he bowed to her greater skill. "I appreciate the use of your gun. I'm glad to know I'm not a complete dunce when it comes to this sort of thing."

''I doubt you could be called a dunce in any area of life,'' she said quietly. ''You're a brilliant man, Max.''

''Maybe,'' he said quietly. ''But not smart enough to keep my wife happy, was I?''

Chapter Seven

"I heard you have a new foal, Faith." Brace stood near the porch, hat in one hand, holding his horse's reins in the other. "Thought I might drop by and take a look, if you don't mind."

She stepped out onto the porch and greeted him with a smile. "You heard right, Sheriff. Nicholas is tickled to death with his filly."

Brace looked past her and lowered his voice. "I wondered if you'd mind writing a letter for me. My family back East is bent on sending out a woman for my benefit, and I need to let them know I'm capable of finding my own wife." He looked subdued, and Faith felt a moment of distress on his behalf.

Mrs. Metcalf, the storekeeper's wife, read his mail to him, but more than two years ago the sheriff had asked Faith to answer his occasional letter and look over any documents he felt might be important. Brace could neither read nor write. He knew some letters, could write his own name and recognize numbers, allowing him to deal with the bank president when he made a deposit to his account.

She might have offered to help him learn, back when she lived closer to town, in the cabin at the eastern edge of

Nicholas's property. Now she decided that it might be better if someone else took on that task. Brace had become more enamored of her than she felt was wise, given her marital status.

"Come on in after you've seen the filly," she told him. "I'd be happy to help you. You know that."

"Walk out with me, will you?" he asked quietly, and she nodded in agreement, lifting her skirt to step down to the ground.

"Is something wrong?" she asked in an undertone.

He shot her an inquiring look. "That's what I was gonna ask you. I don't want to interfere between husband and wife, but you didn't look too happy with that fella you're married to showing up here the way he did. I just thought it might be a good idea to check things out."

"I'm fine," she said firmly. "Max is staying for a while, just so we can sort things out." She was careful to keep a good space between them as they walked to the barn, lest the "fella" in question appear around the corner of the corral and misunderstand the situation.

"He didn't appreciate me being here with you the day he arrived," Brace reminded her bluntly. "I suspect he thinks I'm trying to—" He halted abruptly, as if he thought better of what he'd been about to say, and Faith nodded.

"He wondered if you might not have designs on me, but I assured him you didn't," she said smoothly. Her smile was friendly, but reserved, and Brace only nodded.

The barn door was open and the large stall empty. "I think Max took the mare and filly out to the pasture," Faith said. "He thought he'd try them with the other horses today. He's a bit protective of them both."

"Is he now?" Brace followed her out the back door of the barn and across the corral to the pasture gate. "And why is that?"

Faith related quickly the events of the filly's birth, and again felt a thrill of pride as she recounted Max's efforts. "I don't know what I'd have done if he hadn't been here," she said simply.

Brace seemed properly impressed. "Maybe I'll feel more kindly to him, then," he said soberly. They leaned side by side against the rail fence and watched as Max walked across the pasture, the filly romping at his heels. He had a rope tied loosely around her neck, and Brace grunted in surprise.

"Well, I'll be," he said, shooting a quick look at Faith. "Isn't that foal kinda young to be leadin' around on a line?"

"Nicholas suggested it, and Max agreed to give it a try," Faith said. "There's a school of thought that advocates early training of foals, having them get used to a lead line while they're still very young."

From across the wide expanse of knee-high grass, Max lifted a hand and waved to acknowledge their presence. "You gettin' along all right with him?" Brace asked boldly, and then looked away as if he recognized he'd overstepped his bounds.

"We're fine," Faith told him, ignoring his blunder. "I don't want you to worry about me, Brace. Max is a good man. We had a lot of problems, but they weren't all his fault. And I'm finding out that we need to mend some of those fences."

"I can't imagine you being a bad wife," Brace blurted out, and then halted, a flush climbing his cheeks, as if he had spoken out of turn. "I just want you to know that any time you need me, all you have to do is send a message and I'll be here."

"Thank you," Faith said, aching for the man's embarrassment. She stood upright, dropping her arms from the top rail and smiled at him. ''Are you ready for me to help you write that letter?''

''Yeah,'' he said agreeably. ''It won't be a long one. Just a few lines to let them know I don't need a woman so bad they have to ship one out here.''

''There are several ladies hereabouts who'd welcome a look from you,'' she said quietly. And it was true. The man was good-looking, with a job that paid well, and a house in town that needed a woman's touch.

''None I'm interested in.'' His words were short and clipped and Faith wisely changed the subject, drawing him out about the letter she would be writing to his family.

''What did the sheriff want?'' Max asked, washing up at the sink as Faith placed supper on the table that night. He'd ignored the topic for most of the day, after watching the tall figure ride off after half an hour in the house with Faith. It had been a long thirty minutes, and Max had sat under a tree in the pasture while the two of them had done their business uninterrupted.

Now he asked the question that had burned at the edge of his mind for several hours. And turned to watch as Faith finished placing bowls and plates in their places. She took silverware from the drawer and doled it out next to their dinner plates, then lifted a platter of pork from the warming oven, placing it before him at the table.

''If I give you the carving knife, will you cut up the meat for me?'' she asked.

''Faith? I think you're ignoring me,'' he said quietly. ''Or is there a secret to your rendezvous with Sheriff Caulfield?''

''No secret,'' she said lightly. ''He just asked me to do something for him.''

''Mending?'' Max sat down and picked up the knife and

serving fork she'd provided. The meat was tender and barely needed the touch of the blade to cut it into slices. "Or is this something I don't need to know?"

He reached over to place a generous serving on her plate, and the knife and fork remained upright in his hands.

She looked at him, as if exasperated by his insistence. "Eat your supper, Max," she said after a moment of silence. Lifting the potatoes, she dished a serving onto her plate, then pushed the heavy pottery bowl in his direction. "Help yourself," she said shortly.

The gravy was hot and steaming and smelled like onions and pork drippings and he savored each bite. A jar of vegetables, a mixture of this and that from what Faith said were last summer's end-of-the-season pickings, filled out the menu, and they ate steadily. Faith worked hard and enjoyed her food for the most part, and Max decided she was not about to allow his questioning to spoil this meal for her.

He did not lack appetite, either, and between them they managed to make a good-sized dent in the food she'd prepared. "There's enough left for dinner tomorrow," she said, rising to put the meat and potatoes in a smaller dish, then pour the remaining gravy over the whole thing. "I'll make a pot pie from it."

"Sounds fit to eat," Max said lightly, carrying the plates to the sink. He was careful to help with the dishes and cleaning up the kitchen, aware that she did more than her share both inside the house and out. The chores had been pretty well equally divided between them during the past weeks, and he'd given Mrs. Metcalf a tidy sum when they'd visited the store in town, ordering her to apply it to Faith's account so that she'd lack for nothing.

"Brace can't read or write," Faith said quietly, her back to Max as she entered the pantry.

He was stunned, not only that a grown man in this day

and age would be illiterate, but that Brace should be afflicted so. The man appeared to be intelligent and competent, and certainly held the respect of the townspeople. If it was a secret—and apparently it was, or Faith would not have been so closemouthed about it—then Max would be duty bound to keep the knowledge to himself.

"Have you thought about helping him learn—" he began, only to have her slice a hand through the air as she turned back to him.

"I don't think I'm the one to take on the job," she said. "I almost offered a couple of years back, but he was mortified that he'd had to confess his lack to me, and so I suggested that I write letters for him and look at his bank statement when he picks one up from the manager a couple of times a year." She bent to lift the lid from the food safe in the pantry floor, and Max watched, his gaze caught by the line of her bottom, the lifting of her hemline and the sight of bare feet as she straightened and returned to the kitchen.

She had slipped her shoes off, gotten rid of her stockings in the process, and now walked lightly across the kitchen floor, her toes visible beneath the hem of her dress. It was the most inviting vision he'd seen in hours. Ranking right up there with the sight of her early this morning when she'd arisen and walked from the house in her nightgown just before dawn.

He'd watched from the kitchen, wanting to know that she was safe, heading back to his bedroom when she'd closed the outhouse door behind her and returned through the pale gray light that preceded dawn, to the porch. She'd stayed out there for long minutes, and he'd been tempted to return to the kitchen to make certain of her well-being. But after a bit, she'd come through the kitchen door, careful not to let it slam behind her.

He'd felt like a callow youth still wet behind the ears, peeping at her through the window. Yet she'd seemed caught up in the stillness and early morning sounds, and he'd decided not to disturb her solitude, but had gone back to his bed. Only the start of her rooster crowing minutes later had allowed him to join her in the kitchen as she put a pot of coffee on the stove.

She hadn't been wearing the soft, lacy sleeping garment he'd purchased for her, and for a moment he'd wished for the opportunity to see her garbed in the creation. But even in her simple, nondescript nightgown, with her hair tumbling down her back, she'd been a vision to behold. One he yearned to take as his own—and only her quick retreat to the bedroom to dress for the day had saved her from his impetuous behavior.

Now, he dwelled on the bare feet that carried her to the pantry and back, watched as she swept the kitchen floor and tossed the sand and crumbs off the porch. The broom was deposited back in the pantry, and she sent him a long look. "How about sitting on the front porch, on the swing, for a while?" she asked.

He was only too ready to join her there, and nodded in agreement. They walked through the hallway to the parlor and then out the front door. Trees spread sheltering branches over that side of the house and a breeze blew from the west. It was quiet, peaceful and still warm from the heat of the day.

The swing moved as he settled in one end of it, and Faith held the other side, her hand gripping the chain as she slid back on the seat. "You get to push," she said with a grin. "My legs aren't quite long enough to touch the floor." Her feet hung several inches from the wide boards that made up the porch, and he cast a long look in their direction.

"I can do that," he said with a smile, and nudged the

floor with the toe of his shoe. As if she'd noted his look of interest, she lifted her feet and tucked them beneath her dress, a modest gesture he didn't appreciate.

"Not very ladylike of me, is it?" she asked. "Going barefoot, I mean."

"I'd think you were a lady no matter how much or how little you wore," he told her, and felt a grin take over his countenance. The thought of how little she might wear reminded him of the day the filly was born and Faith had been garbed in the simple dress, with nothing beneath it.

"I know what you're thinking," she declared accusingly, smiling at him as if they were conspirators. "I hope Nicholas wasn't aware of my lack of undergarments the other morning when he showed up to see the filly."

"He was," Max said. "He glanced at you, then looked the other way. I think he didn't want to embarrass you."

Her cheeks turned rosy at his words and he laughed aloud. "I can't believe you're blushing, sweetheart. Nicholas has seen more exposed skin than that any time he walks by the saloon in town. You were well covered."

Faith propped her feet on the swing and enclosed her knees with her arms. "It's been a good day, hasn't it? We've gotten the horses settled all around, and I managed to get my hen sitting on a clutch of eggs in one corner of the coop."

"Isn't it kinda late for new baby chicks?" he asked. "I'd think spring would be better to raise a batch of little ones."

"Not any later for chicks than a mare having a filly in June. Mares are generally bred early on in the year, but when Nicholas found his sorrel last year, he wanted to breed my mare during her next heat. He couldn't stand to wait another six months or so." Faith smiled up at Max, her chin touching her knees, her eyes shining as she spoke of the mare.

"He's an impatient man, I take it," Max said. "And when will you be breeding her again?"

"In less than a month, probably. As soon as she comes in season."

"Will Nicholas bring the stallion here?"

"I think so. And then take the filly home with him sometime before winter."

"I'm surprised he's willing to wait so long to claim her."

"The mother's milk is good for her, though if he had to, he could use cow's milk to feed her."

"When will you be going over there to get a new supply for yourself?" Max asked, drawing out the conversation, enjoying her quiet answers, her quick smiles.

"In the morning. Nicholas brought a jarful for me the other day, but I need cream for butter."

"And you'll take eggs there?" he asked idly.

"Umm..." She leaned her cheek where her chin had been only moments before, and Max thought she looked tired, her eyes closing as if she would drift off to sleep momentarily.

He reached for her and lifted her to his lap, holding her firmly when her eyes flew open and she flailed, her hands coming to rest against his chest. "What are you doing?" she asked sharply, pushing against him.

"Holding you on my lap." And as if that were answer enough, he cradled her gently in his arms, shushing her with quiet sounds that seemed to be effective. She looked up at him, then relaxed against his chest.

"All right," she said, and he smiled into the waves of hair that cascaded down around her shoulders. Her locks caught the glow of the setting sun and he thought he saw a bit of silver here and there in the soft curls. His fingers ran through the length of it, and she sighed, leaning against him more fully.

"You spoil me," she murmured quietly and he nodded against her head.

"I hope so," he said. "You don't get enough of it. I see you working from sunrise to sunset, Faith, and it worries me that you should be so occupied with providing for your own existence."

"And who better to provide for me?" she asked, then lifted a hand to place her fingertips across his mouth. "Never mind, forget I asked," she said. "I already know your opinion on that subject."

"I'd gladly take care of you for the rest of your life," he told her, rocking the swing in a steady movement, enjoying the warmth of the woman he held. He clasped one small foot in his palm and massaged it gently.

"That feels good," she said, stretching out her toes and arching her foot. "If this is taking care of me, I have to admit I like it." And then she considered him, looking up as if she would speak words of importance. "You seem to be doing a pretty good job of looking after me lately," she said. "I've gotten lazy since you're here."

His chuckle was quiet and his fingers firm against her skin as he considered her words. His mother would think Faith was doing the job of a cleaning woman, or housekeeper, both of them positions beneath her status as the wife of a man such as Maxwell McDowell. Yet Max thought his wife had more dignity than any other human being he'd known. Perhaps his mother could learn something from Faith.

And at that thought, he blinked and his hand encircled her foot, stopping its gentle massage. His mother had always been the ideal woman in his eyes. Strong, dignified, a model of womanhood, who helped the poor and took care of her household with an iron hand.

And that iron grip had bruised Faith, if he were to believe the memories she'd related of those days in Boston. Being here with her now, he was inclined to take a second look at the woman he'd revered all his life, the mother Faith claimed had been so cruel. He would hear more about those days of his marriage, if he had to drag the details out of Faith, bit by bit.

His hand pressed anew against her sole, even as his foot ceased the pushing and he allowed the swing to come to a halt. "I think you're ready for bed," he whispered, and was rewarded by a look of sleepy agreement. Faith tilted her head back and smiled, the sight reminding him of other days when he'd held her closely and she'd offered a signal such as this, one he knew would result in their sharing her bed before the evening was out.

If he hadn't had a glut of work to complete in his study before he could climb the stairs to bed. His mother had always insisted that work must come first, and he'd made that his watchword all his adult life.

Now he wondered how many such evenings he'd wasted, leaning over his ledgers while Faith waited in her bed for the husband who tarried too long below stairs. Too many nights, he thought wistfully. But for tonight, he had no choice except to kiss her with a tender touch, release her from his hold and allow her to walk away, into the bedroom she would not share with him.

She rose, as if his thoughts were transferred to her mind, and her hand trailed from his as she turned to the door. "I can't stay awake much longer," she said, her smile sweet, her eyes heavy-lidded. "I'll see you in the morning."

"I'm going out to check the horses before I turn in," he said. "Don't worry if you hear me in the backyard."

"I won't." She drifted through the door, her feet silent on the bare wood, and he mourned her leaving, wishing he had the right to follow after her and claim his due as her husband.

He'd best put that thought aside, lest he foul up what little progress he'd made with her, he decided. And rose to walk around the house and to the barn.

The days passed in a haze of summer. The nights were another matter altogether. For Max, it was pure torture to watch Faith throughout the day, ever yearning for her touch, yet bound by his own rules of behavior. Rules that did not allow him to force the issue of their relationship. Becoming so settled in her life that she would not be able to think of being without him was his first goal. In order to accomplish that, he must be her friend, her constant companion, and to that end, he worked beside her, spoke of the future as though it were a given that they spend it together.

That she sometimes glanced at him with questions in her gaze, that she didn't approach him again with affection, marred his serenity. But he persevered, aware that his time was limited, that the summer was fast fleeting and he must consider the length of time he spent here in terms of the business he'd left behind in Boston.

As he worked with the filly each day, Faith watched him from the pasture fence, and he enjoyed showing off for her benefit. The docile foal was becoming attached to him, recognizing him as he arrived at the gate every morning, ready to provide her with their daily stint of training.

Seeing Faith perched on the pasture fence, he'd grinned and waved that first morning, the day after their evening on the porch swing. He cherished those remembered moments, knowing she had lowered her defenses for that period of time. And as if she had second thoughts, she'd become, once more, a bit reserved, a little removed from him.

But the weeks passed quickly, day by day, Max learning more about the functioning of the woman who spent her time planning for her future. The garden was a top priority, he found, and indeed, he learned the difference quickly between weeds and vegetables. His back ached some nights from hours spent on his knees as the plants took hold in the fertile soil, and his hoe got a workout as he dug weeds from around the hills of corn she had planted.

"Don't be a coward," she'd chided him, lifting tomato worms from the plants and slicing them in half with her hoe. That this woman, raised in the city, trained all her life to be a lady of leisure, could cope with such an ugly specimen of nature was nothing short of impossible for him to believe. But she did it. Firmly, showing no mercy to the critters who would eat her crop, she wreaked vengeance with a wicked sense of humor. And then laughed at him as he attempted to follow suit.

He led the filly beneath one of the trees in the pasture, careful to note where he walked, for the horses spent much time in the shade, leaving a mess behind with no care for his boots. Faith watched him from her perch, and he filled his eyes with the picture she presented. Her skin was tanned, her hair lighter day by day, and even now it shimmered in the noonday sun.

He released the foal from the lead line and wound the rope in a circle as he walked toward his wife. She grinned at him, and he felt a wave of emotion wash over him that made a lump rise in his throat.

I love her.

It was a thought foreign to him. Desire and need had always been enough when it came to his dealings with women. Even when it came to Faith in the early years of their marriage. Now he knew with certainty that the desire he felt trailed far behind the overwhelming love that arose in his breast.

He neared the fence where she waited, and sought for words to speak. "The filly's doing well," he said, stunned by his own inane attempt at conversation.

I've discovered that I love you. It should be simple to say the words aloud, and yet he hesitated.

"You're right handy at the job," she joked, drawling her compliment with slow syllables that made him laugh aloud.

"I'm learning," he admitted, climbing up to sit beside her.

"Yes," she said quietly, slanting a look at him, "I think you are."

"And what is that supposed to mean?" he asked, picking up on her tone.

She shrugged. "Nothing, I suppose. Just an observation."

Deciding to drop the subject, lest he push too hard, he changed directions. "Isn't it about time for the mare to be ready?" he asked.

Faith nodded. "I think so. I need to let Nicholas know she's starting to show signs. Maybe I'll take the wagon over there this afternoon. I could haul some hay for him. He leaves a good share here in the loft, but he may be running low. Even though his animals are all out to pasture, he's bound to have a few head of cattle closer to the house where the grass isn't as heavy. He'll need feed for them."

"I'll help," Max offered, turning to climb down from the fence on the other side, and then reaching up to grasp Faith and lift her down before him. He'd kept his hands away from her with diligence, hoping against hope that she would turn to him as she had once before in an impetuous gesture.

Now, he felt the need for some bit of assurance, and he held her for a moment, his hands around her waist, noting the slender lines of her body where once there had been softness, an added bit of flesh. "You're so slim," he said quietly. "You don't feel the same as you once did."

"I've changed in more ways than one," she allowed, looking up at him, seemingly willing to remain in his embrace.

He took advantage, sliding his hands to her back, urging her forward until she leaned against him. And she did so with alacrity. His heart surged into a faster beat as he felt the pressure of her breasts against him, the scent of her rising to fill his nostrils with sweetness. One hand rose to tangle in the hair she'd scooped high on her crown, then allowed to fall down her back.

It twined about his fingers, clinging to the calluses that covered his palm, and felt like silk threads as he wound it around his hand. He used it to his advantage, tugging her head gently back, until the long, clean line of her throat was exposed to his gaze. Bending to her, he kissed the skin there, touched the soft, vulnerable flesh beneath her ear with his tongue and tasted the faint, salty flavor.

A groan rose from deep within and he allowed it utterance, unable to halt the desire that accompanied it. Within moments, he was as aroused as he'd ever been in his life, as ready for the act of loving as a man could possibly be, and yet only too aware that the woman he held would not follow his lead.

Not now, perhaps not ever.

His mouth left one last kiss against her throat, and without touching the lips that opened for his kiss, without allowing himself the pleasure of coaxing her into submission, he loosed his hold on her and stepped away.

"Max?" She blinked and looked up at him, and he derived one hard-earned moment of enjoyment at the look she wore. He'd left her wanting, and that was a victory he seized on, hoping it would be to his benefit. The presence of his masculinity in full bloom within the confines of his trousers was giving him severe discomfort, and he desperately needed all the advantage he could gain from this encounter.

"I won't put that kind of pressure on you again," he said, noting the rough tones of his voice, aware that desire had manifested itself in more ways than one. "I'm sorry, Faith. I shouldn't have taken advantage."

She nodded, her own cheeks a rosy hue, her eyes shining with passion. "I appreciate your restraint," she said simply, and then turned to walk away. He grinned. The woman lied. As surely as he was standing here with an aching need and the bulge in his drawers to prove it, she'd lied to him. Appreciate? He'd lay odds that she was chewing on her tongue even now.

The woman lied, and he was exultant.

Chapter Eight

Nicholas had decreed the mare was ready to be bred, from the looks of things. Together, he and Max walked from the barn to the back porch, Nicholas leading the gelding he'd ridden over at Faith's declaration of Goldie's readiness. The two men spoke in low tones, their heads bent as if some matter not fit for female consumption was being discussed.

Faith watched from the back door and knew a moment's uneasiness as they approached. A year ago, when Goldie had first been introduced to Nicholas's stud, she'd felt no such compunction at speaking freely to him about the breeding to take place. Now, with Max in the picture, Faith was strangely embarrassed to talk about the stallion in front of him. As if his presence made it unfitting for her to discuss the procedure with Nicholas.

She stepped out onto the porch, her hands shoved deeply in the pockets of her apron, and waited impatiently until the men should notice her. Max looked up first, caught her eye and paused midsentence, nudging Nicholas with his elbow.

''Faith.'' Nicholas spoke her name as a greeting and smiled, his usual, darkly handsome grin. Even as a married woman, she'd found she was not immune to the beauty of the man, admiring him as she might a fine work of art, though she felt not a twinge of desire for him.

Now, with Max in the picture, even Nicholas's strikingly handsome features had definitely taken a back seat. They could have been related, the two of them were so alike in stature, their masculine images cast in the same mold of confidence and arrogance that suited them so well. They stood now, not fifteen feet from her and their eyes met, Nicholas nodding briefly before he climbed up into his saddle.

He turned to Faith and tipped his hat, a courteous gesture she was familiar with, and then rode away. Max watched him go, and she thought he inhaled deeply before long strides carried him to the porch. His boot touched the second step, and he leaned with his forearms on his knee, looking up at her.

"What's the decision?" she asked, although she already sensed what he would say.

"Nick said she's ready," Max told her, tilting his hat back a bit, the better to see her face. He looked sober, his eyes dark, as if he waited for her to deny Nicholas's decision.

"I told him that yesterday," she said sharply. "But he couldn't take my word for it, could he?" She turned and opened the screened door, entering the kitchen without another word.

Men. Once Max had made an appearance at the farmhouse, and was accepted by Nicholas, he'd become just another part of the brotherhood. Between them, they managed to close ranks, not allowing a woman's presence to interfere in manly doings. She slammed the skillet on the stove and turned toward the pantry. The screened door slammed again, and Max stalked across the kitchen, capturing her effectively in the narrow storage area.

''What the hell is all this about?'' he asked gruffly. His eyes were narrowed and piercing, and she met his gaze with anger bubbling inside her, like a geyser ready to blow.

''It's my mare you've been out there discussing, making up your minds like two…two *men,*'' she said harshly.

''We *are* two men,'' Max said quietly, reaching for her. His hands clamped around her waist and he held her before him, immobile and ready for an argument. ''I don't know what's got you all in a dither, Faith. You knew Nick was coming over this afternoon, and you knew I'd be out in the barn with him.''

''I'm not in a dither,'' she said staunchly, sensing the nearness of tears, and totally unable to understand why she was ready to cry and at the same time about to haul off and punch her husband where it would do the most good.

''Well, something's got you all in an uproar,'' he said reasonably. ''And I think I deserve to know what it is.'' He cocked his head to one side. ''Are you mad because we didn't invite you to walk out to the barn while we checked out Goldie?''

''I would have been embarrassed if I had,'' she said, aware that her lower lip protruded just a bit. ''But she's *my* mare.''

He released her and stepped back. ''Yes, she is. And I thought you were all right with her being bred this month. If you've changed your mind for any reason, I'll ride over and tell Nick you want to wait awhile.''

Faith turned and snatched at the new pail of lard, carrying it in one hand as she brushed past Max and walked to the stove. A turning fork in one hand, she opened the pail and scraped out a generous-size nugget of lard into the skillet, where it sizzled over the hot fire.

''You want me to put that back?'' Max asked nicely, holding out his hand for the lard pail.

She handed it to him and turned back to her cooking, placing several pieces of flour-drenched chicken in the hot grease. They sizzled, browning quickly, and she turned them over with the fork, then lifted the pan, moving it aside to a cooler spot on the stove.

''What can I do to help with supper?'' Max asked.

''Just stay out of my way.'' The tears were closer now, and if the man didn't leave her alone, she might just throw something at him. And wasn't this the most foolish position she'd ever found herself in. Arguing for the sake of a mare who probably couldn't wait until that big, hulking brute of a stallion arrived tomorrow to... Faith's mind went blank as the image appeared for a moment, and then disappeared just as quickly.

It was the thought of what would take place in the morning that bothered her so, she realized with a shudder. Aware of a strange warmth within her own body, she recalled that errant thought, that image that had been placed in her mind as she thought of Nicholas's stallion. Imagined him mounting her mare's golden back and taking his pleasure at the smaller horse's expense.

And yet, if the mare was ready, as she'd been a year ago, she would not fight the stallion, but offer herself to him, the foolish creature. No matter that his masculine member would provide her with only fleeting relief from the heat nature had bestowed upon her, in order to guarantee the increase of the population of horses such as Goldie. The foolish creature would allow it, even as she uttered shrill sounds of protest.

And then she would bear a colt, or another filly, in eleven months, and suffer its loss when it was sold or—

''Damn it, Faith. I want you to turn around and tell me what your problem is,'' Max said, his voice rising as he stomped across the kitchen floor and removed the fork from her hand. With his other hand, he pushed the skillet farther to the back of the stove and then tossed the fork into the sink.

His grip was rough on her now, and she looked up at him in shock. Max had ever been a gentleman where she was concerned. Even yesterday, when he'd kissed her in the corral and then allowed her to walk away, he'd apologized for his actions. Now his fingers dug into her waist and his brow was lowered as if he was beset by a fury he was in no mood to control.

"She's my mare," Faith cried aloud. "I'm right back to men making up their minds about my life. You and Nicholas have had your heads together for the past hour, and he's gone off to his nice little wife, who dotes on him, and you've come in here, expecting your supper on the table, and I'm—I'm..."

She felt the tears spurt from her eyes, knew the frustration of salty drops running down her cheeks and falling on her bosom. And saw with amazement that Max was speechless. And then he inhaled sharply, lifting a hand to wipe the tears from her cheek.

"I've never expected you to cook for me if you didn't want to, Faith," he said finally. "And as to Nick going home to his wife, he said he'd better get a move on, that he'd be catching hell from the three women he lives with if he was late for supper one more time this week."

"You know what I mean," Faith wailed, giving up on halting the deluge of tears. It seemed that once she cut loose, she stood no chance of putting a stop to the waterworks.

"No, sweetheart, I'm afraid I don't," he said, settling in a kitchen chair next to the table and drawing her onto his lap. "Why don't you tell me."

She was silent, and he pulled his kerchief from his back

pocket, offering it for her use. She looked it over for a moment, deemed it clean and blew her nose in one corner. Her tears were wiped quickly and she struggled to stand. All to no avail.

"I'm not letting you up until you tell me what's got your feathers ruffled," Max said quietly. "I don't often put my foot down, Faith, but this time I am."

She took a deep breath, and the conflict she'd been chewing on became apparent as she recalled the breeding process just a year ago. It had been at Nicholas and Lin's place, and Faith had been relegated to the house during the actual introduction of mare and stallion. But she'd heard the wild, keening whinny of her mare, had known in that instant what was taking place, and for that small space of time, had rued the notion she'd held dear.

That of breeding Goldie not only once, but twice, to the sorrel stallion that Nicholas had purchased for that very reason.

She and Lin had looked at each other in dismay as the mare sounded her distress, and then Lin's face had darkened as the stallion trumpeted his jubilation at his conquest of the golden mare. "Damn male creatures," she'd said sharply. "I swear, they're all alike. Just listen to that stupid stud."

And they'd laughed then, as if some cloud had passed by. And if Faith thought Nicholas had a darkly determined look on his face when he came into the house and set his gaze on Lin, she'd put it aside, leaving with the mare quickly.

"I remember only too well that Goldie wasn't really keen on this whole business a year ago, and now I've put her in the same position again," she said quietly, looking down at her hands, both of them clutching the kerchief in her lap.

"She's a horse, Faith. A mare, whose usefulness to you is measured by the colts or fillies she can give you. You can't give her credit for having the emotions of a human being."

"I can so," she said, glaring up at him. "She's more than just a brood mare as far as I'm concerned."

His shrug was agreeable. "Well, then I'll just ride over and tell Nick you've changed your mind. He'll understand. Maybe." And then she caught a glimpse of the grin he tried in vain to conceal from her.

She rose from his lap, breaking his hold on her and stomped back to the stove. "You've made me burn the chicken," she said accusingly. "Now, go get the fork you tossed into the sink."

"Yes, ma'am." His voice was meek and she looked up at him sharply.

"If you value your life, you won't make fun of me tonight, Maxwell McDowell."

"No, ma'am," he said softly, rinsing the fork under the pump and returning it to her hand. "Can I do something to help you?"

"Yes," she said. "Go make sure the hen hasn't hatched those chicks yet. I want to know as soon as they've made an appearance so I can take them out of the coop and put them in a separate place."

"All right," he said, turning from her and leaving the house. She decided he'd looked relieved to be rid of her presence, and for good measure she stepped to the door to watch as he strolled toward the chicken yard. It had been just three weeks since she'd put the hen in the nesting box in one corner of the coop. And unless she missed her guess, those little peeps would be chipping their way out of the eggs any minute now.

Max went in through the front door of the henhouse and

closed the door behind him. She knew it was not his favorite place to spend time. The smell was not conducive to improving his appetite, he'd told her one day after cleaning the floor and replacing the dirty straw with a fresh supply.

For whatever reason, he'd gone there gladly now, and she suspected it was to get away from her and her tears. She turned the chicken in the pan again and recalled her claim. It had not burned. Indeed, it looked crisp and brown and ready for the oven. She liked to bake it once it had browned, leaving her free to put together the rest of her meal. Tonight was no exception. She had potatoes cooking slowly and a kettle of green beans that had been simmering on the back burner for three hours.

The chicken was in the oven and she'd mashed the potatoes and set them aside to stay warm when Max came back in the kitchen.

"You've got a whole boxful of baby chicks," he announced. "What do we do with them now?"

"I'll move them after supper," she said. "I have a small pen by the woodshed, with chicken wire over the top and an old doghouse for shelter. The varmints can't get at them there, and it keeps the little ones away from the rest of the flock."

"I'll wash up and set the table," he volunteered, casting her an inquiring look, as if wondering if he was welcome at her table.

"All right," she told him, deciding that being agreeable was the best route to take for now. If she decided to change her mind about the mare, she still had time to let Nicholas know before morning. And if the truth be known, she was just a bit embarrassed at having made such a display over the breeding and Max and Nicholas spending time together.

They sorted out the hen and chicks before dark, toting the babies out in a basket, Faith carrying the hen in her apron, where the creature squawked and set up a ruckus Max said was enough to wake the dead. Once the little yellow chicks were settled, and their mother had looked them all over, they hustled into the old doghouse, and Faith bent low to see them there. The hen had her feathers ruffled, covering them beneath her skirt of dusty gray, clucking quietly as she squatted in the bed of fresh straw Max had carted in at Faith's bidding.

"You want to take another look at the mare and filly?" he asked after she had pronounced the chickens safe for the night.

"Probably not," she told him. "I'll just have second thoughts again, and it's too late now to change my mind."

"It's never too late to change your mind, Faith," he told her as they walked back to the house. "I keep hoping you'll have second thoughts about me, you know."

She glanced up at him and frowned. "I told you when you arrived here that I wasn't going back to Boston with you, Max. I haven't given you reason to think otherwise, have I?"

He followed her onto the porch and then into the dark kitchen. The sun had set and the house was silent and shadowed. "Do you want me to light the lamp over the table?" he asked, ignoring her query.

"No, I'm almost ready to go to bed," she told him. "I'll need to be up early."

And then she lay awake in the wide bed, her gaze fixed on the midnight sky, agonizing over the diverse emotions that tore at her serenity. Max was worming his way into her heart once more, a position she'd sworn would never be open to any man. She found herself looking forward to each morning as a gift to treasure, a time wherein she might store up memories to keep her company during the long days of winter, when Max would be gone and her life would be empty once more.

I've never stopped loving him. The thought was alive in her and she recognized it as truth. All her talk, her denial of her need for the man, were as naught in the dark hours of the night. Perhaps, she thought, she might better rise from her solitary bed and seek him out. He would welcome her, of that there was no doubt, and she would once more know the joys and pleasures to be found in the arms of Maxwell McDowell.

And then what? Once he staked a claim, he would never give up. She'd find herself beset by his coaxing, his loving, and eventually would concede defeat to his greater, overwhelming presence in her life. She rose from the bed and stood at the window, aware of the soft breeze that caused her nightgown to outline each curve and hollow of her body.

Max had bought her this garment, and she'd refrained from wearing it, aware that to do so would be a concession to his influence. Now she stood in the midnight hours, craving the blessed sleep that would not come to her, aware that his presence in this house had changed her in a way she had not thought possible.

It had seemed so simple. Allow Max to share her days for a week or so, and then send him on his way, with the knowledge that she'd given him a fair chance and found him wanting.

Wanting. Such a complex word, she thought, leaning her forehead against the windowpane. Encompassing her with his tenderness, surrounding her with his humor and touches of elegance, the man had her almost panting at his heels.

Wanting. She was filled with it, suffused with a yearning for his arms that brought her to the very edge of desire, almost to the brink of passion.

Her behavior in the corral brought flaming color to her cheeks, and she pressed her cool palms against them, recalling her need for him in those few moments. Remembering his cool apology as he set her aside and watched her walk away.

The only redeeming feature of the whole episode had been the knowledge that he was aroused, that the shape of that male member had, for one long moment, been pressed against her, and in that she had reason to rejoice. He was not as aloof, as uninterested as he'd seemed to be in those moments.

She smiled, hugging herself. It was a decision she must set aside for now, with the knowledge that the morning was fast approaching and Max would rise early to await Nicholas's arrival with the stallion. There was much to be done to prepare for the breeding process, and she set her chin, aware that she would not be involved this time.

Let the men handle it. She would comfort the mare afterward, as she had the last time, currying, brushing and spending long minutes with her.

For now, she must seek her bed and close her eyes.

Breakfast was a silent affair, Max eating steadily, thanking her nicely for the meal, then leaving the house without explanation as to his whereabouts or intentions. Nicholas had given him instructions yesterday, and he sought out the mare, checking her once more for her readiness.

He led her to the corral, fixing two ropes in place so that she would be tied to opposite sides of the enclosure once the stallion arrived. Then, covering her with two heavy blankets, he fastened them beneath her belly with big, metal safety pins, to ensure that the stud didn't mar her glossy coat with his urge to bite the mare he mounted.

Max had never been a part of such a procedure, yet Nicholas seemed to know what he was doing, and Max was willing to bow to the man's greater knowledge in this case. He'd barely fitted out the mare and secured her as Nicholas had directed before he heard the trumpeting sound of the stallion from the yard.

Max grinned. It seemed Goldie's scent carried to where the horse waited, and he'd be willing to bet that Nicholas was having a hard time holding the stallion down. Leaving the mare where she stood, Max passed through the barn to the front door and greeted the neighbor.

"I heard your stud. He sounds impatient," Max said with a grin.

"You don't know the half of it. I think he knew when we left home what he was going to find here. He about wore me out, holding him to a nice, steady canter."

The sorrel stallion tossed his head, flecks of foam flying, and his eyes were wide as he whinnied again. Nicholas undid the cinch and slid the saddle to the ground, standing it on end near the barn door. "I want to pad his hooves out here," he said. "He was a little rough last time we tried this, and Faith will have a fit if her mare gets marked up."

"I've already covered her the way you told me," Max said, in awe of the magnificence of the animal before him. The stallion was big, his haunches thick and powerful, and his red coat gleamed in the morning sunshine. His neck was arched and his mane flew as he lifted his head abruptly, nostrils flaring as if the mare's scent was carried on the wind.

Max looked toward the house and saw Faith in the kitchen doorway. She seemed small and delicate from this distance, and he thought of the mare he'd just spent half an hour preparing for the taking by this mighty horse before him. The mare, too, had seemed smaller than usual, somehow. More vulnerable, tied in place, with no chance of escape once the stud was brought to her.

The urge to conquer was inbred in all male creatures, Max decided. For as he watched his wife, he felt a surge of lust that had nothing to do with his usual desire for the woman. He looked away, shocked by his own emotion. He'd tried to be a gentleman with Faith. Perhaps she, like the mare awaiting the mating ritual—

He shook his head, setting aside the thought that had provoked the blood to rush to his loins. There was work to be done.

When all was said and done—when the breeding had been accomplished, with only a few seconds of peril to the mare as the stud rushed his fences at the last moment—Max felt exhilarated. And it was obvious Nicholas shared his thoughts. His grin was wide as he led his stallion from the corral and through the barn.

The mare was turned out to pasture after a quick grooming, and Max watched as the other man saddled his horse, preparing to leave.

"Tell Faith it went well," he said, climbing into the saddle. "I suspect she was upset this morning, wasn't she?"

Max nodded. There was no point in elaborating on the issue. Surely Nicholas was familiar with women's moods, and if Max was any judge of things, Lin stood to be rushed into a private place once Nicholas arrived back at his home. There was something about the whole situation that called for action, and Max wondered glumly how he would handle his own problem.

He watched Nicholas ride off, one hand lifted in a quick wave toward the house. And then Max turned toward the woodshed, ostensibly to check on the hen and her clutch of chicks in the enclosure beside the structure. In reality, he knew there was merit in the idea of staying removed from Faith for a while, at least until his male impulses were under control.

He stood at the chicken wire fence and watched as the hen dusted her feathers in the dirt and pecked idly at a bug that had ventured too close, providing a part of her breakfast. Perhaps Faith was intending to bring feed to them. With a quick movement, he went to the henhouse and found the pan she used, filled it partway with chicken feed from the barrel and returned to the little family.

He tossed handfuls through the wire fence and watched as the hen clucked to her little ones, calling them to the breakfast table. They responded like small, walking balls of yellow fluff, and he grinned at the sight as they scampered around, pecking and squeaking like miniature windup toys he'd seen in an exclusive toy store in Boston.

"They need water, too," Faith said from behind him, and as he turned to her, she undid a piece of the fencing to bend low and enter the enclosure. The shallow pan of water in her hand was placed in a secure position, and the hen went to it, dipping her beak in the water, then tipping her head back to swallow. He watched in amusement as the chicks followed her lead, and chuckled as they backed off when the water splattered them.

"Now you're going to tell me you'll butcher these cute little things and put them in jars to eat next winter," he said, humor lacing his words.

"Only the roosters," she said. "The pullets will be laying hens next spring. One rooster is all any henhouse needs on hand. And even one is too much sometimes."

"You don't hold your resident rooster in high esteem?" he asked, grinning at her.

"Right now, I'm not too fond of any male creature,"

she said sharply, turning aside to stalk back toward the house.

She'd apparently not gotten over her snit from the night before, and he considered her back as she stiffened her shoulders and held her head high. Her hips swayed a bit beneath the drab dress she wore and he wished for a moment to see her without the heavy, unattractive garment.

As if called to attention, he felt the same heated response he'd struggled with earlier. Noted its rise as it claimed him once again, and his lips thinned, even as heat climbed to burn his cheekbones. The breath he sought did not come easy, and he felt his nostrils flare with the effort. She was bending over now on the porch, sliding off the work boots she wore while in the yard or tending to her chores.

Bare feet entered the kitchen and the door slammed behind her.

Without thinking, acting as might an adolescent boy, he stalked across the yard, took the steps with one long leap and followed her inside. She turned quickly to aim a startled glance at his face, and he thought her face became pale, except for two bright spots of color high on her cheeks.

"What's wrong?" she asked sharply, her hands busy untying the apron she'd worn during the morning's work. She hung it on a handy nail near the pantry, her gaze trained on him, her look wary.

And well she might be, he thought. He'd kept his hands off long enough. He'd played the part she seemed to have cast him in, given her the room she needed in order to reacquaint herself with him again. And for what? She looked at him as if he were an interloper, a stranger, a man she barely knew.

"I think you need to go back outside and find something to do," she said quietly. "I'm going to change the beds and sort out the washing for tomorrow. I have the cream ready to churn, and I'm certain you can find chores enough to keep you busy for the rest of the morning."

"I've already decided what I plan on doing for the rest of the morning," he said, his voice almost unrecognizable as the words poured forth in a harsh utterance.

She backed against the wall, her hands flat on either side, and her chin rose in defiance. "I think not," she said, the words clipped and cool. And yet within the depths of her eyes he saw a flash of heat, of promise, and he advanced on her steadily.

"I can't believe you're going to force me to do this," she said, her words delivered from between lips that barely moved. Her hair was caught high on her head with a ribbon, and as he paused before her, he reached for it, tugging it free and allowing the heavy, golden fall to cover her shoulders and breasts.

"I don't intend to force you," he said. "I remember too well how you clung to me, Faith, how you made soft, pleading sounds when I loved you. I have no need of force with you, sweetheart."

Her voice was a whisper, her words a litany of appeal, as if she beseeched him for mercy at his hands. "I've never asked you for much, Max. But I'm begging you now not to do this to me."

"I'm not going to do anything to you, sweetheart. I'm going to do it *with* you. And therein lies the difference. You'll have a choice. Will it be your bedroom or the one I've been sleeping in? I warn you, the bed you allotted me is too narrow for comfort for what I have in mind. You might do better to allow me into your virginal chamber."

She shook her head. "You sound foolish, Max. I'm not a virgin, not by a long shot. And even though the law stands behind you in this, I won't agree to submit to your high-handed methods."

"I don't want you to simply submit," he said, and recognized that truth even as he spoke it aloud. Total surrender was what he was after. The giving of herself, the opening of her body to his claim, the submission of her will to his. And he would use all of the skill he'd set aside over the past three years to bring it about.

A sound from her throat called to his senses, a whispering murmur he could not ignore and he reached for her, holding her curves against his straining body. She was all that was warm and beautiful in his life, and even as he looked down into the brilliant blue of her eyes, he thought of the mare he'd held steady as the stallion staked his claim.

There was much the same acknowledgment of her fate in Faith's gaze as he'd seen in the dark, soft eyes of her mare. Even her hair clung to his skin as had the mare's mane clung to his hand as he'd held her halter, tossing her head in a final burst of defiance at the breeding she was being prepared to endure.

Except that he would be certain Faith did not merely endure, but would lift to his touch and exult in the joining of their bodies. He took her mouth in a kiss that brooked no denial on her part, his lips parting over hers, his tongue claiming the soft parts of her cheeks and the tender tissues inside that dark cavern wherein lay a member much like his own. She was slow to respond, her tongue battling with his as if she would force him to abandon his game.

And then she slumped against him, as though she knew defeat at his hands, allowing him to plunder the depths, opening for his advances. Her fists were clenched against his chest, her eyes closed, and as he lifted his head to look down at the flushed features of the woman he had chosen to wed, he saw slow tears wash the rosy hue from her cheeks.

"Don't cry, sweetheart," he whispered, knowing the

words resembled nothing so much as the begging he'd vowed not to stoop to. He would take her to bed, claim her as his own and then set about the process of carrying her back with him to the home that waited them in the city.

"Max." She spoke his name, the single syllable a pleading note that touched him as could no other word she might utter. And then she opened her eyes, and the fear and disgust he'd thought to find there did not exist. Instead, he recognized a depth of desire he could barely countenance.

He lifted her in his arms, carrying her with a lack of delicacy through the kitchen and into her bedroom. The bed was made, the quilt pulled taut across the feather tick, and big, fluffy pillows were propped against the tall headboard. The open window allowed the morning breeze to drift across the room, the white curtains billowing as a draft of air caught them, tossing them adrift.

She was light in his arms, her weight not nearly that of the woman he'd married, and his hands were impatient as he stood her beside the bed and began removing her clothing with swift skill. The buttons gave way to his practiced fingers, and he slid the dress over her hips to settle on the floor.

She wore a petticoat, and he untied the tapes, watching closely as it followed the dress to circle her with a cloud of creamy fabric. Beneath it she wore drawers, the hems trimmed with lace—lace he recognized from the emporium in town; drawers he'd purchased for her use. Through the sheer material of her vest, he saw dark circles where her breasts pressed tautly against the fabric to gain his attention, the crests already puckered and visibly taut, moving as she caught her breath.

He closed his eyes, fearing the rush of blood to his arousal. It was almost more than he could cope with, this sight of the woman he'd allowed to walk away, the wife he'd come to love over the past weeks with a passion he hadn't known himself capable of.

His hands trembled as he lifted the vest over her head, eschewing the tiny buttons as too much of a good thing. Next time he'd spend long moments undressing her. Later on, he promised himself, he'd give her more of the attention she deserved, noting each inch of skin as it was exposed to his avid gaze.

For now, he could only remove her clothing as quickly as possible, and watch her as he stripped off his own shirt and trousers, tugged his drawers down and stepped from them as her eyes traveled his length to settle there, where he was most vulnerable.

She shivered before him and he stepped back, viewing the slender lines she'd developed since their last such encounter. Slim and supple, her breasts formed before his eyes into two spheres of rounded temptation he could barely resist. Her hands rose, her arm crossing to cover herself, and he growled out a warning.

"Don't do that. You're beautiful, Faith. I want to look at you." Surprised at her slow obedience to his words, he enveloped her with his gaze, pleased at her acquiescence. Arms falling to her sides, her fingers lax, she lifted her chin, holding it high as if she invited his scrutiny.

The sunlight bathed her, the breeze touched her hair and as she lifted a hand to brush it from her face, he was stunned anew at the beauty before him. He'd thought her lovely, had been proud of her appearance in those days of their early life together. Now he recognized a depth of character, a strength of purpose she had not owned as a younger woman.

Pride filled her bearing, and he delighted in her obedience to his wishes. She chose to do as he asked, giving him the right to love her. Exultation filled his veins, heating his blood and bringing him to full arousal. His hands were firm, yet gentle as he lifted her, placed her in the center of the wide bed, then stepped back.

Flinging his boots from his path, he tossed his clothing from the floor at his feet to the general vicinity of the chair. And then he bent over her, more aware than ever in his life of the size of his manhood, proud and prominent as he knelt beside her on the bed.

The soft mattress gave way beneath his weight and he recognized her scent, the warmth of it rising from her body as he lowered himself against her. She was at once soft and yet gifted with the resilience of well-toned muscles and the long sleek lines of a woman who knew hard work and did it well. Her arms were strong as they circled his neck, and the fine, womanly shape he settled against fitted itself to his longer, larger frame.

He brushed back curls and waves from her face, gripping with both hands the abundant golden locks, watching as tendrils wrapped around his fingers and clung to callused flesh. ''I've always loved your hair,'' he murmured. ''When you used to wear it up for evenings out, I'd imagine pulling the pins loose, thought about it falling to cover your back and your breasts.'' His smile felt taut, straining against his teeth. ''There were times I barely made it home without undressing you in the carriage.''

''I never knew you thought those things,'' she whispered, one hand lifting to touch his cheek. ''You were always so...well-behaved.'' Her mouth curved in a secret smile and he bent to touch it with his own.

''I was a fool,'' he muttered. ''I never let you know how much I wanted you. I didn't want to frighten you, I think.''

''I'm not frightened now,'' she said, catching her breath in a sudden gasp as he leaned closer, pressing against her breasts. Her mouth was open a bit, as if she must take in long, slow breaths and he lifted slightly.

"Am I crushing you?" he asked, and wondered at the stark harshness of his voice. His jaw was clenched with the effort he made to keep from seeking out the heated flesh he yearned to touch.

Wait. Wait. The words hummed in his mind, and he fought to set reins on the passion flowing throughout his body.

She was warmth and fire beneath him, and his masculine need was urgent against her belly, yearning to encounter the warmth she sheltered between her thighs. As though she knew, as though she sought to please him in this, she moved her legs, opening to him, allowing him space to settle there.

Yes. As if he'd arrived home after an endless journey, he fitted himself against her, then bent to take her mouth. His kiss was openmouthed and avid, taking the blend of lips and teeth and tongue with the skill of a conqueror long denied his rights.

She cried out once, a keening moan, and he lifted from her. His eyes narrowed as he sought the source, only to find her eyes closed, her hair a golden cloud about her head and her mouth swollen from his attentions. Her lips parted again and a murmur escaped, a whimper as she tugged at his shoulders, shivering at his touch.

"Did I hurt you?" he asked, and again barely recognized his own voice, so harsh and driven were the sounds coming from his throat.

She shook her head, the sharp, negative movement a denial of his horror at the thought of bringing pain to her lissome body.

And then he spoke to her, his whisper harsh, his words a prediction of what might come to pass. "I will, I fear," he said, barely capable of holding the reins on his passion, feeling already the pulsing rhythm that preceded his release. "It's been three years, Faith."

"For you? Three years without..." Her voice was soft, the words demanding his reply as blue eyes opened to swallow him in their depths, and he nodded in a silent response, knowing he had no reason to query her in the same manner. Faith was as faithful a woman as the day was long. She had not strayed from her wedding vows, no matter her anger with him or her disappointment in the hash he'd made of their marriage.

And he had not sought out another, had not slaked his desire for Faith in the body of a stranger. She was all he wanted, all he had ever yearned to possess.

And now he reached between their bodies, sensing her indrawn breath as she stilled beneath long fingers that fondled her soft folds. His index finger moved gently, with tender care around the pulsing bit of flesh that cried out for his touch. She was damp there and he stroked with a circular movement of that lone finger, his eyes intent on her face.

Her hips lifted to his caress, and as he watched, soft color bloomed across her skin, her nostrils flared and she murmured beneath her breath. It was a revelation, a glimpse of the heaven he had once held as his own and then allowed to escape. Now he bent to her, savoring these moments of loving, with the sunshine pouring through the open window, the breeze cooling his hot flesh.

His gaze feasted on her, adoring the woman he held beneath him, the wife he'd come so close to losing forever. Now, for whatever reason, the Fates had smiled on him this morning, granting him the exquisite thrill of watching as she allowed him access to her moments of release.

And then she cried aloud, and he leaned closer to hear

her words. "Not without you," she whispered. "I need you, now, Max." Her breath caught, and her head tossed to one side, then the other, as a thin, wailing cry rose from her lips. He sealed them with his own, swallowing the gasping, passionate pleas.

And then, as she fell back against the bed, he rose to kneel above her, placing her thighs over his own, leaning forward as he slid one large hand beneath her to lift her for his taking.

Chapter Nine

His hands were warm and familiar beneath her, yet Faith knew a moment of panic as Max lifted her to him. It had been so long—three years since she'd been this close to him, long enough to blur the memories of the pure ecstacy of their coming together in that bed in Boston. Now, even though she ached for his possession, she felt a pang of unease as he nudged against that most feminine part of her and then leaned forward.

"Faith?" His whisper was harsh in her ear, his unspoken query loud in her mind. *Are you sure?* And she could only nod, gripping his shoulders as his penetration registered, at first a moment of taut resistance as her unused body rebelled against the invasion.

"Please, sweetheart. Relax for me. I don't want to hurt you." He murmured the words against her ear, and then he groaned aloud and shifted, easing back from the dominant position he'd chosen. He rolled with her until she was sprawled across his big body, her legs straddling him. His chest heaved beneath her as he struggled to control the automatic flex of muscles.

She nestled her face against his throat. "I'm sorry, Max. I thought—"

"It's all right, sweet," he murmured. "I rushed you too quickly. You're not ready for me."

"I thought—" His mouth halted her words as he lifted her and clasped her face between wide palms, touching her lips with soft kisses and hushed phrases of comfort.

"Don't think," he told her. "Just feel how much I want to please you, sweetheart."

He lifted her above him and nuzzled the fullness of her breasts as they hovered just above his face, his mouth feasting on one tight, nubbed crest, then the other, until she cried out with the aching need his lips and tongue brought into being.

With another quick, smooth movement, he rolled with her until, side by side, they embraced and he found once more the sensitive peaks of her breasts, those nubbins of flesh that seemed attached by some slender, shimmering bridge of nerves to the even more responsive parts between her thighs.

His hands moved over her, caressing her back, her waist, the smooth curves of her bottom, and then he lifted her leg and sought the hidden folds that lay open to his touch. She was surrounded by him, by hands and mouth and the pressure of his manhood resting firmly against her belly, reminding her of its aching need.

And yet the man who was even now spending long minutes patiently wooing her reluctant flesh seemed capable of ignoring that firm part of his body that surely was craving a satisfaction her taut flesh had denied him. In all of their times together, he'd never been so long-suffering, so ready to please her, and she sighed with the pure pleasure of knowing he would have her find satisfaction before he sought his own.

His hands were deft, knowing where to touch, how to press firmly and then with tender, teasing skill as he searched out each crevice and fold of her womanhood. His fingers slid with ease wherever he chose to explore, and she felt the wet, heated response that came from deep within her body to ready her for his final taking.

A spiraling warmth possessed her, and he whispered soft words of encouragement against her throat. Then, opening his mouth over her breast, he suckled deeply and she shivered with the corresponding quiver of female flesh where his hands formed her to his purpose.

As the waves wash the beaches and then reform to splash again on the sand, so his coaxing touch brought her wave after wave of perfect, ascending sensation, building to a final climax so sharp, so piercing, she cried aloud.

"Max." She repeated his name, whispering, then sobbing incoherent phrases as she repeated that beloved name. As if she could not speak it enough, could find no other single syllable to express the joy he brought her with the magic of his touch, the caress of teeth and tongue and lips against her flesh.

He turned her beneath him then, and lifted her legs again, this time seeking and finding the welcome he'd insured by long moments of loving. Faith clung to him, her legs circling him, her arms clutching at his back, as if she could not be close enough to the solid, muscular form that pressed her against the bed.

He was deeply within her, and she knew a moment of panic as his possession of her body threatened to seek out the very limits of her womanhood. He was there, at the entrance of her womb, and she sensed the moment when his seed was deposited, knew the instant he began within her another precious bit of humanity.

I'm going to have his child. As surely as she knew her name, so she was aware in that moment that Max had once more bequeathed her with the most priceless, beloved gift of all.

He would leave her. That was a given. But when he did, when he was gone from her, she would forever be in possession of a part of him. Whatever their future, she would receive another chance, another child to love.

"Faith? Are you all right?" His words were slurred, his breath escaping in great gasps as he lifted to look down at her. His hair was damp with perspiration, his eyes dark and exultant, and his face was set in harsh lines that told of passion spent, and desire sated. Even as she watched, his lids dropped to half cover his piercing gaze.

"I'm fine. More than fine," she managed to whisper. And she was. He'd taken her with care, with tenderness, with all the skill of a man well-versed in the art of loving, and she had been the recipient of all that was good and gentle in Max McDowell.

"I was too fast," he muttered, rolling with her, and cradling her as though he could not conceive of releasing her from his embrace.

"You were wonderful, Max," she said, lifting her face to reach for his lips, kissing him with a mouth that was soft and swollen from his touch. He tasted just a bit salty, and his scent was of a man spent and satisfied. She nuzzled his chest, touched the puckered nipples with her tongue and tightened the muscles deep inside her body, lest his manhood leave her empty.

"You're going to be in trouble," he murmured, sliding his hands to hold her bottom tightly, so their bodies remained linked.

"I think I like the sort of trouble you're offering," she said, leaning her head back to send him a look of challenge. "You are offering, aren't you?"

He rolled her to her back and seated himself deeply

within her once more, adjusting to her as she lifted her hips to capture him. "Can you already?" she asked, pleased at his obviously quick recovery.

"It seems I can," he answered, withdrawing and then sliding forward to fill her again.

She was taken prisoner by his skill, unable to deny him his place there, where she had been hollow and empty for so long. It would not last forever, she thought, turning her face up for his kiss, but while he was here, she would accept what he offered, and be glad. She'd been a fool to hold him off so long, to deny herself this pleasure, given on her behalf with all the generosity he possessed.

And then her thoughts were set aside, replaced by the pure joy of this moment, a gift from the man who knew her body and used that knowledge to grant these moments of ecstacy and passion. She closed her eyes, reveling in his possession, her hips rising to meet his every thrust, her hands clutching at his shoulders. Her legs holding him fast, and her soul singing a silent melody as she knew again the thrill of loving the man who owned her heart.

They slept, curled in the middle of the bed, and when Max awoke it was to the wakening murmurs of the woman beside him. She roused from sleep slowly and he curved her against himself, his hand buried in the length of golden hair, tilting her head back to rest his lips against her brow.

He felt her breathing quicken as she woke fully and then she lifted a hand to his face, her palm curved against the length of his jaw.

"Can we talk about the baby?" he asked, and Faith stilled, her hand clenching as it dropped from his face to rest against his chest. He'd put it off since his arrival, yet had recognized that the time would come when they must face the death of the baby boy who had lived so short a while. And left such pain behind with his passing.

Perhaps now was not the ideal moment to face her with it, but while he held her close, while their hearts still beat as one, he pursued the subject he'd set aside during the past weeks.

"What can we say?" she asked, and he heard the sorrow she made no attempt to hide. "What is there to discuss? We had a child and he died. I failed you and I failed our baby."

"You have it backward, Faith. I was the failure. I didn't realize it then, but I see now that I should have insisted on bringing things out in the open, on telling you how I felt. Instead, I grieved alone and left you to do the same. I can't forgive myself for hurting you that way."

"Did you grieve?" she asked, and then lifted her hand to press her fingers against his mouth when he would have responded. "Of course, you did, Max. I didn't mean for that to come out the way it did." She seemed to shrivel in his arms, and he tightened his hold so that she could not escape, then reached for the sheet to cover her.

"I grieved," he answered, the whisper slipping past her restraining fingertips. "But I know you must have felt a deeper sense of sorrow than I. It was only later, when you'd gone, that I realized how devoid of feeling you seemed, how vacant your eyes had become. I remembered then how listless and helpless you were in those days, after it was too late to repair the damage I'd done with my neglect."

He sighed deeply and felt that same hopeless, empty emotion he'd lived with during the years without Faith in his life.

"And then I regretted all the words of comfort I hadn't said, all the long nights I'd left you alone because I thought you had forbade me from your bed."

"Your mother..." Faith allowed her voice to trail off, and stiffened in his embrace. "I'm sorry, Max. You'll think I blamed her for everything. But in this one thing, she hurt me beyond measure."

"I want to hear it," he said, even as his mind rebelled at words of blame his mother could not refute because of the distance parting them.

"She told me it was my fault, that our son died because I couldn't nurse him, that I didn't have enough milk, and so he was forced to live on milk from the grocery store. Cow's milk that surely was not fit for a baby to drink." Faith ducked her head and Max felt her breath against his chest, knew the hitch in her breathing as she shivered. "I *didn't* have enough milk for him. She was right about that. But the doctor told me that sometimes women who are under a great deal of strain have problems nursing their children, and that cow's milk does very well for those babies."

"And my mother didn't agree with him?" Max asked quietly. Even as he remembered her words of censure when bottles were purchased and nipples boiled in a kettle on the kitchen range.

I never had a bit of trouble providing for my sons. He recalled her words as if she whispered them in his ear, even now.

"She was right, Max. He died of milk fever, and if I'd been able to feed him as a normal mother could, he—"

It was his turn to halt her words and he did it by placing his lips over hers and sealing the hateful, blame-filled phrases from his hearing. "I don't want you to talk this way," he said finally. "You were a good mother, Faith. If you weren't able to produce enough milk, and if the doctor was right, that you were under a lot of strain, then it was my fault for not providing you with a home in which you could be safe from a woman who didn't understand you."

"Oh, she understood me, all right," Faith said, bitterness filling her voice. "She knew exactly how to hurt me, how to make me feel the pain of my loss, and own it as my own fault."

"Hush, sweetheart. Don't let it cause you any more grief. Our next child will be born in a different home, with different surroundings, and we'll be on our own, without anyone else there to cause you distress."

"Our next child?"

"I want another child, Faith. I want it from you. I can't imagine another woman in my bed or my home. I'm willing to buy a house for us, something outside the city, maybe, where you can have some land around you, instead of the sounds of passersby through the windows and the grocer's cart rolling down the street."

"Have you looked for such a place?" she asked, and he was pleased at the lift in her voice, the hope manifested in her query.

"I saw thirty acres just outside the city, with a large home and outbuildings," he said. "The owners had been raising horses there, and they moved to Kentucky where they would be closer to the center of horse-breeding country."

"Is it empty?" she asked, and he nodded. She snuggled closer and was silent.

After long moments he whispered the query that well might make a new beginning for them both. "Will you consider it?" he asked, then held his breath as he awaited her reply.

She sighed, then murmured against his chest, and he felt the soft brush of her lips against his skin, her fingers lifting to spread across his shoulder. Her eyelids fluttered and he knew their presence as if butterflies touched him there. And then she slept once more.

The setting sun found them, blessed their union as they dozed, and then sank below the horizon as Max reached for the quilt to draw it over the woman in his arms. She whispered his name and curled closer, and he smiled, closing his eyes as he joined her again in the restorative sleep that claimed them both.

They had settled nothing, but she'd given him much to consider, and even as he slept, his dreams were filled with the home he'd left behind, the woman who was his mother running the house he'd lived in as both son, then husband. It was time for sweeping changes, he decided.

Once he returned to Boston, with Faith at his side, he would form a new life in which his wife's happiness would be uppermost in his heart and mind.

"You got a letter from back East," the postmaster said as Max opened the door of the general store and ushered Faith inside. The gentleman who tended the mail had a corner of the large room for his own, and it was there, from behind a grilled opening, that he doled out the letters, newspapers and occasional packages that arrived daily on a westbound train.

"I have?" Faith asked, surprise obvious in her words.

"No, ma'am, Miss Faith. It's your husband who got a letter," Titus Liberty said with a smile. "If his name's Maxwell McDowell, that is."

"That's me," Max said, striding up to accept his mail. He glanced at it for a moment, then stuffed it in his pocket. Bending, he whispered in Faith's ear, "Let's go on over to the bank first, and I'll just sign over these papers to you so you can deposit your money in your account."

"I don't have an account, Max. I haven't any money in

the bank,'' she told him, looking up into dark eyes that seemed to have become veiled, hiding his emotion. ''I'll have to open one.''

''You can do that without me, sweetheart,'' he told her. ''It's all yours, anyway.''

With a wave at Mr. Metcalf, they left the store and walked across the street toward the wide doors of the bank. Max stepped up and held the brass panel for Faith to pass through the doorway before him, then walked to the high table provided. Picking up a pen, he dipped it in the inkwell. With a flourish, he signed his name in two places, then blew on the signature and handed her the papers.

''It's all set. You go ahead, and I'll step outside and read my letter.''

She shot him a curious glance, then nodded. ''All right. I'll be out presently.''

The president of the bank looked through his spectacles at her papers and nodded, then reached into his desk drawer for a form. He studied it for a moment, then pushed it across the desk, handing her a pen.

''If you'll sign that right at the bottom, Miss Faith, I'll open your account for you.'' He glanced once more at the document he held, then at the bank check Max had brought along with him.

''This is a considerable amount of money, you know. Are you sure you don't want your husband's name on the account with yours?'' he asked.

''He told me to do with it as I please,'' she said crisply. ''And I'd like it in my name alone.'' Recalling the day she'd signed all the documents Max had placed before her, then shoved them helter-skelter to the floor as she turned her back on the legacy from her father, she focused on the dollar amount this transaction represented. Her eyes widened as she read the figures, and then counted the zeroes that followed the number three.

Thirty thousand dollars. Her father had left her a small fortune, a veritable gold mine, an amount from which she could draw interest and still hold the major portion untouched. Her life would change immeasurably with this much money at her fingertips. And Max was allowing it to take place.

Her sensible mind recognized his strategy. He would turn her loose, in order to free her from any restraint on his part. And then she would make up her own mind as to her future. He'd stepped back, and she wondered at his motives.

He'd presented his case, leaving her the choice. *Will you consider it?*

Had she even replied before sleep captured her in its web? Was that to be his final plea? Was he satisfied to leave her here now that she was endowed with sufficient funds to survive on her own?

Faith signed the papers and sat back in the chair while the banker rose and approached his teller. The two men put their heads together and the documents Max had signed were examined again. In a few minutes, the banker returned and held out a small, black book for Faith's use.

"Your balance is on the first page," he said. "We'll catch it up to date whenever you bring it in, adding your interest to the base amount. If you choose to add any more funds or take out money for whatever reason, it will be kept track of in this book. You'll want to keep it in a safe place, Miss Faith."

He smiled at her as she took possession of the pasteboard-covered record book. "Did you want any money today?" he asked, and she shook her head. Max had been paying for everything at the general store since his arrival, and she was left with what must surely be a considerable amount of credit on her account there, what with the eggs she'd delivered several times into Mr. Metcalf's keeping.

"Thank you," she said politely, then turned and left the bank, aware of the man's gaze fixed on her as she walked away. He'd no doubt not met another woman in town who had this much money at her disposal, she thought, and that fact brought a spring to her step as she opened the door and walked into the sunlight.

Max was sitting on a bench in front of the bank, and as she stepped into view, he folded his letter and replaced it in the envelope he held. Rising, he held out one hand, and looked into her eyes.

"Is everything all right?" he asked. "Did you get a receipt for the money?"

She nodded. "I suppose it's as good as a receipt. He gave me a little book with the amount written in it, and he initialed it himself." She held it out to Max, but he shook his head.

"I don't need to see it, so long as you're satisfied," he said.

"I want you to look at it for me," she told him, aware that his pride needed a bit of bolstering right now. He'd effectively turned her loose, and if she felt independent, it was all right to allow him to think she still needed his advice and cherished his concern.

He took the bankbook and opened it, scanning the figures, then closed it and handed it back to her. A grin touched his lips. "Do you feel like a woman of means?"

"No." She considered a moment and then changed her mind. "Yes, I suppose I do," she said. "I don't have to worry about money for food or more canning jars or oats for the horses this coming winter."

"Speaking of the cold weather that's sure to come before long, I'd like to check at the general store and see about getting you a wool cloak,'' he said. ''I was thinking last night that you don't have a really warm wrap.''

''I get along,'' she said, facing him proudly. ''You don't need to spend any more money on me, Max.''

''I know that. But I want to, Faith. I'd like to know that you're wrapped in soft wool, with a hood over your head when you go out in the cold.''

She shook her head. ''Not today, Max. I don't need it, and it's foolish to spend money on something I'll only hang on a hook in the wardrobe.''

He lifted a brow and considered her for a moment, as if he debated arguing the point. And then he took her elbow and turned her back toward the general store. ''Can I buy some coffee, anyway?'' he asked. ''And another slab of bacon for the pantry?'' If he was attempting to be meek, he was doing a poor job of it, she decided as she eyed him with a sidelong glance.

''You buy it and I'll cook it,'' she said, allowing him to win this small battle.

It wasn't until they were on the way back to the farmhouse that she remembered his letter. ''Was your mail something important?'' she asked.

''My brother wrote,'' he told her. ''Asking some questions about financial matters. I'll need to answer it and send a reply in a few days.''

She was silent for a moment and then looked up at him from the wagon seat beside him. ''Does he want you to come home?''

''He didn't push for it.'' And it seemed that was all he had to say on the subject.

Max moved his satchel from the spare room into her bedroom, and it was obvious he wasn't about to ask permission for the change in their relationship. He stood in the doorway as she prepared for bed that evening. She turned quickly on her bench before the mirror to face him, her hair flying in a shawl of gold around her.

"Are you going to ask me to leave?" he asked quietly, leaning against the doorjamb as she dropped her brush with a clatter on the dresser.

She shook her head. "No, I think you know better. If I'd wanted you to stay in the other room I'd have stopped you while you were moving in your things while I fixed supper."

He nodded and she watched him a moment, then lifted a hand in welcome. "I'd be a bit tardy telling you now I don't want you in my bed, Max. Anyway, I'd be lying if I said such a thing."

His smile was slow and his steps were casual as he walked toward her. "Do you mind if I undress you?" he asked, taking the hand she offered, lifting her to her feet and pulling her close. His hands slid up her back and into the mass of curls and waves of waist-length hair, gathering its length into his hands.

"I don't mind," she said. "But I was about to get my nightgown out of the drawer."

"Would you mind leaving it there?" he whispered, leaning to take her lips in a kiss that spoke of passion. A passion that had lain dormant throughout the long day, and now was allowed free rein to make itself known.

He kissed her thoroughly, taking liberties as if he'd been set free from constraint, tasting the tender inner surface of her lips and then probing with gentle movements of his tongue, past the barrier of her teeth to the sensitive flesh of her mouth.

Tilting her head for his pleasure, and her own, she obeyed his silent coaxing, tangling her tongue with his, aware of his growing ardor. And then it seemed he'd had enough of this dueling they'd begun, and he forsook the playing field, retreating to the softness of her throat. As his hands leisurely opened the first few buttons of her dress, he leaned to kiss the exposed skin, leaving dampness in the wake of a mouth that seemed set on discovering each part of her body.

She was backed to the bed, and he lifted her until her feet dangled inches above the floor, then turned her until she lay before him as she had the day before. His gaze did not leave her as he stripped off his clothing. His boots had been left by the back door, and he eased off trousers, drawers and stockings with a smooth movement, then shed his shirt, allowing it to fall unhindered behind him.

Faith lifted her hands to finish the unbuttoning process he'd begun minutes before, but he halted her, his movements efficient as he sat her upright on the bed, made short work of her remaining buttons, then drew her arms from the sleeves. He relieved her of her vest, pulling it over her head, and then eased her back down, until her head was on the pillow. Gathering her petticoats and dress in his fists, he drew the yards of fabric down her body, his palms shaping the skin he exposed, pressing into her resilient flesh.

She lifted her hips from the bed, easing his way, and his fingers snagged in the top of her drawers, taking them along with the assortment of garments he'd managed to strip from her. In mere seconds she was exposed to him, naked except for her stockings. One knee on the bed beside her, he bent to loosen her garters, then rolled the brown coverings from her legs and tossed them aside.

"Now we're even," he murmured, dropping fully onto the sheet and leaning to touch her breast, watching as his fingers caressed the swollen peak. "I like this," he said, bending to take it in his mouth.

"I noticed," she said, choking back a laugh. And then flinched as he suckled.

"Too much? Too hard?" he asked, looking up through lashes that hid his expressive eyes from her sight. He watched as she lifted a hand to brush his cheek with her fingertips. "Faith? I don't ever want to hurt you."

"It won't be too much a little later on," she said, thinking of the night before and the strength of his desire, the feel of his hands and mouth on her flesh.

She thought his eyes flared with a dark fire, and then he lowered his lashes and used his tongue to rub against the peaked nub. "Better?" he asked mildly, and she could only nod as her body responded to the teasing touch.

"I won't hurry you along tonight," he promised quietly, leaning to kiss her again, allowing his fingers to trace her waist and hips, the flat of his palms shaping her flesh as he took note of each hollow and curve that made up her slender form. "This may take a while," he mused, his mouth paying homage to her temple, then sliding the length of her cheek to settle for a moment in the hollow beneath her ear.

"Max?" She spoke his name as if it were a query and she needed an answer.

"What is it, love?" he asked, inhaling her scent as if it were a fine perfume and he found it to be the source of all that was sweet. Tasting her skin in small increments, drawing out the exploration of her breasts until she wondered at his patience.

"You needn't worry about me not..." She halted, unable to be as bold as he, unwilling to speak of her desire and readiness for his loving.

"Are you ready for me?" he asked, as if he knew her thoughts and read her mind.

"I can't lie still any longer," she confessed, shifting her hips, aware of the fine tension that built between her thighs with his every whisper of breath against her flesh. "I think I need you now, Max."

"We have all night," he said quietly. "When I come into you, I want you to be aching for me, Faith. I want it to be perfect for you."

And it was.

Chapter Ten

Nicholas's arrival before breakfast was a surprise. As was his reason for showing up at such an early hour, Max decided. And yet he could not help but be pleased by Faith's neighbor seeking his help. After an invitation to join them at the table, Nicholas refused a meal, settling for coffee instead, and then set about asking a favor of Max.

It was a heartening event, Max decided, as Nicholas described his problem. To be considered worthy of Nicholas's esteem, to the extent that it involved his family and home and their safety, added a new depth to their friendship.

"I know it's a lot to ask, but I haven't much choice," Nicholas said bluntly. "Other than the protection of the law—which isn't a feasible option since Brace isn't living next door—you're it, Max. I can't ask the sheriff to ride out to the ranch every day, and even if I could, I'd still be leaving Lin and the others alone for much of the time." He drew in a breath as he finished his lengthy explanation.

"Where are you going?" Max asked.

"Collins Creek. The reason for all of this has to do with my business. There are a couple of problems at my bank there that require my presence. Taking my family along isn't a good idea. I'll save time by traveling alone and handling things quickly."

"How far away will you be?" Max asked. "And what do you want me to do?"

"Just that easy?" Nicholas asked, one brow lifting as he surveyed his neighbor.

"I don't have any reason to turn you down," Max told him.

Nicholas nodded. "It's about fifty miles or so," Nicholas said. "Not a tremendous distance by any means, but it's not a trip I want to subject Lin and the children to right now. Jonathan is cutting his molars, which is an experience that seems to involve a lot of sleepless nights for his mother. Katie is up to her neck with the garden, which is coming in nicely and she's not about to leave with the canning underway."

He sighed, leaning back in his chair. "I try hard not to ruffle Katie's feathers. I don't know what we'd do without her, and I don't even want to think about it. If she says she's had enough of town life and isn't about to venture back there, then I have to accept that."

He picked up his coffee cup and drank the last swallow, then gestured with one hand. "Bottom line is that Lin is a homebody. The thought of lugging two children to Collins Creek makes her cringe, especially when we'd just be turning around and heading back in a day or so." He glanced at Faith. "Do you mind sharing your husband with another household for a few days?"

"No, not at all," she said readily. "You know better than that, Nicholas."

The big man's smile was warm, and Max felt his hackles rise. Only the knowledge that Nicholas was besotted with his own wife allowed him to ignore the close relationship between Faith and her neighbor. ''What do you want us to do?'' he repeated bluntly.

Nicholas looked his way. ''Not a whole lot. Just be available. Check on them every day and make sure they're all right.''

''We can stay there if you like,'' Faith offered. ''It wouldn't be any problem to come here for chores and spend the nights at your place.''

Nicholas nodded, and relief flooded his features. ''That would be even better. There's room for everyone. We have a couple of bedrooms we don't use.''

''We'd need only one,'' Max said with no inflection in his voice, but Faith's color rose as he made the forthright statement.

''That figures,'' Nicholas said, shooting him a knowing glance. ''I assumed you weren't a man to forfeit your rights, McDowell. A fella would be a fool to let a woman like Faith get away a second time, once he was back in her life.''

''We're working things out,'' Max said, looking up at Faith as she set his plate on the table with a clunk. He thought she looked like a thundercloud, and his arm slid to circle her waist. Her eyes glittered, blue ice offering him a glare that promised retribution.

''If she's anything like Lin, you'd better watch your step,'' Nicholas advised him. ''I found a couple of years back it didn't pay to get her dander up. I still don't risk it.''

''I hate it when I'm invisible,'' Faith said shortly. ''If you gentlemen want to discuss me or Lin, you need to find some privacy to do it in.''

Nicholas shot her a teasing look. ''You and my wife make a pair, lady. And I'd be willing to bet you lead this fella a merry chase. Don't look for sympathy from me. I know you, remember?"

Max cleared his throat. "I suspect we'd better get plans ironed out," he said, feeling Faith's aggravation like an icy shower, threatening to give him grief once Nicholas had gone on his way.

"Which would you rather do, Faith? Stay here or over there, and then trot back and forth a couple of times a day?"

"We'll be running one way or the other no matter where we sleep. I'd feel better, and I think Nicholas would, too, if we bunk with Lin."

Max picked up his fork and worked at the pile of eggs on his plate. "When are you leaving?" he asked, between bites.

"This afternoon," Nicholas answered. "As soon as I can get my gear packed and clean up a couple of things I've got going."

"What's happening over there?" Max asked.

"I've hired three men to help with rounding up cattle and sorting out the herd. That's part of the problem. They're not known to me, and I don't feel comfortable leaving Lin to deal with them.

"We're in the process of culling out the steers for shipping down to Dallas. The men can handle things while I'm gone. I just need you to keep an eye on the place, and make sure Lin and the children are safe."

"I can ride with your men if you need me to," Max offered.

"Can you handle that sort of work?" Nicholas asked. "I wasn't sure of your background."

Max shrugged, an offhand movement that signified confidence. "I can ride. I haven't done any work with cattle, but I'm pretty sure I can manage to fill in and see to whatever you need to have done."

"The main thing is to keep them contained for now," Nicholas said. "We've rounded them up out of a series of dead-end canyons, and there'll be hell to pay if they wander off again. My men are setting up a temporary corral tomorrow to hold them while we sort through the lot."

"I imagine I can lend a hand with that," Max said. "I'm a fair hand with horses."

"He's a good shot, too," Faith volunteered. "Taught him myself."

Nicholas grinned. "That's a high recommendation, my friend. Faith is handy with a rifle. Sometime I'll have to tell you a story."

"I may have heard part of it already," Max said. He spread jam on his toasted bread and drank the last of his coffee. "I'll come over this afternoon and you can show me around."

Faith rose to refill their coffee cups, but Nicholas covered his with his palm and shook his head. "I probably will have left by then," he said. "I'll only have time to ride out and talk to my men before I do. Why don't you bring the wagon along, Faith? Your mare and filly, too, if you like. I have plenty of room in the barn for the extra stock. That way all you have to do is come back here to feed chickens once a day."

Faith considered him a moment and then nodded in agreement. "I suppose that'll work. I'll get our things together while Max does the chores." She smiled sweetly. "It's time to clean the chicken house, and that'll keep him busy for an hour or so."

"I knew she'd get me," Max said glumly, shooting Nicholas a glowering look as the men rose to leave the kitchen.

"Thanks for the coffee," Nicholas said, reaching for his hat as he pushed the screened door open. Max's hat hung on a handy nail, and his long fingers snagged it by its wide brim as he followed.

Faith lost no time in picking out several changes of clothing for each of them, stuffing them into a valise and then adding small personal items to the assortment. She folded her new nightgown and smiled as she thought of Max. Since stowing his belongings in her bedroom, he'd decided the gown should be left permanently in the drawer. Sleeping in Lin's home would put a damper on his behavior.

Her hands slowed as she considered the change in her life over the past few days. Max would be heading east before long if the problems in his family's business couldn't be solved without his presence there to handle things. He'd written his brother a reply and had planned on riding to town to post the letter today. It wouldn't be any great problem to do that and then head on to Nicholas's place after she'd tidied the house and readied the horses for the trek.

Dinner was a hurried affair, and Max prepared to set off on horseback to town after they'd eaten. The valise was on the wagon, the horses hitched and ready to leave when Faith deemed things to be in order, and she had only to tie the mare and filly on behind for the short ride to the big house next door.

At the last minute she picked up the crock of eggs from the pantry to take along, and then looked around the kitchen. "I think that's all of it," she said as Max came through the kitchen door.

He reached to take the crock from her, then held her in the bend of his other arm, leaning to kiss her briefly, holding her close for a long moment as he admonished her to take care. Her patient smile told him without words that she was hiding amusement at his concern. And he sighed.

"I know you think you're invincible, sweetheart, but I'm allowed to worry about you if I want to. Just be sure you have your gun with you. It doesn't hurt to be cautious."

"I know," she said, and her lips curved. "I kinda like you looking after me, Max. It's been a long time since I was the focus of anyone's attention. It's growing on me."

He held her tightly and bent to drop a series of kisses across her face. "I hope so. I intend to spend a lot of years looking after you."

He deposited the eggs in the wagon near her feet and she waved as he rode off. Her rifle lay on the wagon floor, and the mare and filly trailed behind on lead ropes as she traveled the short distance to the house Nicholas had built for his wife.

It was truly lovely, Faith decided, as her wagon rolled past the back porch and on to the open barn door. A man emerged, looking up at her with admiration as she drew the team to a halt. He reached for the nearest horse and held his harness firmly while Faith climbed down from the wagon seat.

"Ma'am?" he said, the greeting traditional, and Faith nodded.

"You must be Billy," she said. "Nicholas said he'd hired a stockman."

"I kinda do it all, at least the chores up close to the barn. There's two others that are workin' the herd right now," Billy said, after acknowledging her remark with a nod. "Nick told me to get your animals settled in, and then when your husband shows up I'm to head on up to the north pasture and help with rounding up the cattle we're takin' to Dallas in a couple of days."

"Max should be here in a few hours," she told him,

gathering her valise and the shawl she'd brought along. "I'll be in the house with Mrs. Garvey and the children."

"Yes, ma'am," Billy said, tugging at his hat brim as he turned to strip the harness from her team of horses. "I'll put these animals out in the pasture, and the mare and filly with them." He cast an admiring look at Goldie. "Sure is a pretty little thing. Nicholas is tickled with his filly. Told us all about her."

"Thank you," Faith said briefly, heading for the house. The man was filled with admiring glances, she decided, and a wariness she was not familiar with settled within her. She'd cast it aside within minutes of seeing Lin on the back porch, and soon was deeply involved in holding the baby, whose teething problems had kept Lin up most of the night before.

"I'm so glad you're here," her neighbor confessed as Faith settled into the rocking chair, the baby snuggled in a blanket and held close for comfort. For an instant, as she hugged young Jonathan close, Faith had a flash of the future. She soon might be holding her own child this way, if her deeply ingrained knowledge of coming events was to prove true.

"This could be good practice for you," Lin said slyly, shooting Faith a sidelong look, as if she sought confirmation of her theory. "Wouldn't you like to have a child one day, Faith?"

Faith's reply stuck in her throat and then was offered as a casual statement of fact as she rocked slowly. "I had a little boy," she said quietly. "He died of milk fever when he was two months old."

Lin gasped and approached her with open arms, then bent and embraced both her friend and the baby she held clutched to her bosom. "I'm so sorry," she whispered. "I had no idea. You never said anything before."

"It isn't something I talk about much."

Lin stood beside her and chose her words with care. "Was that part of the problem in your marriage? Or would you rather not speak of it?"

Faith looked up into eyes that pleaded for understanding, and Lin smiled, a faint movement of her lips. "I'll understand if you tell me to mind my own business," she said.

"No, it's all right. I blamed myself for a long time for the baby's death, and Max's mother helped me along that path."

"Max's mother?"

"She lived with us. Or rather, we lived with her, in the family home."

"It doesn't sound like a good situation. We have Katie here and she's been like a mother or favorite aunt to Nicholas for a long time, but she's been my right hand all along, and she's definitely my ally. I don't know what I'd do without her."

"I'd like to have done without Max's mother, believe me," Faith said, lifting a corner of the blanket to peek within its folds at the baby, who seemed to have settled down. "I wasn't very good at mothering, but she wasn't any encouragement. I seem to have done everything wrong when it came to tending my child, beginning with my lack of nourishment for him."

"I find that hard to believe," Lin said staunchly. "As to not having sufficient milk for a baby, it's something that happens on occasion. You weren't the first woman to have problems. I think you'd be a fine mother. And I hope you get another chance to prove it. Without Max's mother in residence."

"That's not about to happen anytime soon," Faith said quietly. "I'm living in Texas, and Max's family home and business are in Boston. And never the twain shall meet,'' she quoted softly.

''If Max is half the man I think he is, he'll work something out,'' Lin predicted. And Faith was left to rock quietly before the parlor window as her friend left the room in silence to tend to chores that had been neglected for the benefit of a teething baby.

Max rode into the yard an hour later, and with a quick glance at the house, where Katie sat on the back porch and shelled peas, he headed for the barn. A wave of her hand from the woman who ran Nicholas's house was his only welcome, but once he caught sight of the wagon near the barn, and a glimpse of Goldie in the pasture beyond, he knew Faith was not far away.

The stockman Nicholas had hired was named Billy, and seemed to be knowledgeable about the roundup and the chores that needed tending to. He spoke highly of Faith's mare and admired the new filly. ''Sure wouldn't mind havin' a horse like that myself,'' he said cheerfully.

And Max was left to silently agree with the man. A whole stableful of such animals would be to his liking. If he could only persuade Faith to come to Boston, he'd do whatever it took to provide her with space to house her animals. Perhaps that would be the deciding factor. And with that in mind, he began forming the artillery he would use to persuade her to his purpose.

It was not to be a topic of discussion, as he'd planned. Faith stayed up late with the baby so that Lin could sleep, and he was barely aware of her presence when she slid into the bed beside him, well after midnight.

Daylight found him seeking out Katie in the kitchen, who quietly placed his breakfast before him, then fixed a plate for Billy when he appeared at the back door. Together, the men went to the barn, and Max began a day of chores that gave him a taste of cattle ranching. He worked with the men, building a temporary corral where the cattle would be held, stringing new rope from trees and hastily erecting fenceposts.

He left them in late afternoon and rode toward the house, aware of muscles that ached and blisters that had formed in new places on his hands. Gloves were a hindrance sometimes, he'd discovered as he worked, and he was filled with a new respect for Nicholas and the life he'd chosen.

Faith helped Katie with supper and then joined him on the back porch after the dishes were washed and put away. "Are you all right?" she asked, sitting on the top step beside him.

"Just tired," he told her. "I didn't know there was so much work involved in raising cattle. I guess I thought they just ate until they were big enough to butcher and then trotted off to the stockyards." He groaned and smiled at her, with a wry twist of his lips that told of a hard day in the saddle.

"You have blisters," she said, touching his palm. "You'll need to let me put salve on them for you."

He shook his head. "They're fine. I'll wear gloves tomorrow."

"Why didn't you today?" she asked, her fingers gentle on the swollen areas.

"It wasn't handy," he said with a shrug, "and by the time enough rope had run through my hands to make me aware they were getting raw it was too late to do much good."

"Men." The single word was a tender condemnation, and he lifted her face to his, pressing a kiss against willing lips.

"You like men," he teased.

''Just you.'' Her mouth opened beneath his, and he hesitated.

''Can we continue this inside?'' It was a coaxing whisper, and she laughed beneath her breath as she nodded.

The next day was more taxing than Max had bargained on, but the smile of gratitude on Lin's face as he returned to the house at suppertime was payment enough for his hours of labor. And then Faith whispered in his ear as he paused at her side for a welcoming kiss, and the massage she promised him made him feel refreshed at the mere thought.

He was fresh from a bath when she arranged him on the bed, and the cool touch of her hands was welcome against his back. She turned down the lamp and blew it out, and he heard the rustle of her clothing as she undressed.

The mattress moved as she lowered a knee beside his hip. A fragrant oil met his skin and slender fingers fed it into his sore muscles. Then, with a lithe movement, she was astride his back, leaning forward as she worked, lending her strength to the task. Her fingers followed the long lines of sinew and tendon as she spoke quietly of the happenings of her day, and he listened, bemused and half-asleep.

He drifted in a world of pleasure, half listening to the words she whispered, her tone as soothing as her touch. And then she rolled to one side and he turned his face toward her. ''Thanks,'' he murmured, replete with satisfaction.

''You're welcome.'' Her hand touched his jaw, brushed a stray lock from his forehead and then slid to his nape, where her fingers played in the length of dark, waving hair. ''We'll probably be leaving here by day after tomorrow,'' she said quietly.

''You think so?'' His eyelids were heavy, but he fought

the urge to doze off. ''Are you tired?'' he asked, stifling a yawn.

''Not as tired as you,'' she said, smiling tenderly. And then she leaned toward him and her kiss was warm, lingering and damp. ''You need to sleep,'' she told him.

''Maybe in the morning...'' he murmured.

It seemed they'd barely slept when the distant sound of gunfire brought him to his feet beside the bed. Donning drawers and a pair of trousers and shoving his feet into his boots, he snatched up a shirt. Aware of Faith at his heels, he sped to the back porch and turned. Faith was behind him, her nightgown a pale shadow in the darkness.

He stepped onto the porch, tugging his shirt in place and buttoning it rapidly. His eyes narrowed, searching the shadowed outline of buildings and the stretches of pastureland toward the north. Silently, he waited, watching for any visible movement.

Inside the house, Lin spoke, and Faith's reply was quiet. ''No lights,'' she said. ''We don't want to make Max a target on the porch.''

He opened the screened door and went into the kitchen. ''I'll need my revolver,'' he told Faith and she went to the bedroom quickly, carrying it back to him in moments. ''Is there a long gun I can use?'' he asked Lin, and she led him to the locked cabinet in the pantry where Nicholas kept extra weapons, opening it with a key from the top shelf.

''Take what you need,'' she said quickly. ''I'm sure Billy will be in to let us know what's happened. I'll have Katie watch the children, and Faith and I will arm ourselves.''

But there was no sign of Billy, and the barn was dark and silent. Within minutes, Max headed across the yard, opening the door and easing inside. Working in the moonlight that filtered through behind him, he readied one of

Nicholas's horses for riding, unwilling to expose himself by lighting the lantern hanging from the ceiling.

Behind him, a sound caught his attention, and he turned quickly, then relaxed as he recognized Faith in the doorway, her pale hair gleaming. "What are you doing out here?" he asked quietly, noting the rifle she carried.

"I came out to see if Billy was here, but apparently he's not. Can I do anything to help?"

"I'm going to ride north and find out what's going on. I want you to go back to the house and stay safe. I'm wary of Billy not being here."

"Nicholas seems to trust him," Faith said slowly, and Max waited for her next words as if a second shoe were about to fall to the floor. She did not disappoint him, her face somber as she looked up. "I don't like the man, Max. I can't say why. Just a feeling, I suppose. Watch your back."

He frowned at her warning, and yet he had no reason to doubt her instincts. "Nick wouldn't have a man so close to the house if he couldn't trust him," he told her.

She shook her head stubbornly. "I don't care what Nicholas thinks. I don't have good feelings about the man."

Faith was not given to rash statements. If she felt so strongly about this, it would pay him to heed her words. "All right," he said. "I trust your judgment, sweetheart." He bent to snatch a quick kiss. "Be safe," he murmured.

"I'll be fine. Lin has a shotgun at hand, and I'm not afraid to use my rifle if I have to."

"My wife the sharpshooter," he teased, casting her a last look. His left foot lifted to the stirrup and he was in the saddle and out the door, riding swiftly across the pasture, and beyond it to the wide meadow to the north. Within moments he was at the eastern edge of the meadow, where a hedgerow rimmed the side.

He rode along it, counting on the bushes and tall trees to conceal him. He pulled his horse to a halt, then blended into the foliage, intent on the horizon, where, farther to the north, he knew the men were watching the herd of cattle.

Whoever had pulled a trigger was in hiding, but the fact remained that something was not as it should be. It would not be wise to rush in. Better to stay back until he surveyed the lay of the land. It took on different forms in the night, the familiar acreage becoming a mystic landscape in the dark.

Her rifle at her side, Faith went back to the house, aware of every shadow, her hearing attuned to each sound from the trees. There was a hush she was wary of, as if the night birds had drawn into their nests. Even the owls were silent, and the usual soft rustling sounds of small night creatures were missing.

"Will he be all right?" Lin asked from her post beside the kitchen window.

"He's a man," Faith said sharply. "They all think they're invincible, don't you know?"

Lin chuckled in the darkness. "He's capable, I'm sure, Faith. Nicholas trusts him. He told me he thinks Max is a warrior in civilized clothing."

Faith considered that thought and nodded. "He may be right. I just never considered him in that light, I suppose. But he's fearless, I'll give him that. He's never run up against an enemy he couldn't best, or a foe he couldn't run to ground, so far as I know."

"It took him long enough to find you," Lin said.

"He's never told me much about how he managed to track me down," Faith said. "Only that he paid good money to locate my whereabouts. It makes me wonder if my face was on Wanted posters that circulated among lawmen between here and Boston. I've meant to ask him, but we've always found something else to talk about."

"I imagine you've had a lot of catching up to do."

In the dark, it seemed easier, somehow, to speak of Max and the problems they'd faced during the past weeks. Faith chose her words carefully as she confided in her friend. "We had to start from scratch," she said. "Right back at the beginning, with his mother and my unhappiness, and Max's inability to understand my problems."

"Has he seen the light?" Lin asked.

"Apparently so," Faith told her. "He's done a lot of backtracking, I think. And I've decided that if I ever plan to make any sort of life with him, I'll have to face his mother down someday."

"Will you go back to Boston with him?"

The silence was long as Faith considered the implications of that decision. And then she spoke slowly as she faced the decision she must make. "Not yet. Maybe never," she said. "I can't go back until I'm sure it will be different. And I don't know how I can ever reach that point."

"You don't trust him?" Lin's query was touched with sadness.

"Yes." It was a quick reply, an admission of her bone-deep knowledge of Max's honesty and trustworthiness. "But I'm afraid of getting back into the same mess I walked away from. In fact, I'm just about ready to put my roots down here, and let Max make up his mind what he wants to do."

"Is that fair?" Lin asked.

"To me? Or to Max?" But before Lin could form a reply and voice it aloud, a gunshot resounded from afar followed by a volley. The noise echoed in the kitchen and sent both of the women to the floor.

Lin lifted her head to peer through the window first, and Faith joined her there. "Can you see anything?" she asked.

"Nothing. But someone out there has a rifle, and I gave Max a shotgun."

He'd ridden through the woods, confident that his movements were hidden by the wealth of trees and undergrowth he traveled past. Max halted as he caught sight of a herd of cattle, heads down as they grazed. And then he saw two riders traveling in wide circles, passing each other at the far side of the herd. They halted for a moment as they met, and then rode on.

Max watched as, near a small campfire, a third man stepped from the shadows to bend low, lifting what appeared to be a coffeepot from the fire. Billy, from what he could make out. And there was no way of knowing who had fired the shot that had alerted him, not more than a half hour ago.

And then one of the riders approached the campfire and the two men spoke, their words carrying on the night air to where Max watched. "Any sign of trouble?" Billy called, his voice muted.

"Don't know who fired the shot," the rider answered. "Probably trying to stir up the cattle. We're lucky we didn't have trouble on our hands."

"Well, keep on riding. I'll spell one of you in a while." Billy's words were distinct in the night air. As the cowhand rode off, the other man's gaze followed him closely, and then he replaced the coffeepot over the fire and stepped away from the smoldering wood. His head turned, and it seemed his eyes swept the horizon, as though he searched the darkness with purpose.

A small flare of light caught Max's attention, a barely perceptible flash that disappeared as quickly as it had been born. Beyond the herd, where hills rose in a hulking silhouette against the horizon. Apparently the area Nicholas had described, Max thought. And if those hills concealed dead-end canyons, it stood to reason that men might also have chosen them as hiding places.

As if the flaring glow had been a signal, Billy lifted a hand, a seemingly idle gesture, and yet one with purpose. For a metal object in his hand caught the firelight and glowed momentarily.

The man was sending a signal, and Max felt his skin prickle in awareness at the sense of danger. From the hills came another, longer flash of light, and Billy responded by circling the campfire to search out his horse. Already saddled, the animal was quickly mounted and Billy turned its head sharply to trot in a wide circle to the west and then north around the milling herd of cattle.

Max watched, uncertain as to his goal. Billy was surely up to no good, but whether or not the other two men were trustworthy was a question Max had no way of answering. Better to watch and wait, he decided, and he backed his horse into the undergrowth beneath tall trees.

The three men met at the north side of the herd and then Billy rode on, riding alone, his horse moving slowly as he circled the area. His partners headed back to the campfire separately, riding on either side of the herd, meeting finally near the smoldering fire. They murmured quietly, and one of them dismounted, tying his horse loosely to a rope corral.

From his vantage point, Max watched, narrowing his gaze to keep Billy in sight, losing track as the moon went behind a cloud and the lone rider disappeared from view for a moment. And then, as if firecrackers were set off in a flurry, there was a quick volley of gunfire and several riders appeared, traveling rapidly from the shelter of the hills to encircle the herd of cattle. Max nudged his mount into motion and bent low over the horse's neck as he headed for the lone rider, who had begun another circuit.

"Rustlers." The single word resounded in Max's ears as the man shouted the warning, and Max pulled the shotgun from the sheath behind his saddle. From behind him, he heard the man left by the campfire shout another warning, and then another hail of bullets shattered the night air, and Max knew a moment of panic as his horse collapsed beneath him.

He jerked his boots from the stirrups as he hit the ground, rolling away from the animal as it whinnied, a shrill, piercing sound that told of pain. The animal lay on its side, and Max crept up to lie in the shadow of his saddle, lifting to peer over the heaving side of his mount.

The herd was moving, and as he watched, several mounted men circled to control the direction of the milling cattle. Their shouts were muted, yet carried on the night air, and he caught a glimpse of Billy in their number. The cowhand by the fire had disappeared, and the second rider lay beside his horse, a hundred feet from where Max sheltered.

"Let's move them out," a man shouted, and the others obeyed, tightening the herd as though a noose surrounded the cattle, herding them toward the east, where a flat pastureland beckoned.

Max weighed his options. If he could make it to the riderless horse, he could follow. But doing so would expose him to the men who had already shot his horse and apparently killed the other rider. He watched instead, his anger rising as Nicholas's cattle were taken in hand by Billy and his henchmen.

* * *

"There's no way of knowing what's going on," Faith said, her ears straining lest she miss any further sound from the area north of the ranch house. "I'm going out there." She turned to face Lin, gauging her response.

"I doubt it would do me any good to try stopping you," her friend answered. "Just let me get another gun for Katie and I'll post her at this window while I stay in the other room with the children."

"Can she shoot?" Faith asked, twining her light-colored hair into a knot atop her head, then tugging her hat in place, lest the moon cast its glow and expose her. Her fingers were nimble, filling her pockets with ammunition for the rifle she held. There was enough firepower in her grasp to back up Max should he need her help, and the thought of him on his own out there in the dark lent speed to her movements.

"She can aim and pull the trigger. That's all we need for now," Lin said. "You go on ahead as soon as I call out."

Faith stepped out onto the porch, aware that the light from inside the house made her a ready target. With a long leap to the ground, she set off for the barn, and slid through the door, flattening herself against the wall as she listened intently to the sounds of horses and the rustle of straw where the cow was bedded down for the night. Satisfied that there was no alien presence within the confines of Nicholas's barn, she felt her way down the aisle to where her horse was stabled.

By the time she reached the stall, her eyes had become more accustomed to the faint moonlight shining through several windows, and she spoke quietly to her mare, then led her from the stall to stand in the aisle. Her saddle was nearby on a sawhorse and she quickly lifted it to Goldie's back, then located the mare's bridle and bit. Within minutes

Faith had led her mare from the barn and mounted her, half-hidden beneath the shadow of wide eaves.

The horse was pale, visible beneath the moon, but there was no help for it, she decided. She wasn't familiar with any of Nicholas's animals, and Goldie was to be trusted. Almost soundlessly, Faith found her way into the woods and lingered among the trees, traveling slowly so that her horse would not come to disaster on the uneven ground.

It seemed an eternity before she caught a glimpse of a campfire in the distance, and she nudged her mare to a quicker pace, riding in shadowed depths beneath low-hanging limbs.

The herd of cattle ebbed and flowed in the distance as several horsemen circled them, keeping them together as they edged them to the east. And then she caught sight of a large heap beyond the campfire, and noted the form of a man crouched behind the shelter of a fallen horse.

The cattle began moving more rapidly, and her heart skipped a beat as she recognized the man's peril. Should the herd be swept in his direction, he might be trampled by their hooves, having little protection to keep him safe. He lifted his head a bit, turning until his back was to her, and she stifled a gasp. Broad shoulders and the tilt of his hat proclaimed his identity.

Max. It was Max. Without forethought, without hesitation or examination of her own peril, she dug her heels into Goldie's sides and bent over the mare's neck. "Go," she whispered, the single syllable harsh and rasping. The horse obeyed, her ears flattening, her haunches propelling her forward as Faith clung to her back.

That her golden horse was a brilliant silhouette in the moonlight was of no matter to her. The man who needed her help was her only concern, and her heartbeat matched the sound of Goldie's hooves as the mare raced across the grassy pastureland toward Max.

"Damn." The single word was guttural, and Max felt his jaw harden, his eyes narrow as he glanced toward the men who herded the cattle, the bulk of the herd slowly turning toward him. He'd thought to run to safety, but knew full well he didn't stand a chance with numerous guns able to aim and fire before he moved more than fifty feet. It was a lost cause. His next best bet was to huddle behind his downed horse and hope its body sheltered him.

Now, as he watched the flying horse, her rider bent low over the shimmering mane, it seemed he stood a good chance of seeing Faith shot from her saddle instead. His muscles tightened, his hand clutched the stock of the shotgun Lin had given him, and he readied himself for the leap that would enable him to escape, should the element of surprise be in his favor.

Faith's hat flew off, her hair streamed out behind her and he heard the call of one of the men who rode closest. "It's a woman." As if it were a signal, the others turned their horses and headed toward the golden horse.

"Get back! Get back!" A loud, angry voice cried out the order and the men hesitated, unwilling to obey as they watched Faith ride across two hundred yards of prairie toward the man who had risen from behind his fallen horse. The herd shifted, stragglers making a bolt toward the north, and one rider, then another turned back to round them up.

As if they'd been prodded by an unknown force, the cattle broke into a full run, and the men who fought to control them suddenly had their hands full. Shouts and cries of anger rose in the air as Faith drew back on her reins, and the golden mare slowed beside Max's position. A shot rang out and Max swore, a violent oath.

His foot touched the stirrup Faith had vacated for his

benefit, and he swung up behind her. As Goldie felt the release of her reins, she surged ahead, and Max bent low over Faith, hoping to cover her back and present his own as a target to the gunman who was aiming in their direction. Twice more a shot rang out, and Max gripped Faith by the waist and lifted her from her seat, aware that her balance was skewed as he slid over the cantle and into the saddle.

She settled against his thighs, and Goldie sidestepped, as if protesting the shift of his added weight, then moved forward at Faith's urging. Again shots rang out and as Max ducked his head and held a protective arm around Faith, they reached the edge of the pasture and surged into the deeply shadowed woods.

He felt a stinging sensation high on his arm and pressed closer to the woman in front of him. If Faith should be shot… He could not tolerate the thought of such a thing, and yet she'd left herself exposed to the threat of death when she'd charged across open ground to snatch him up.

Behind them the cattle pounded the ground, and the sound of men shouting provided a background for their own frazzled breathing and the snorting of the mare beneath them. Faith slowed the horse and spoke quietly to her, leaning to rub her hand along the animal's neck as they rode even farther into the trees.

"Will they go back to the house, do you think?" she asked, gasping for breath. "I've left Lin and Katie alone with the children."

"No, I think they've neatly disposed of the other ranch hands. The other two men apparently weren't in on the raid," Max said. "It seems Billy was definitely in cahoots with the gang. I doubt if the rest of them fear being identified by us."

He felt Faith trembling, drew her back against his chest and supported her with one arm. "You weren't shot?" he asked, and waited as she struggled for breath. Her head shook, a negative reply, and he felt a weight lift, even as he noted with renewed intensity the throbbing pain of his wound.

"We need to get back to the house," he said. "There's a small matter for you to tend to."

Chapter Eleven

Max clutched the glass in his hand as he tilted his head back to swallow. Nicholas's whiskey was potent, and Max closed his eyes, hoping for immediate relief from the fire in his arm, relishing the smooth glide of aged liquor as it slid down his throat. It was a celebration of sorts, he figured, aided and abetted by the women surrounding him. Still being alive, after the events of the night, was reason enough to offer a toast.

His mind far from alert during the long ride back from the north range atop Goldie's saddle, he'd held tightly to Faith, allowing her the reins and simply clinging to consciousness. Making his way into the house and slumping into a kitchen chair had required an effort almost beyond him, he realized.

And then he'd been taken in hand by Lin, swallowing without argument the double shot she offered him. Now he settled back to numbing the misery that lanced his upper arm. His glass was quickly refilled as Lin reached across the kitchen table with a dark bottle in her hand, apparently intent on bringing him to a sedated state that would allow the tending of his wound with little pain.

If she only realized how close he was to dropping his

head on the tablecloth and closing his eyes, she'd snatch the glass from his hand, he thought with a grimace. And then he felt the touch of Faith's hand on his shoulder. Beside him, she waited, and he felt the weight of her gaze warming him, drawing him to her, the craving for her touch causing him to shiver at the caress she bestowed as her fingers threaded through his hair.

She'd hauled him almost bodily into the house, leaving the horse tied in front of the porch, and then left him to Lin's care while she found a fresh shirt. He'd heard her movements in the kitchen as she gathered hot water and clean towels for her use. Now she was once more at his side and he tilted his head to view her through eyes that narrowed as he focused on her.

Her lips formed a thin line as she lifted a pair of scissors from the table and prepared to seek out the wound that continued to seep blood, matting his shirt and the remains of her own. "What are you doin'?" he asked, his voice slurring the final word.

"I'm going to look at your arm," she said calmly, though even to his blurred vision she seemed more than a bit pale.

"You're not a doctor," he protested mildly, and looked around the kitchen as if he expected one to appear from the woodwork.

"No one ever said I was," she retorted. "But I'm all you've got, mister."

"Hmm..." His considering murmur made her smile, and she looked at him with a grin. "You know what you're doin'?" he asked, focusing on her soft lips.

"You'd better hope so." And then she set to work, and he closed his eyes.

The horse had not been able to keep up a prolonged gallop, and Goldie's trot had jarred him painfully. So they had ridden slowly in the light of dawn. Max had been thankful for Faith's calm demeanor, watching as she shed her own shirt, tearing it into a rough bandage, then halted her mare long enough to press the thick pad to his wound.

Now her calmness was focused on his shoulder, and her words were accusing. "You call this a *small matter?*" she asked, quoting him as she cut away the bloody fabric, allowing the tattered material to fall from Max's arm. She lifted a clean towel, wet it in the basin of hot water and then motioned for Lin to hold the lamp nearer.

"You consider a bullet tearing a hole in your arm a minor detail, do you?" As she spoke, her voice rose in volume, and Max looked up at her in surprise. The woman sounded angry. He could understand concern, even a certain amount of horror as she faced the result of the bullet's fury. But anger was useless at this point.

And then he looked closer, into blue eyes that held tears in abeyance. Faith was struggling to keep from shedding those salty drops, biting at her lip, then blinking rapidly as she paused in her chore of washing away clotted blood, revealing the extent of his wound.

"I'll need to get out all those bits and pieces of fabric from your shirt, or they'll cause infection."

"I may have the very thing to do the trick," Lin said quietly, turning to the silverware drawer in her buffet and sorting through its contents. "Try this," she suggested, handing Faith a silver nutpick. Without comment, Faith dipped it into the small cup of whiskey beside her.

The pointed tool was out of its element, Max decided, and he frowned as he watched his wife, her hand steady as she used the slender instrument to remove small bits of fabric from his raw flesh. Blood welling from the wound hid her prey, but Faith was relentless, bending close to probe about, lest stray bits of fiber remain. A rim of perspiration stood out upon her brow and her complexion seemed ashen to Max's discerning eye.

"Are you all right?" he asked, wincing as her instrument touched raw flesh while lifting a bit of thread from the bloody mess.

"This isn't the high point of my week," she admitted, her voice trembling, as if her throat were filled with aching tears. She looked up into his gaze and he was stunned by the pain that blurred the depths of her blue eyes. Wiping the latest bit of flotsam on a clean towel, she bent low once more, peering into his wound.

"Let me give you a hand. I'll wipe the blood away while you tend to the rest of it," Lin said quietly, reaching with a clean bit of cotton to soak up the oozing residue. "There," she murmured after long moments. "I think you've got it all, Faith."

Max turned his head sharply to see for himself, gritting his teeth as he recognized the havoc a bullet could bring about, and thankful for the numbing effect of whiskey. Faith was cleaning the edges of the wound, examining the raw area with an intent look. She straightened as she soberly assessed the damage.

"I think we'd better stitch it up," she said finally. "It'll heal better if we pull the edges together, don't you think?" Her query was addressed to Lin, and from the doorway the housekeeper added her opinion.

"I've got some good silk thread, Miss Faith," Katie said, bustling toward the group around the table. The woman had faded red hair, combined with a rounded figure and bluer than blue eyes that twinkled in Max's direction. She blurred a bit, and he blinked to focus on her, squinting his eyes. Tucked neatly into a dark dress beneath the long apron she wore, she looked the picture of a typical Irish grandmother, he decided. She placed a sewing basket on the table and opened it, drawing forth a spool of black thread.

"That looks fine," Faith said. "Cut a length, and we'll soak it in the whiskey before we use it."

Max watched her closely, noting the steady movement of her hands, hearing the calm tone of her voice through a fog. He reached with his free arm to circle her waist as she stood between his parted thighs, and she glanced down quickly, her eyes still dark with concern. Beneath his palm her flesh trembled, and he felt her heart beating unevenly, there where his hand rested beneath her breast.

"Sit on my knee," he said quietly, needing her close. "You look wiped out, sweetheart."

"You're the one who's been wounded," she snapped. "I'm fine."

"Are you?" He looked up at her, noting the single tear that trailed from the edge of her eyelid to slide the length of her cheek. If he could only think straight, he'd be able to offer comfort, he decided. But it seemed all he could do to sit upright for now.

"I will be, once I have you stitched up and bandaged," she told him. And then she turned a bit and perched on his thigh, and he felt the shuddering breath she drew. Her head drooped a bit and she leaned her forehead against his for a moment. "You frightened me half to death," she said quietly. "I was so afraid I wouldn't get to you in time. And then I feared we'd not make it without both of us getting killed by a stray bullet from those men."

"Nicholas is going to raise the roof when he gets back home," Lin said glumly. "Not only has he lost a herd of cattle, he's lost two of the men who hired on to work for him. Not to mention that his neighbor took a bullet."

"The one fella Mr. Nicholas hired is still alive," Katie stated. "He just got a crease in his skull that knocked him out cold. But the other one got nailed in the chest. Poor man didn't know what hit him.''

''Where are they?'' Max asked, aware that he'd missed out on the flurry of excitement following the rustler's raid, and more than aware that the whiskey he'd consumed was taking its toll.

''The sheriff came by and said that he'd had someone take Shorty into town to the doc,'' Katie told him. ''The other man doesn't have any family hereabouts, and unless they can find out where his kin might be, he'll be buried in the churchyard.''

''Has anyone found any trace of the rustlers?'' Max heard the slurring of his voice as he felt Faith's weight shift against him. He eyed the needle Katie offered; then, as if pronouncing judgment, he nodded approval. With a long look in his direction, Lin chuckled, then dropped the needle in the cup of whiskey, and Max set his mind to considering something other than the mending of his flesh that was to come.

Katie glanced at him, her gaze taking in his grip on Faith, her eyes registering approval as she nodded at his inquiring look. ''A hired hand on the next ranch to the east saw the herd being driven across Joe Filer's land, and he had a notion things weren't what they should be. So he hightailed it to town to let the law know what was goin' on,'' she told him. ''The sheriff's got a posse out right now chasing down the gang. If anybody can catch them, it's Brace. He's a good man.''

Max grinned, reaching for his whiskey glass with shaky fingers. ''You had Billy spotted right off, didn't you?'' He looked up at Faith, watching as she held a pad against his wound, waiting while Lin threaded the needle with care and drew out the silk thread into a double strand.

''I had a bad feeling about him,'' Faith said quietly. And

then she stood as Lin held the needle out to her. "This isn't going to be pleasant," she told Max. "Do you want to lie down?"

He shook his head and, leaning his right elbow on the table, propped his brow against his hand, giving her a clear field in which to work. "I'm about at the point of feeling no pain," he said. "I'll just sit here and behave myself. Go ahead."

She drew in a deep breath and began, whispering beneath her breath, giving instructions to Lin to blot the blood from the wound, halting to tie off the stitches as she went. Drawing in a quivering breath, she tied the last knot, then soaked a clean cloth in the small cup of whiskey before her and held it against the mended skin.

Max inhaled sharply, then uttered an oath beneath his breath, stunned by the intense burning of the alcohol against raw flesh. "I'm sorry," Faith whispered, bending to touch her lips to his cheek. "It has to be clean. I don't want to risk infection. The back of your shoulder, where the bullet entered looks pretty good. I've washed it out as well as I can and I think just a bandage will suffice. It went in at an angle, and it seemed to have missed the bone."

"I've learned lately to be grateful for small things," Max said with a shaky grin, the pain producing a sobering effect.

"I can't thank you enough," Lin told him. "You went beyond the call of duty, Max. Nicholas will be indebted to you for your help."

"I didn't do a hell of a lot of good," Max grumbled. "They ended up with his cattle, and he lost a man, not to mention a nice piece of horseflesh."

"You did all anyone could have," Lin insisted. "And now I think you'd do well to crawl into bed. We'll find you something nourishing to eat, and Faith can stay with you and keep an eye on things."

"I'm well enough to sit up to the table and have breakfast," Max said. "At least some coffee." And perhaps coffee was exactly what he needed, he thought.

He was still there when a horse bearing the sheriff appeared at the foot of the back porch steps. Brace tied his reins to the upright post and made his way to the door, rapping once before he opened it. "How bad is it?" he asked Max, his gaze narrowed as he searched out the wide bandage.

"I'll live," Max told him. "The question is whether or not you came up with any of Nicholas's cattle."

"I've got men out searching the canyons between here and the railroad lines to the north. I had a wire sent directly to the railroad to be on the lookout for cattle with botched brands. They may try to split up the herd and sell them off in small pieces. But I'll tell you one thing. Those fellas will have a hard time burning over Nick's brand. And any steer with a fresh iron mark is gonna be suspect.

"Unless they keep them in a canyon for weeks, we may get a line on the gang. They won't make any money unless they can sell the herd, and we're a step ahead of them, I think."

"What about Billy?" Faith asked.

"He's the only one we managed to get hold of," Brace said. "Silly fool got himself wounded and fell in front of one of the steers. I think one of the gang turned on him, after he'd outlived his usefulness to them. He was singing for all he was worth when we tossed him into a cell. The doc patched him up and he's probably facing a long time in prison, maybe even a rope if the judge isn't in a good mood when he sees him in court."

The sheriff looked at Lin. "When is Nick coming home?"

"Not for a couple of days, I suppose," she said. "He

just left day before yesterday. I haven't decided yet whether or not to wire him the news. There isn't much he can do from Collins Creek, and his business there is pretty important."

"He'll find out soon enough," Brace agreed. "Maybe we'll have some good news by the time he gets back. I'd sure like to get my hands on that gang. I'd thought we had the rustlers in this area all cleaned out. But I reckon there's always another batch of fools waitin' to take the place of the last bunch."

Max felt weariness overtake him as the conversation moved on, and when Faith touched his arm and offered him her hand, he rose and allowed her to lead him out of the kitchen and down the hallway to the big front bedroom.

"Isn't this Lin and Nicholas's room?" he asked as Faith turned down the quilt on the wide bed.

"It will be when the children are a little older. For now Lin and Nicholas use a room at the front of the house upstairs. Directly over this one, in fact," Faith said, fluffing the pillows and piling them in place. She turned to him. "I'll help you undress," she offered.

He glanced to the door and then grinned at her. "I think you ought to close that first," he suggested. "I'm not real fond of exposing myself to a houseful of womenfolk."

She shot him a dark look, but moved to the open portal and swung the door into place, then leaned back against it. Her scowl faded as she searched his face, and then she walked slowly toward him.

"I was worried, Max. All I could think of was that you'd come all the way out to Texas for me, and then ended up getting shot. I had this vision of your mother reading me the riot act and your whole family after my hide for exposing you to danger."

He held out his good arm in her direction and she slid

her hands around his waist and clung to him unashamedly. Her head leaned against his shoulder and she cried silent tears, her fingers digging into the muscles of his back. Holding her closely, he leaned his cheek against her hair and shut his eyes. If he'd doubted it before, the certainty of her love became apparent in a new and clear revelation now.

"I'm all right, Faith," he assured her. "A bit banged up, but I'll be good as new before you know it." He felt weakness, invasive and quick, as he whispered the words, and as if she sensed the faltering of his strength, she turned to loop his arm around her shoulder, and led him to the bed.

"Will you lie down with me?" he asked, sitting on the edge of the mattress as she bent to remove his stockings. His boots were by the back door, his shirt a pile of tatters on the kitchen floor when he'd last seen it, and now he dreaded the effort involved in standing to remove the trousers he wore.

"As soon as I get you out of these pants," she said, hauling him to his feet and undoing the belt he wore. The heavy denim pants fell around his ankles and he kicked them aside, then dropped weakly to the mattress again. Faith watched him closely and bent to lift his legs to the bed.

"I'll be fine. I just need to sleep awhile," he told her, aware that his words were slurring even more, the aftereffect of the whiskey he'd downed.

"I know," she said, tucking the sheet over him, reaching for a damp cloth she'd placed on the nightstand. Her hands were gentle as she wiped his face. The cloth was cool and she wielded it with care, cleaning the dust from his skin, wiping his temples and forehead. Then she rose to carry it across the room, wringing it out in a basin on the washstand.

She returned and used the refreshing cloth on his chest and neck, and he sighed, accepting her touch and the peaceful sound of her murmurs as she tended him. ''I could get real used to this,'' he said softly as she left him again, returning in moments to sit beside him.

''Did I tell you I love you, Max?'' she asked quietly.

He felt his heavy eyelids twitch, and he lifted them to peer up at her. ''Not for a long time, sweetheart,'' he replied, feeling that he walked on shaky ground. The admission she made so gravely was one he'd waited for over the past weeks. That it might come on the tail of his brush with death made him wonder about the reason for her decision to announce her devotion. He'd rather have heard it when he was hale and healthy.

His eyes closed again and he murmured her name, ''Faith,'' and then opened one eye to seek her out. ''Stay with me.''

''I'm not going anywhere,'' she said with a smile. And then her face blurred before him and he allowed the darkness to sweep over him.

She'd come close to losing him. The thought vibrated in Faith's mind throughout the next three days as she kept watch in the downstairs bedroom. Fever was her enemy and she slept but rarely, and then as close to Max as she could get. Rousing when he stirred, she bathed him when the heat of his body alarmed her, then forced Katie's brew of herbs and tea down his throat when he would have refused a less hardy soul.

Max's healing was rapid once the fever abated, and when Nicholas arrived home on the third day since the shooting, he was greeted with a barrage of greetings, all of which led him to the room where Max was recuperating. He rapped once on the door, then entered, his gaze seeking out the man who had laid his life on the line for a friend.

Faith watched through the window as the two men clasped hands, her eyes tearing as they exchanged a few low words. Not for these two any suggestion of emotion, but beneath their brief touch of hands and their bandying remarks, she sensed an underlying bond of friendship that would no doubt withstand the years.

Max needed a friend like Nicholas, she decided. He could do no better if he were to search far and wide for a man to stand at his back.

She'd pronounced him able to return to the farmhouse today, and he was eager to do just that, after the noon meal. Their few belongings were packed and ready. A man, newly hired by Lin in order to fill the gap, had been instructed to harness the team and ready the wagon for the trip, and once Max and Nicholas caught up on the news, Faith would be loading him onto the high wagon seat for the short ride.

Brace arrived as they sat down at the table, and Katie brought forth another plate for the lawman. "I've never yet turned down a meal you cooked," he announced, bending to plant a kiss on her cheek. "You're the best cook in the county."

Faith laughed aloud as Katie blushed, pushing Brace toward his chair. "What a lot of malarkey," she said, concealing her pleasure with a great flurry of apron flapping. And then they ate, Brace describing in detail the rounding-up of Nicholas's herd.

"There were over a hundred head in one spot, inside a shallow box canyon. Those jackass rustlers were just about to begin branding the bunch, had their irons all hot. I don't think they'd figured on having such a tough time of it, wrestling full grown steers to the ground." He laughed, reaching for the platter of fried ham and serving himself a second helping.

"We saved them the trouble, just swooped in from three sides and nailed 'em good. The sheriff from over in Garrison brought his men along for the ride, and between us we got a dozen or so men in jail." He chewed for a moment and then waved his fork for emphasis. "This is a bigger gang than we'd thought at first."

"Any idea where the rest of my cattle are?" Nicholas asked. Faith watched him, noting the harsh set of his mouth, the taut line of his jaw. Nicholas did not take kindly to being robbed.

"The man from Garrison said he'd do some scouting in that area. We've probably lost a number that got sent to the stockyards right off. But the best of the bunch are those they were gonna brand and sell to dealers. They should be back on the range by now. The men were herding them in this direction when I rode out.

"And that reminds me," Brace said suddenly, reaching into his shirt pocket. "You got a letter, Max. Titus Liberty flagged me down when I left my office and asked me to deliver it when I saw you." He drew forth a cream-colored envelope with sealing wax on the back flap and placed it in Max's outstretched hand. "Hope it isn't bad news from back East."

Max shook his head, glancing quickly at the handwriting and stuffing it into his own shirt pocket. "Just some of my family catching up with the latest news, no doubt."

And then he changed the subject, turning back to Brace and asking quietly, "What about the men who were shot?" That Max was in that same group was not the issue. Faith recognized his true concern for those hired hands who'd been in harm's way and met a fate worse than his own.

Brace's eyes darkened as he shook his head. "It sure is

a thankless job, deliverin' bad news to a family. We found out about the dead man. Seems he was alone, but for a sister down south of Dallas. Doc sent her a wire and told her that her brother was buried in the churchyard in town. On the other hand, Shorty is doing fine. He said to give you a message, Nick. He'll be comin' back this week, soon's his head is healed enough for him to ride out.''

''Where'd you get the new man?'' Nicholas asked Lin as she stood behind his chair, coffeepot in hand.

''He was asking in town about work and Brace sent him out. I told him I didn't know how permanent the job was, and he'd have to talk to you about it when you got back home.''

Nicholas shot an inquiring look at Brace and received a nod. ''Seems like a good man to me,'' the lawman said. ''I figured he'd fill the gap, anyway, till you got things under control again.''

The sound of a horse outside the house caught Faith's attention and she looked out the window, where her wagon and team were being driven toward the back porch, Max's horse, her mare and the filly tied behind. ''I think your chariot awaits,'' she told Max. ''I'll go in and fetch our things.''

They were silent as they traveled the shortcut across the fields toward the farmhouse. Max made no offer to hold the reins, and Faith handled her team with automatic movements. The presence of Max's arm behind her was welcome, and the warmth of his thigh pressed to hers was a comfort, she decided.

She thought of the letter he had yet to open, and discretion dictated that she not inquire as to its sender. He'd let her know soon enough if it was news she should be privy to. And yet a niggling doubt circled in her mind. The envelope was heavy; the writing, at least as much as she'd seen, had been in a feminine hand.

Probably from his mother, she thought, a feeling of gloom resting on her shoulders.

She accepted Max's help with the animals and didn't protest when he carried the valise to the house. The door opened with a creak, and she crossed to the windows to lift them wide, allowing the breeze to enter.

"It's stuffy in here," she said, heading for the pantry. "I'll go on out and feed the chickens. They'll be wondering if they've been forgotten."

"Didn't Lin take care of them yesterday?" Max asked. "I thought I heard her say she was riding over in the morning."

"She did, and she gathered the eggs and brought them back to their place. We'll be starting fresh today." The egg basket was handy and Faith reached for it, then slanted a look in Max's direction as she went toward the back door. He'd settled at the kitchen table and held the letter in his hand, a somber expression on his face.

"Are you all right?" she asked, hesitating on the threshold.

He glanced up quickly and a smile appeared, his eyes brightening as he offered reassurance. "I'm fine, just wondering what my mother wants." He drew in a deep breath. "Might as well open it and find out, hadn't I?"

Faith left the house, a premonition of dread settling in her stomach. Whatever the woman wanted, it would mar the day for them. She trudged across the yard to where her chickens waited, gathered by the fence. The barrel of feed was topped by a rock, holding down the lid, and she tossed it to the ground, then bent to fill the basin with chicken feed. Opening the wire gate, she slid inside the enclosure, scattering feed before her, smiling as the hens scratched to get their share. When the basin was empty, she tossed it over the fence and went into the coop where the laying boxes held the day's bounty.

The eggs were still warm and she piled them gently in the basket, then let herself out the front door of the coop. Replacing the feed basin in the barrel, she headed for the house. It was time to face whatever Max's mother had up her sleeve.

"You're telling me I have three days to prepare for company," Faith stated quietly. She sat before her dressing table, brushing her hair, watching Max in the mirror as he sat on the edge of the bed.

"She'll be here on Saturday," he told her. "It's too late to stop her, Faith. Even if I sent a wire now, she'd already be on her way by the time it arrived. Or else she'd just ignore it. When my mother gets a bee in her bonnet, there's no stopping her."

"So she'll show up here on Saturday, and then what?" The brush was placed carefully on the dressing table, when Faith's first inclination was to throw it across the room. She scraped her hair together and began braiding it.

Max frowned. "Do you have to do that?"

She felt ornery, she decided. Max liked her hair loose, but she wasn't in a mood to make him happy tonight. It was utterly foolish. She was aware that he had no jurisdiction over his mother's comings and goings, but there was no one else to vent her anger on. Max was the target, like it or not.

"She won't be happy when she finds out you were wounded," Faith said, ignoring his disapproval. "I'll bet she has you on a train back East lickety-split. You'll be hauled off to the finest doctor in Boston."

"I had fine care right here," he said mildly. "I don't need a doctor in Boston, or anywhere else for that matter."

Well, that was one point in her favor, Faith decided silently. She'd proved to be a worthy nursemaid, whether his mother approved of his care or not. "What did she say in the letter?" Faith asked finally, unable to bear his silence.

"Just that she's coming here and hoping to settle on a time for me to return home."

Faith dropped her eyes and turned aside, aware of Max's ability to gauge her mood should he take a good look at her face. "And when will that be?" she asked sharply.

He rose from the bed. "I don't know, Faith. But I'll have to go back sometime. You know that. I've already stayed longer than I'd planned when I arrived."

"I haven't tied you down," she told him, bending to pick up her house shoes and tossing them toward the wardrobe.

"I'm here because it's where I want to be."

Faith heard the words as if through a whistling wind, so rapidly did her heart beat in her ears. Fear raced the length of her spine, sending chills to dwell in the depths of her being. He would leave. As surely as she was alive and breathing, he would pack his bag and turn away from her at his mother's bidding. And she would be alone once more.

Her head lifted, her chin tilting upward. She'd been by herself before. She'd survived without him for three years, and she could do it again. She'd known this was coming, had recognized that she couldn't leave with him, would be unable to accept the life he offered her in the East. It was pointless to grieve for what could not be.

"Faith?" He was behind her, lifting her from the bench, easing her into his embrace. "Don't turn away, sweetheart. I can't stand it when you freeze up this way. I can only think of those dark days in Boston when you retreated from me and I was at a loss as to what to do to reach you.''

''I have to protect myself,'' she said quietly, barely recognizing the sound of her own voice. Harsh and chill, her words were a shield thrown up to hide the aching heart that threatened to burst within her breast. ''I should have known better than to let you find a place in my life again. There was no doubt in my mind when you came that I'd be left holding the bag one day, Max. And now I can see it happening.''

He gripped her shoulders with hands that didn't allow escape. ''I told you when I got here that I wanted you back, Faith. I told you my aim was to bring you with me to Boston. I haven't changed my mind on that score.''

She jerked futilely in his grasp. ''And I haven't changed mine,'' she retorted. ''The only thing I left behind when I left Boston was my baby's grave. I don't need to go back there to remember him. His memory will always remain in my heart.'' Her voice rose in a spoken vow. ''I won't ever go back and live in that...that mausoleum again.''

''Mausoleum? Is that what you call my family home? A tomb?''

Her jaw was taut, her teeth clenched, and she glared in fury as she spat out the words that fought to be uttered. ''Yes. A tomb. A place where your mother would have buried me forever. I was one of the living dead, Max. And you were too thickheaded to recognize how terribly unhappy I was.''

She wrenched away from him and he caught his breath sharply, growling an oath. His hands dropped from her and he stuffed them in his pockets. The bandage on his arm stood out, bringing her attention to the wound as his muscle twitched and his mouth twisted in pain.

"If I hurt you, I'm sorry," she said politely. "I didn't mean to put strain on your arm."

"I'll live," he told her, snatching up his shirt from the chair where he'd dropped it only minutes before. He slid his arms into the sleeves and, leaving it to hang open, turned to leave the bedroom.

Faith pressed a hand against her lips, unwilling to ask his destination, unable to keep back the sobs that ached to be allowed out. Tears ran unchecked from her eyes, and with blurring vision, she watched him stride from the room.

Chapter Twelve

Faith changed the dressing on his wound in silence, each evening carefully unwrapping, then inspecting the stitches she'd set in place. A healing poultice was applied, then covered with fresh bandages. "You'll need to have these stitches removed when you reach Boston," she told him on the second day. "It's healing well."

"You can take them out before I go."

"I doubt they'll be ready." His skin was warm, his scent that of a man in need of loving—a faintly musky, delicately tinged aroma that enticed her to glance toward his lap as she stood between his thighs. As she did, he dropped his hands to rest there, and she felt her lips twist in silent laughter.

He tilted his head and caught her eye. His wry grin acknowledged her amusement, and he murmured words she bent to hear. "See what you do to me?"

"Not on purpose." Her smile disappeared, and she was irritated with her own response. Thankfully, a woman's arousal was easier to conceal than that of a randy man. A taut fullness in her breasts and a warm tingling in the depths of her belly told the tale of her newly awakened flesh. It would never do, she decided grimly, and, gritting her teeth, she banished it to oblivion, ignoring her body's awareness of the man before her.

"Obviously, you can get along without me, Faith. I never doubted that. But I'm bright enough to know that you've enjoyed what we've shared."

"I haven't denied that." She wrapped the bandage firmly in place, holding it with a large piece of adhesive plaster.

"And you can forget me when I'm gone, never think about me?" He shifted, his muscular thighs enclosing her. "You won't miss me?"

Exasperation chilled her words. "I managed before you got here. I'll do just fine when you leave."

"I'll be back," he promised.

"Will you?" She moved to step away from him, and his legs parted, releasing her.

"Not till spring, probably. I have things that require my presence over the autumn months, and winter makes travel difficult. But when the weather breaks..."

Faith turned aside as his voice softened. "Don't make promises to me, Max."

"All right." He rose from the chair and gathered the soiled bandages, rolling them into a tidy bundle and then placing them in the stove for burning. "Thank you." His words of appreciation followed her as she left the kitchen, and she nodded, barely able to see where she walked because of the tears blurring her vision.

It wasn't fair that she should be so foolish over the man. That she should ache so at the thought of his leaving. Reaching the sanctuary of her bedroom, she closed the door and leaned against it, allowing the tears to run unchecked down her cheeks, until sobs began to choke her and she dived for the bed. A pillow muffled the sounds she would not allow him to hear, and it was the middle of the night before she rose to undress and crawl beneath the sheet.

Morning brought birdsong and the sound of her rooster greeting the dawn. Max had slept somewhere in the house for the past two nights. Probably in the spare room, she decided, although the sofa in the parlor was a possibility. One thing was for sure—her bed was a lonely place during the long night hours, and she'd hugged the pillow against her breasts to ease the pain of Max's absence.

Heartache was not a stranger, but Faith's familiarity with its presence didn't make it more palatable. She'd almost forgotten the long days and nights three years ago. Her chest had ached with a constant misery, even though all her intelligence told her such a pain had no real relationship to the physical organ that beat there. A broken heart was a figure of speech, a term used by those who felt pangs of rejection or the pain of loss when a lover fled from their lives.

The loss of both her lover and the child she'd borne him had created in Faith almost unbearable anguish—that of a woman betrayed and then left alone to mourn.

She shook her head at the fanciful thoughts that filled it this morning. Max had not intentionally betrayed her. She couldn't hang that particular sin on him. But he had allowed his mother to dictate the terms of their marriage. And for that, Faith found herself unwilling to forgive him.

Perhaps… She shook her head. No, he would never turn his back on the woman who had raised her sons to be loyal to family and business first and foremost. His wife must make her own life, fitting it around that of Maxwell McDowell, businessman. And in her heart, Faith knew she could no longer fit that pattern.

He would leave—he'd said as much. She looked into her own eyes as she sat before the mirror, drawing her hair up into a knot atop her head. It was part of the armor she donned today. Hair tightly controlled, dark dress buttoned to the throat, her apron tied about her waist to keep her full skirts away from the stove.

If Max's information was correct, Hazel McDowell would arrive today. And when she walked through the door she would see a no-nonsense woman in place.

Faith rose and inspected herself. She was about as unattractive as she was likely to get, she decided. Max would find little to inspire him to seek her out now. No longer was she casting smiles in his direction. The small byplay they'd indulged in was over. Once his mother arrived he'd no doubt be more than ready to take his leave from this primitive way of life she had chosen.

Within twenty minutes, the kitchen was redolent with the scent of coffee brewing and bacon frying on the back of the stove. From the open doorway, she spotted Max striding toward the house, egg basket slung over his arm, Wolf gamboling around his feet. As if begging for attention, the dog darted before his erstwhile playmate and barked sharply. All to no avail. Max was not playing games today.

His brow was furrowed as he entered the back door and cast her a long look. "I took care of the horses and gathered the eggs."

"Leave the basket on the table. I'll take care of them." Faith's words were terse and to the point, and Max did not argue. Depositing the wicker basket, he walked to the sink and washed his hands, then bent to splash water on his face, running long damp fingers through his hair to tame its waves.

Faith wiped the eggs with a clean, wet cloth and placed them in the crockery bowl she used for storage. Five of them were broken quickly into another dish and whisked to a frothy foam. In moments she had lifted the bacon from its pan and drained off the grease into a cup, then spilled the eggs into the skillet to cook.

Bread was sliced, coffee poured, and still she was silent. Max took his cue from her and worked around her, setting the table and bringing the butter and jam from the pantry. Seating herself at the table, she pushed the bowl of scrambled eggs in his direction and busied herself with buttering a piece of bread.

"She's due to arrive this morning, Faith. There are things we need to talk about," he said, serving himself and lifting his gaze as he settled the dish before her.

"What would you like me to say?" she asked, her gaze averted. "I'll put clean sheets on my bed for your mother to sleep on while she's here, and I'll try to cook meals that will suit her refined tastes."

Max felt a chill touch his spine at her words. Faith was not going to give an inch, and he was caught in the midst of a storm that was almost guaranteed to leave victims behind. His mother was a known factor in this situation. Faith, on the other hand, had changed so drastically over the past years, he wasn't sure just how she would cope with Hazel McDowell's presence in her home. At least it wouldn't be a long visit. If he knew his parent as well as he thought, she would be champing at the bit to return East by Sunday.

"I'm getting used to the parlor sofa after the last couple of nights," he said dryly. "And I'm sure you or my mother will be equally comfortable in the spare room. Unless you'd like me to join you upstairs. I'm sure that bed will hold both of us."

"Us?" Faith's brow rose scornfully. "There is no *us,*" she told him. "There is simply Maxwell McDowell and his estranged wife. And if I have to I can even manage to sleep on the floor in one of the empty rooms upstairs for a couple of nights."

"What are you talking about? You needn't sleep on the floor." He felt his irritation with her grow by leaps and bounds. The woman was deliberately inciting him to anger, and from the gleam in her eye, was enjoying his frustration.

"I'm giving her my room," Faith said. "She won't be here long enough to inconvenience me. I'd say twenty-four hours should about do it."

"Do what?" He heard the tenor of his voice change, noted the gruff tone he employed and caught a glimpse of Faith's superior expression as she cast him a long look.

"It should be just about long enough for her to have you hotfooting it off to Benning to catch the Monday afternoon train."

Max tilted his chair back a bit. "Ah, I see," he said quietly, proud of the light inflection of his words. "You've already got me on the train, have you?"

She met his gaze fully and nodded. "I don't see that you have any choice," she said politely. "You're going back to Boston...and I'm not."

The front legs of his chair hit the floor with a bang. "What I want from you doesn't matter, does it? What I see as a future for us together doesn't mean anything."

Her brows lifted and she feigned surprise. "Oh? Did you have a future planned with me in mind?"

Hurt gathered under his skin like prickly heat, and he stood abruptly. "You don't recall, I suppose, the description I gave you of the house and property I've been looking at outside of the city. Nor do you consider the nights we've spent together in your bed as a change in our status, do you?"

"We haven't been sleeping together lately." Her eyes were cool, yet there was an underlying shadow in them as she responded. "I'm very aware of the depth of our relationship. I was here and you were in need of a woman's touch, Max. I didn't make you any promises, and you certainly didn't aim any in my direction."

"I told you I'll be back. Damn it, Faith! You told me you loved me." The words were a shout, punctuated by the sound of his chair hitting the floor as he shoved it aside.

"Yes, I did," she admitted agreeably. "I've never claimed not to be gullible. And you've always been very talented when you set your mind to it. I was caught up in the moment, I suspect."

A spasm gripped his chest; his heart pounded with a heavy beat and the realization that unless he was able to change Faith's opinion of him, all was lost. He would once more forfeit the joys of claiming this woman as his own, would face the future without her presence in his life.

"You don't give your love lightly, Faith. I know better than that. You care about me, and you know how I feel about you."

She tilted her head, and his gaze feasted on the clean line of her jaw, the wide, full stretch of soft lips that firmed even as he watched. Her blue eyes were sharp, yet their radiance was blurred by anger, and as he focused on her mouth again, he saw it tremble.

"I feel like I'm singing the same song over and over again, Max. I can't fit into your way of life," she said carefully. "I doubt your mother has had a change of heart where I'm concerned, and I'm not equipped to handle living in her home and changing myself to fit into the mold she tried to force on me."

"You don't have to be anything but what you are right this minute." He felt a sense of desperation seize him as Faith rejected him and all he offered. In a few words, she had denied him the chance to make a new life for them, and if the stubborn tilt of her head and the set of her mouth were any indication, she was not about to be swayed.

Her laugh was strained, a harsh sound that held not the slightest degree of humor. "What I am is a farm woman,

Max. What you need is a city wife, a woman with social aspirations and the ability to help you further your career in business.'' She met his gaze with eyes that blazed with determination. Then, with a quick movement, she rose from the table and gathered dirty dishes.

''Your mother was right,'' she said, heading for the sink. ''I'm the wrong woman for you. I don't want the same things you do, and I'll never belong in her home.''

''I don't want you in my mother's home. I want you in my life,'' he said quietly. ''And it doesn't matter where we live.''

''So long as it's in Boston.'' Her words were a statement of fact as she saw it, apparently, and too close to the truth to be ignored.

''My work is there,'' he said bluntly. ''It's a family business, and I have a certain amount of responsibility to the people who work for me and depend on the business for their living.''

She shrugged, as if dismissing the problem with a simple lift of her shoulders. ''Fine. We've gone over this time and again, and I understand. I know you'll be leaving. I've known it all along.'' And still she stood at the sink, gripping the edge of the wooden countertop as if she needed it to bear her weight.

He felt a helpless surge of despair rush through him, as though a dam had broken and the water was carrying him into a current he stood no chance of escaping. ''There's no give to you, Faith. You want it all your way.''

She turned then to face him, frowning, and as he watched, he thought he caught a glimpse of sorrow in the depths of her blue eyes. ''I'm selfish, I suppose, Max. I've discovered that I'm important. Maybe not to you or your mother or the Boston business community, but to myself. I have to consider my own happiness this time.''

"Will you give her a chance?" he asked, rising to approach her. "Will you listen to her when she arrives? Try to get along with her, and see if we can reach a compromise?"

Faith's smile was tinged with pain, her mouth trembling. "Sure. I can do that, Max. I'll get along with her. I'll keep my mouth shut and let her set the rules again, and then when you leave with her, I'll wave goodbye."

He felt the anger surge anew. Faith in a cynical mood was more than he could handle right now. "I don't know why I'm trying so hard to find a middle ground here," he said finally. "You're not willing to try, are you?"

She looked into his eyes as though she searched for something, and he reached for her, grasping her narrow shoulders, drawing her close. His head bent and he captured her lips, desperation driving him to form some sort of connection that would link them as one.

For a moment she was pliable in his embrace, her mouth softening beneath his. He heard her breath catch in an audible sound of surrender and she leaned into his chest, her hands sliding to his back. Holding him close, tilting her head to one side, the better to accept his kiss, she opened her lips as if inviting his invasion.

For that few seconds his heart sang within his breast. *She's mine.* The thought raced exultantly through his mind, searing a path that brought him to immediate arousal. And then she tensed, straightening her posture and dropping her hands, and a soft cry escaped her lips.

"Faith, I love you," he said, holding fast to her shoulders, as if he could somehow draw her back into an embrace she seemed bent on escaping.

She shook her head and wrestled against his grasp. "You're hurting me, Max," she whispered. "Let me go."

Her eyes were bleak as they lifted to meet his gaze. "I'm

sorry. I know you love me, at least right now. And I love you, Max. But I was wrong to give in to my need for you, even for those few moments. It's become a habit to turn to you lately, and I can't afford to be that weak-kneed woman any longer."

"Weak-kneed? I don't think so," he said harshly. "You have the strength of ten in your little finger. You work from dawn to dark, you've carved out a life here that would have daunted many a man bent on living in this backwoods community. Allowing me to help, letting me close to you, giving me the rights of a husband—all of that doesn't make you weak or puny, Faith."

He held her at arm's length, and his laughter was scornful as his voice rose in volume. "You've had me dangling at the end of your string for weeks as I've tried to bring us to some sort of an understanding. I'm the one who has been out of whack. I've been dreaming foolish dreams, hoping for the impossible."

The sharp rap of knuckles against the back door caught his attention, and he turned his head abruptly. "Sorry to interfere, folks," Brace said quietly, "but I've got a passenger in a buggy out here. She'd like to see you, Max." A tapestry valise in one hand, Brace stood outside the screened door.

Dropping his hands from Faith, Max turned to the sheriff. "I'll be right out," he said. And then glanced back at the pale countenance of his wife. "Do you want to join me?" he asked.

She shook her head. "No, you're the one she wants to see. Bring her in, and I'll freshen the coffee. If she hasn't eaten breakfast, I'll cook something."

The door opened at the touch of his hand and he stepped onto the porch. From the buggy seat, his mother watched, her mouth pinched, her eyes raking his length as if she sought some sign of the civilized man who had left Boston months before. As never before, he was aware of his clothing, the rough denim trousers and simple cotton shirt he wore. He looked down at scuff marks on his boots and for a moment saw himself through the eyes of Hazel McDowell, and knew she found him lacking.

And then he met her gaze. ''Mother,'' he said, greeting her with an uplifted hand. He noted Brace's keen glance, the hesitation in the lawman's movements as he held the door ajar to peer into the kitchen, and then step inside. Max took the steps easily and crossed to where his mother waited.

Holding out a hand, he offered to lift her from the high seat, but she shook her head, a silent denial of his help. And then spoke, her tones familiar. ''I seem to have interrupted something. Shall I wait until you've solved your problem inside the house?''

''That problem is ongoing, I fear,'' he admitted. ''Come in, Mother.''

She reached out her hand, seeking his, and peered over the side of the buggy, searching for a step. With a quick movement Max clasped her firmly about the waist, then lifted her to the ground, wincing as raw pain shot through his shoulder.

''Have you been hurt?'' she asked.

''Just a slight wound,'' Max told her. ''Faith has been tending it.''

One hand rose to clutch at the brim of her hat, the other brushed at her skirt, and Hazel cast him a long, assessing look. ''I knew no good would come of you being here,'' she said bluntly. ''You must tell me later what has happened to you.''

He nodded, then, allowing her a moment to regroup, spoke of her journey and referred to the business of breakfast. As she completed a quick visual tour of the yard and outbuildings, they turned toward the porch.

"Faith is waiting to greet you," he said, his hand beneath her elbow as she climbed the steps.

"I doubt she's overjoyed at my presence." Her voice was clipped and terse, and he did not have it in him to disagree with her deduction.

Brace stood inside the kitchen door, hat in hand, the valise against the wall, his gaze fixed on Faith. That they had been speaking in low voices was apparent, Max decided, and he felt a twinge of jealousy cut through his chest like a sharp blade. The lawman cleared his throat and nodded at the older woman.

"I hope you have a pleasant visit, ma'am," he murmured, and then lifted a brow in Max's direction before he headed out the door. At the sink, Faith seemed to shrink into herself as the door closed behind the man, and Max shot her what he hoped was an encouraging look.

"Mother would probably like some coffee," he said. "She got in on the early train, and there wasn't time for breakfast."

"Just a piece of toast will do very well, and a bit of cream in my coffee," Hazel said coolly, settling herself in a chair. Her fingers worked at her gloves and she tugged them off, then placed them in her reticule, closing it with a resounding snap. "I don't want to put you out, Faith."

"I have bread for toast and the coffee's already hot," Faith answered, crossing the kitchen to where her dishes were stacked in the dresser. She opened the door and removed a plate, then a cup and saucer from the matching set.

Max smiled to himself. He'd been drinking from a thick mug, as had Faith. Apparently, the dishes she'd chosen now were for company usage. And certainly his mother qualified on that account. The two heavy, plain plates Faith kept on a shelf were for family, he thought, and congratulated himself that he'd acquired that status, at least for a little while.

"I'll have more coffee, too," he said smoothly, and watched as Faith hesitated, then withdrew another china cup and saucer from the dresser. He'd just lost his position, and been relegated to observing his wife's company manners, he decided.

Hazel was grim, her eyes following Faith's every move and Max felt irritation creep over him. "I don't really think it was necessary for you to travel all the way out here, Mother," he said bluntly. "I'm happy to see you, but the trip was obviously hard on you. I'd have been returning shortly."

"Your brother was still waiting for word when I made my decision to come," she said. "Things must be taken care of, Maxwell. There are decisions to make and you know your brother is not capable of doing more than maintaining the situation. It is your place to be at the helm of the ship, so to speak."

"Only by virtue of my age," he said. "If Howard had been born first, he'd be in charge."

"Well, he wasn't, and you *are* in charge, so there's no point in discussing the issue," she said sharply. "There are contracts to be signed and a new shipping line inquiring about the company using their services. They've given us a better opportunity in the Far East, and it bears investigation before winter arrives."

Max sat down and leaned back in his chair. "It seems you have the whole thing under control, Mother. If you think it's an advisable move, why didn't you tell Howard to sign the paperwork and get things underway? He has my power of attorney."

"You know he depends on you, Maxwell."

"I know he's a capable man. The problem is that you don't give him the chance to show his worth."

Hazel's eyebrow winged upward and her mouth grew taut as she formed a reply. "I think this discussion could be handled privately."

"Faith is my wife," Max said bluntly. "She doesn't have to leave the room just because we're discussing business."

"She has no understanding of—"

Coffee splashed into the saucer as Faith plopped the hot beverage on the table in front of Max, then delivered the second cup to his mother. "I'm leaving," she said, casting him a long look.

I told you so. As surely as if she spoke the words aloud, he heard them in his head, and felt her anger as a wedge between them.

Her skirts swayed as she walked out the back door, and the sound of it slamming vibrated in the air. "At least she knew enough to make herself scarce," Hazel said firmly. "I don't think the woman has changed for the better in any other way, though. She's certainly abandoned her upbringing, hasn't she?"

"Faith is my wife, Mother," he said quietly. "I will not listen to you speak of her in such a manner."

"I only speak my mind," she answered. "And the truth as I see it."

"We don't always see alike," Max reminded her. "And this time I think you're wrong. Faith is a lady. She may wear simple clothing and work hard in order to make a living, but she's proved to me that she has more courage than many men I've known. I admire her greatly, Mother."

Her eyes narrowed as they took his measure. "She's managed to wind you right around her little finger, hasn't she? I suppose, being a man, you couldn't resist all that blowsy yellow hair and those big blue eyes she turns in your direction.'' As he began to speak, she lifted a hand to halt his words of denial. ''Never mind. I'll say no more. I just want to know when you're coming home, Maxwell. I came here to remind you of your responsibility.''

''I'm very aware of my obligation to the business,'' he said. ''I'm going back to Boston. The plans were already in motion before your arrival. If I'd been able to stop you from leaving there, I would have.''

''Well, I'm glad you've come to your senses. I told your brother you would remember your upbringing and do the right thing. I suspect you needed to get Faith out of your system. I'm sure you can see now that she doesn't belong in the position you placed her in. Perhaps she can't help it. Maybe there's a weakness in her that doesn't allow her to fill her place as she should.'' His mother sighed. ''A pity, I suppose.''

''She's more woman than I'd ever hoped to have as mine,'' Max said bluntly. ''The problem is that she hasn't agreed yet to return with me.''

''That's her loss,'' Hazel said, her eyes lighting with what appeared to him to be a glow of success. ''Leave her here and get on with your life. Divorces can be obtained. It may be messy for a while, but I'm sure we can keep it quiet, and certainly public opinion will be with you.''

''I'll take your bag to the bedroom, Mother,'' Max said, biting his tongue against the words that begged to be uttered. It was hopeless, he decided. There was no changing her. He was between a rock and a hard place, and right now he wasn't sure which was which. Faith was about as stubborn as a body could be, but his mother was running a close second. Getting the woman out of here was a priority.

* * *

Meals were cooked and eaten, chores accomplished with a minimum of discussion, and nightfall found Faith in the yard, standing beneath a tree, hoping to fade into oblivion beneath its branches. It was not to be.

"I wondered if you had retired early," Hazel said, her voice preceding her.

Faith looked up from her contemplation of the dirt beneath her feet and saw the majestic shadow of Max's mother approaching through the darkness. "I like to take a bit of fresh air in the evening," she said. "I appreciate the quiet and the opportunity to be alone for a while."

"And I disturbed you," Hazel said, apparently without apology. "I felt we needed to spend a few minutes together, Faith. I know you aren't fond of me, but we do have a concern for Max's well-being in common, I believe."

Being *fond* of Hazel McDowell was about the last emotion Faith could have dredged up at this moment. The woman was a thorn in her flesh and not for the life of her could she drum up any degree of politeness right now.

"I'm concerned for Max, yes," Faith said finally. "Whether or not you can understand my feelings on this subject, let me tell you a couple of things. First, Max is a grown man. He is capable of deciding where he wants to be without his mother hunting him down like a runaway child. Second, I have no hold on the man. Whether he leaves here tomorrow or the next day is up to him. Third, and finally, I am no threat to you, Mrs. McDowell."

The laughter that greeted Faith's final words was light and gleeful. "Oh, I'm well aware of that," she said. "Maxwell is well-bred and even though he has come here to tie up loose ends, he'll go back to his own place in society and make his life there. You could never hold a man like Maxwell."

The urge to dispute that particular claim rose within

Faith, but she bit her lip and held her tongue. *I could if I was willing to tag along tomorrow.*

"In fact, earlier today we were discussing his obtaining a divorce," his mother continued.

"A divorce?" Faith's heart began an erratic beat as she spoke the words.

"Yes. I'm sure you realized it would come to that eventually."

"I suppose so," she said quietly, even as the word resounded in her mind. *Divorce.* And Max had discussed it with his mother.

"I understand there is a train east on Monday. At noontime, I believe Max said," Hazel continued.

"Yes." Her voice sounded dull, withdrawn, and Faith couldn't find it in herself to care. She stepped from the shadow of the tree into the moonlight. "I think I'd better go in now. Morning comes early in the summertime."

"Good night." Hazel's final words were soft, filled with satisfaction, and Faith did not reply, only walked toward the house, then climbed the steps to the porch.

"What's wrong?" Max stood in the shadows, and his words were quiet, but intense. "Did Mother upset you? What did she say, Faith?"

"Nothing. She told me good-night." And so she had.

"You look...strange." His words were hesitant. "I was just coming out to speak with you when I saw her there. I didn't want to interfere if you were having a private conversation with her."

Faith cast him a long look. "Didn't you? Or were you throwing me to the wolves?"

"And what is that supposed to mean?" His voice was soft, carrying only to her ears, but she cared little if his mother overheard them talking.

"It doesn't matter, Max. None of it matters. Come inside, and I'll dress your wound one last time. You can find a doctor in Boston to treat it when you arrive there. And then I'm going to bed.

"Tomorrow is going to be a long day. You'll have to sort out all your things and get packed up. I'll take you to town early Monday morning. Or I can run you in to the hotel tomorrow if you like. That way you won't have to worry about missing the train."

"Faith." It was harsh, his utterance of her name. "Will you reconsider?"

She shook her head, and brushed past him. His hand rested against her arm for a fleeting moment.

"Don't touch me, please," she whispered. "Let me tend your shoulder and then you can get your mother settled in her room."

In ten minutes she'd accomplished her task, aware when Hazel entered the back door and watched from across the room. Leaving Max to clean up the mess, Faith left the kitchen.

Chapter Thirteen

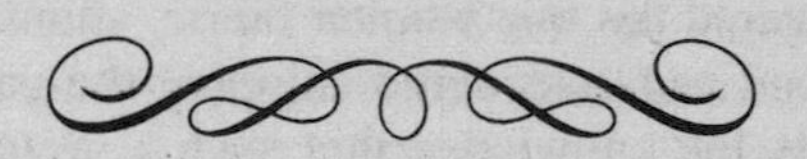

"I don't like to see you out here alone. It doesn't seem as if things are as safe as they used to be." His jaw jutted forward, and Faith had to smile.

Brace could be as stubborn as a mule, she decided. Somehow he'd managed to appoint himself as her guardian angel, and if his furrowed brow was any indication, he was set on resolving the issue of her solitude at the farmhouse. He stood on the edge of her porch, hands stuck in his back pockets, looking distinctly uncomfortable.

"I'm quite handy with a gun, you know, and I've been alone before," she said calmly. "Having Max here for a while didn't make me suddenly helpless, Sheriff." What it had done was make her dependent on the man, but that was a weakness she wasn't about to admit.

"He knows I'll look after you," Brace told her, shifting his stance. His gaze focused on her as if he found something vastly fascinating about her face and form. He'd been her friend for a long time, but since Max's departure more than three weeks ago, Brace had almost made a pest of himself, showing up at the farmhouse door several times.

There was always a viable excuse for his visits. Then, once his business was done, he'd manage to make himself helpful, lingering to talk as long as he could to keep Faith in conversation.

Once it was to bring her newspaper from town. Another time to deliver a catalog order that could just as well have waited for her next trip to Benning. Today he'd snatched the excuse to deliver a warm winter cloak from the general store, one Max had ordered for her before he left town.

She'd fingered the fine woolen fabric, admired in silence the lined hood and considered shipping the garment off to Boston. Only the knowledge that such a gesture would be childish and only cause him pain kept her from indulging herself with the whim. Hurting Max was not her aim in life.

So instead, she folded it and held it against her breast, where it warmed flesh that had been chilled by bereavement. The day was warm, yet held a hint of autumn, and she felt oddly cold, deep within where lay a dark, forbidding chasm. She might never again know the warmth of a man's embrace, and that knowledge made her ache.

It seemed she was doomed to carry night and day the pain of Max's leaving her. Pale and drawn, she'd peered into the mirror this morning and recognized misery staring back at her. No wonder Brace watched her with such obvious concern.

"Are you feeling all right?" he asked, shifting away from the edge of the porch to stroll to the far end of the wooden structure. He turned and lowered himself into the swing that hung there. Long chains held it dangling from the porch roof, and he set it moving with his foot, then patted the cushion beside him. "Come on and sit down for a minute, Faith. You look like you're about whipped."

"Thanks," she murmured, crossing to take her place on the other end of the wide seat. "I'm not sure that's much of a compliment." She placed the cloak on the seat between them and laced her fingers together in her lap. "I've been working in the garden. The sun always wears me down."

"I'm thinking it's more than heat that's got you looking so weary," Brace said quietly. He touched her shoulder with his fingertips. "I don't mean to pry, but I'm thinking you're unhappy, Faith. I had a hard time believing that Max would just go off and leave you here alone."

He leaned his head back and examined the batten board porch ceiling. His words were musing, and a glimmer of a smile curved his mouth. "You know, old Max's mama is a right hateful lady from what I saw of her. She acts like she'd lead Max around by the nose if he let her. I'll warrant he'll be happy to get her home and off his hands."

Faith fervently hoped so, but was having a hard time working up much sympathy for Max's dilemma. "It was his choice to travel back across the country with her," she said with a shrug. "She told him that his business was in serious disorder without him there. I suppose his mother was right in reminding him of his responsibility."

Brace glanced at her and shook his head as he rocked the swing with his foot. "I don't know about that. I don't see how he could just walk away. You deserve better than being left alone, Faith." A calculated look touched his face, darkening his eyes as he took her measure.

With a candor she had not expected, he made a deliberate suggestion. "Have you ever thought of ending your marriage?"

She caught her breath, meeting his gaze, then shook her head. "I considered it was pretty well ended when I left Boston. I really never expected Max to show up here, you know. To tell the truth, I'd probably have been better off if he hadn't, if he'd sought a divorce three years ago and freed himself to marry again."

"I'm just surprised it took him so long to hunt you

down,'' Brace said sharply. ''I don't know how any man could have a woman like you in his life and then just let her walk away without doing some fancy footwork to get her back.'' His gaze softened as he spoke, touching her with admiration, resting for a moment on her hair, then lowering to where her fingers twined together in her lap.

''You're not wearing his ring,'' Brace said quietly. ''Does that mean anything?''

She shook her head and grimaced. ''Not really. But to be honest with you, I don't feel very married right now.'' Though I should, she thought. Now that I have every reason to believe Max left me with a part of himself to keep me company. Her monthly was late enough to make her condition a fact, yet even before she'd missed it by one day, she'd known.

From that magical moment in Max's arms, when her heart had still beat with the rapture of loving and being loved, she'd known. And the conviction that their time together had borne fruit had not faltered.

''Faith…'' Brace looked at her with a hunger he made no attempt to conceal. It was a look she recognized, and she ached at the denial she would voice aloud. Abruptly, he repeated her name, and his voice was raw, roughened by emotion.

She inhaled, perceiving the bent of his thoughts. ''Don't,'' she said softly.

''I'm not trying to force myself on you,'' he told her, his hand leaving her shoulder to circle her wrist, as if to reinforce his words. ''I wouldn't do anything to bring you harm or to shame you. I think you know me well enough to realize that.''

She found tears blurring her vision, and she cleared her throat. ''I like you, Brace. You've been a good friend to me. But I'm a married woman. Unless, or until, Max dissolves our marriage, I can't look at another man. I can only be your friend.''

He was silent for a moment, his fingers releasing her, only to caress the back of her hand with an almost absent gesture. Rocking the swing in a steady movement, he turned to scan the yard and the trees beyond.

''You're gonna have a good crop of apples this fall,'' he said quietly. ''I'll come out and give you a hand when it's time to pick them.''

''I'd appreciate that,'' she whispered. And then she dredged forth the memory of an earlier conversation they'd shared. ''Have you heard from your family about the woman they were wanting to send out here for you?''

As if relieved at her query, he chuckled, breaking his contact with her as he turned a bit in the swing to face her. ''Yeah. My sister wrote me another letter, a couple of weeks ago. I've been meaning to ask you to read it over and help me think of something to tell her, kinda help me get her off my back.''

''Bring the letter out, and we'll come up with a good excuse,'' Faith said. ''I've been neglecting something else we spoke of. I haven't looked at your bankbook lately.''

''And that reminds me of something else,'' he said, enthusiasm touching his words. ''I was thinking maybe if you have the spare time we could start some reading lessons. I'm pretty good with numbers, but I've got a craving to learn from books.''

''I have books aplenty in the parlor, Brace. We can spend a couple of hours a week, whenever you have the time to spare.'' She shot him a warning glance. ''But let's not speak again of paying me for being your friend.''

''All right.'' His eyes lit with pleasure. ''I enjoy spending time with you, but I won't take advantage of you, Faith. I hope you know that.''

"That's the least of my worries," she said, and recognized it as truth. Brace was a man to be trusted.

As if it were a signal, he stood, drawing his pocket watch out to flash it before her. "Bought me a watch," he said, grinning boldly. "Remember when you told me about telling time on the big clock in town?"

She nodded, pleased that he'd taken her suggestion. "You have a brain like a sponge," she said. "Reading will come easy, once you put your mind to it." As he stepped to the ground, she stood and followed him to the hitching rail where his horse waited.

"Thanks for bringing the package," she told him. "When you see Mr. Metcalf, tell him I'll be in to deliver eggs on Saturday."

Brace nodded, lifting himself into the saddle with an agile movement. Tilting his hat a bit over his eyes, he gathered his reins and turned his horse toward town.

Faith watched his back, noted the width of his shoulders, the easy way he sat in the saddle, and wondered why he had never appealed to her as more than a nice man, a friend to be cherished. Max had spoiled her for anyone else, she thought gloomily. The cloak drew her gaze and she walked to the swing, picking it up and holding it once more against her breast.

Dark blue, with crimson cording down the front and edging the collar, it boasted intricate fastenings, six in all. She'd seen their like in the catalog among the best quality ladies' fashions, and admired them, even as she'd known such luxury was beyond her reach. Now she held a garment that was top of the line, if she was any judge of such a thing. And Max had seen to it that she would be warm in the winter to come.

The house was silent as she passed through the rooms, and as she knelt before a cedar chest beneath the bedroom window, she pressed her lips against the fine material of Max's gift. The lid was heavy and she held it open with one hand while she placed the cloak atop two quilts.

Smoothing it with her palm, she sighed. It wouldn't do to be prideful. She'd wear it for warmth and think of Max when the nights grew cold and harsh winds blew around the farmhouse. When she slept in her bed it would cover her, lying atop the quilt, and when she went to town she'd wear it with pride.

She'd be grateful for its folds. They would help conceal the child she would bear, come spring.

Boston, Massachusetts—October, 1898

"This beats being in cahoots with another shipping line, Max. Buying our own ships will make a difference all the way around," Howard said firmly. "We'll increase our import capabilities, and on top of that, we'll no longer be paying out good money for someone else to oversee the transport of goods."

"And what is that going to mean, as far as additional work in this office?" Max asked. He leaned back in his desk chair, resplendent in another new suit. His summer's work had put additional muscle in his shoulders, making new clothing necessary. A visit to the tailor had solved that problem, and his first new suit had been sent to his home within two days time, allowing him to relax once more in clothing that fit well.

He was tanned and trim, his trousers having to be altered to fit as well, and his brother had viewed him with a lifted brow the first day back in the office building the family owned. "It doesn't appear that the wilderness did you any harm," Howard had said with a laugh. "You're looking like a sodbuster, brother dear. Brown as the proverbial berry."

Max had plowed through the backlog of work, doggedly clearing his desk, aware that Howard lurked about, ready to propose a new venture for the business that had been in the family for almost a century. Now his brother stood before him and waffled a bit, as if he disliked admitting that his plan would produce problems.

"We'll have to buckle down for a while," he said finally. "Both of us, Max." His voice became defensive as he stood firm. And then he added a final thrust. "I've done double duty for the past months, you know."

"And I did more than my share while you were ill three years ago," Max stated mildly, "not to mention the late hours I've worked since I got back in town." Defensive himself, he held up a hand to halt the hasty words that were sure to come. "I know. I know. You couldn't help being laid up for six months. But then I couldn't do much about the family emergency that took me away, either."

"Emergency?" Howard asked, doubt ringing in the word. "It took you three years to get around to finding your wayward wife, and suddenly it was an emergency?"

"She wasn't *wayward,*" Max said quietly, his tone a warning.

Howard backtracked readily. "You know what I mean. Wrong choice of words, I suppose."

"I'm going to have her back here," Max told him. "And I'm not going to sacrifice my marriage a second time to this business. If we have to hire additional supervisors, so be it. I'll put in my work week, and expect you to do the same, but no more late hours and weekends at my desk at home."

Howard sat down in a leather chair and considered his brother steadily. One leg crossed over the other. "I take it you've done a total about-face—reformed, so to speak. I feel like I've lost track here somewhere. Mother didn't mention the fact that you were bringing Faith back to the fold. What did I miss?''

Max stifled the urge to vent his anger on the man before him. ''Mother has caused a bundle of trouble all the way around,'' he said after a moment. ''Apparently, she was not kind to Faith during the years of our marriage, and I was too thick-skulled to catch on to the problems.''

''You know she's an interfering creature,'' Howard said with a shrug.

''More than I was aware of, apparently,'' Max admitted. ''Has she interfered in your marriage?''

Howard grinned widely. ''Why do you think I chose to build a house all the way across town when I walked down the aisle with Melissa?''

''I should have been so intelligent,'' Max said morosely. And then he straightened in his chair. ''Spilled milk,'' he said firmly. ''Not worth fussing over.'' His gaze was sharp as it focused on his brother. ''But know this one thing. No matter what it takes, I'll be making a home for my wife and somehow coaxing her to live in it with me. That's my first item of business.

''You,'' he said firmly, ''can be in charge of hiring a new agent to keep track of shipping and schedules. Someone dependable and honest, with some experience behind him. I'll look over the paperwork for the loans we require this afternoon, and we can get this thing set in motion by tomorrow.''

''We'll need to set up a new office on the docks,'' Howard reminded him.

''That's up to you,'' Max said with a wave of his hand, already engrossed in the sheaf of papers he held. ''Find a clean place with enough room for three or four desks, in a safe area.''

''That's it?'' Howard was nonplussed, his mouth twitching in amusement. "You sure don't fool around once you make up your mind, do you?"

Max looked up, impatient with the delay. "See if you can locate that captain that left Pacific General. Buy him away from wherever he's working. We'll offer him enough money to insure his agreement to work for us. Tell him he'll have the first ship to sail with our flag on it."

Max narrowed his eyes, examining his memory. "What was his name? Richard Weathermore? Something like that, if I recall." He waved a hand, pointing at his office door. "Get on with it. If you've settled this in your mind and made the decision to do it, then get it underway."

Howard rocked back on his heels, his hands thrust into his pockets. "I just thought you might want to argue about it a bit, cringe a little at spending such an inordinate amount of money. At least waffle over the expense."

"You have to spend money to make money sometimes," Max said bluntly. "It's a solid idea. Should have thought of it myself, I suppose. But since you're the one with the intelligence this week, I'll give you the credit." His grin was sudden and rare, and Howard responded to it.

"Damn, it's good to have you back, brother." He turned on his heel and crossed the Aubusson carpet that covered the floor. At the door he turned back, his hand on the brass knob. "Congratulations on resolving your problems with Faith, by the way. Melissa always liked her, you know. So did I. Felt sorry for her during all the mess—"

He broke off as Max frowned. "I mean when the baby died, and all. And then to have her just walk away." His grin was faint as he spoke his mind. "I didn't think she had it in her to leave you, Max. I think she shook you up a bit."

"You don't know the half of it," Max said quietly, leaning back in his chair, the sheaf of papers clutched in one hand. "Now make tracks, partner. There are things to be accomplished."

Benning, Texas—late October, 1898

My love, the letter began. Faith felt a tear trickle down her cheek, and she brushed at it with an impatient hand. Brace stood in front of her and she glanced up.

"I'm sorry. I'm rude to read this in your company." She folded it back into the envelope and stuffed it in her pocket.

"That's all right, Faith. I knew when I saw it was from Max that you'd want to get your hands on it right away."

"Come in and we'll have some coffee," she said, feeling the warmth of the missive in her pocket as if it were a burning coal.

Brace stepped onto the porch and held the door open for her, then followed her into the kitchen. "I'll put the coffee on," he offered. "You sit down and read your letter, why don't you?"

Faith gave in to temptation. It was the first correspondence she'd received from Max. In almost two months, she'd written and torn into shreds several notes of her own, determined that he should break the silence first. And it had paid off. She carried the proof in her pocket.

There was enough sunlight shining through the window to see by, and she settled in a chair beside the glass panes. She thought there was a faint scent of *something* on the paper. Some trace of shaving cream, perhaps, or maybe it was the smell of the hand soap Max used in his office. Stifling the urge to lift the paper to her nose, she inhaled deeply, hoping to recognize the drifting aroma, but to no avail.

It was but a single page, the writing distinctive and bold—Max's own hand, not a note dictated to his secretary. Faith wasn't surprised. Max was too private an individual to place his thoughts before a third person. Her eyes lingered on the heading once more.

"My love," she read, savoring the salutation. "My work is heavy and time has passed quickly. Forgive me for not writing sooner. We left with harsh words between us, but I refuse to leave things unsettled. There is a great deal I would like to say to you, and many problems yet to be solved, but perhaps time will heal some of the wounds we managed to inflict in our last encounter. Know that my thoughts are with you."

He'd signed his name in slashing letters, and the letters were blurred as if his hand had smudged the ink.

She looked out the window to where the garden lay brown and bleak, only the dried potato vines clinging to the fruits of her harvest. Autumn was upon them. Already the nights were chilly, and even though the days warmed up and the final crop of hay in the fields between the farm and town wasn't yet cut, there was an air of preparation in the days that passed.

Winter would be here soon, making travel difficult. Max would not be coming back, she realized. He'd said he would in the spring, but she'd hoped—oh, how she'd hoped that before the first snowflakes fell, he would find his way to her. It was not to be. And her heart sank at the knowledge.

You could have gone with him. The words rang in her head, a much repeated refrain of regret, and she considered them honestly. No, she thought, I couldn't. Not the way things were. I took a stand, and Max made his choice.

He didn't have a choice. Again she heard the inner voice of reason and dismissed it with a shrug. "We all have choices," she muttered beneath her breath.

"Did you say something?" Brace stood at the stove, looking at her over his shoulder, a concerned expression on his face.

"No, I was just thinking aloud," she said, and then turned to him, forcing a smile. "Why don't we take a couple of hours and work on your reading, Brace?" she asked brightly. "Are you in a hurry to get back to town?"

"No, ma'am," he replied, and his smile matched hers. "I'll go get the book from your parlor."

She watched him go, and felt a pang of regret. Why couldn't a man like Brace be the one to make her heart beat faster, her breath catch in her throat at the sight of his dear features? And then, as he returned with the simple, easy-to-read book they used for their times together, she crossed to sit at the table and smiled at him as he sat at an angle, always careful to keep his distance.

"We're on page sixty-four, if I remember right," she said, and watched as he found the place with ease, pleased at the rapid progress he'd made over the past weeks.

Boston, Massachusetts—November, 1898

"You're about as happy as a fish out of water," Howard said glumly. "You've made all our employees walk around with frowns. It used to be almost a decent place to work until you came back from Texas, Max."

"I didn't guarantee our employees a party every day when they hired on with us," Max said sharply. "I'm working my way through all the snags you've thrown at me over the past weeks, and I'll be the first to admit that the bluebird of happiness is not sitting on my shoulder."

"You need to get your nose out of that stack of work, if you ask me, and think of something besides the business," Howard said forcefully. "Melissa asked you twice last week to come by for supper, and you brushed her off with a feeble excuse."

Max leaned back and eyed his brother ruefully. "I'm not good company right now. I want to get things straightened up here so I can spend more time getting my personal life in order."

"If we didn't need both of us here right now to get this whole situation in hand, I'd send you back to Texas," Howard told him.

"And if I didn't feel compelled to be here, I'd be on my way right now. Nothing would make me happier."

"Have you heard from her? Or aren't I allowed to ask?"

"Yeah," Max said, his voice a disgusted growl. "She's fine. The chickens are fine. The mare is fine, and even the sheriff is fine." He looked up and displeasure was dark on his countenance. "If it weren't for a note from her neighbor, I'd wonder if the woman had more than one set of words in her vocabulary. According to Lin, everything is *not* fine. Faith is tired all the time, and isn't any happier than she was when I left. Lin fears she's not eating properly. And she said her face is drawn and pale."

"And what are you going to do about it?"

Max spread his hands on top of his desk blotter. "Nothing for now." He looked up and focused on his brother. "There are too many people depending on this business for me to walk away when things are precarious. Once we get the shipping line organized and the office running smoothly, I'll have a longer stretch of days to myself."

He pointed at a file on one side of his desk. "I'm in the midst of negotiations for the house, and that's going slowly. It's difficult to deal with owners who live halfway across the country."

"Have you told Faith about the place you're buying for her?"

Max shook his head. "I wanted it to be a surprise. Oh, we spoke of it when I was in Texas, but nothing definite was in the works then. I couldn't make any promises."

"And now?" Howard sat down in the chair across from Max's desk. He tilted his head to one side and scanned his brother. "I'll tell you, Max. If ever a man looked in need of a woman's touch, it's you."

Max looked down at his spotless cuffs, the splendid weave of wool that made up his suit. "I look all right to me."

"It's your eyes, Max. The pallor of your skin. You've almost totally lost the tanned look you sported when you arrived back in town two months ago. And your mouth is drawn."

"Maybe Faith and I make a good pair," Max said with a hollow laugh. He held up a hand. "Tell you what. I'll make a vow to travel before Christmas. Bad weather or not, I'll get on a train and head for Dallas. The train doesn't run well from there to Benning in winter, but December shouldn't be too bad. Gives me six more weeks to get things in order here. And then I'm going to get her."

"Will she come willingly?"

Max set his jaw, knew a moment of panic as he considered that very shaky possibility, and then he spoke, his words harsh and without compromise.

"She'll come. If I have to carry her over my shoulder, kicking and screaming, she'll come with me. This has gone far enough."

Benning, Texas—November, 1898

My love, it began. It seemed that Max was fond of the salutation, Faith decided. And then she halted in the middle of the sidewalk, right in front of the bank, to read the letter she held. Good manners decreed she be alone to peruse her mail, but she'd decided that waiting until she headed for home to read his words was not an option.

Her hands trembled as she held the paper before her. He wrote of work, of Howard and his wife. It seemed Melissa had given up on her brother-in-law, having invited him to supper numerous times without an acceptance from him. The new shipping line was shaping up. Spring would tell the tale, Max said.

And then there was a blot, as if he'd sunk into deep thought, resting the nib of his pen on the paper, allowing the ink to flow onto the page. He'd scribbled a note beside the smudge, circling it and asking her pardon for failing to use his desk blotter. She smiled at his foolishness, as he'd probably wanted her to.

Not a word of Hazel McDowell. And Faith wondered at that.

Not a whisper of love, no aching words telling of his need for her. And for that fact, she mourned.

She crumpled the paper in her hand, and then laboriously straightened it, smoothing it between her fingers.

"Did he make you angry?" Lin stood beside her, a frown gathering at her brow.

"Who?" Faith raised wide eyes to her friend.

"Max, I assume," Lin said dryly. "That is a letter from him, isn't it?"

"This?" Faith looked down at the wrinkled mess she held. "Yes, it's from Max. And yes, he made me angry." She inhaled deeply. "I'm so mad at him I could spit."

"Well, at least you're feeling *something*," Lin said. "It sure beats that placid, calm look you wear all the time. I was beginning to think my friend Faith had been taken over by the man in the moon."

"I haven't been that bad," Faith said quickly. "I even ate supper at your house last week," she said, recalling Max's letter and Melissa's spurned invitations.

"Correction," Lin said. "You pushed some food around on your plate. Katie said you must be sickening with something."

"I'm fine."

''Hmm...'' Lin murmured. ''And then Katie said she thought maybe you were in the family way. Apparently, sometimes that affects women's appetites.'' She shot Faith a piercing look, and then continued on, her gaze watchful. ''With me, it just increased my appetite. Nicholas was certain I would turn into a butterball by the time Jonathan was born.''

''Family way?'' Faith repeated, latching on to the phrase that described her problem exactly. ''Why on earth would she think that?''

''She's a canny lass, according to Nicholas. Knows things before I do sometimes.''

Faith was silent, her gaze fixed on the sidewalk at her feet. And then she lifted her head and met Lin's inquisitive look. ''Katie is one smart lady. Tell her I said so.'' Her whisper was almost silent, but her smile spoke volumes.

Immediately Lin wrapped her arms around her friend and held her close. The paper Faith clutched crinkled loudly, and Lin backed away. ''I've crunched your mail,'' she said, grabbing for the single sheet of paper and smoothing it with quick touches.

''It's all right. I already read it.'' Faith took it from her and folded it, replacing it in its envelope. ''I'll probably read it over when I get home, just in case I missed something.''

''Come home with me,'' Lin begged, holding Faith's hands in her own. ''Katie's making pot roast for supper, and you know how you like it. We're having the last of the garden vegetables and a fresh apple pie.''

''I have things to do,'' Faith began, her words vague as she sought for an excuse.

''I'll bring her,'' said a male voice from a nearby doorway. Brace stood just a few feet from where they stood, his gaze locked on Faith's pale features. ''She looks like a strong wind would blow her away, Mrs. Garvey. I'll see to it she's at your table at suppertime."

"Thank you, Sheriff," Lin said with a grin. "I knew I could count on the law to take a hand in things when this woman gets ornery. We'll lay a place for you, too."

"That would be fine, ma'am," he said, tilting his hat at a jaunty angle. And then he reached for Faith's arm. "Come on, my friend," he said quietly. "Let's gather your things, and I'll tie my horse to the back of your wagon and drive you home."

Faith looked up at him, her eyes filling with tears. "You're a wonderful man, Brace. Have I ever told you how much I appreciate you?"

"No, I don't believe so," he said with a grin. "But I'll give you an hour or so to do the job. Now, let's get you together and you can wait on the wagon while I pick up your supplies from the store."

Faith frowned. "How do you know I have supplies waiting for me?"

"I saw you come out of there empty-handed, and I figured old Mr. Metcalf was putting them together." He searched her face and apparently saw something that pleased him, for he smiled. "Was I right?"

"Frequently," she said, turning back to Lin. "It seems I'm to be a guest at your table for supper this evening. Thank you for the invitation."

Brace was quick, loading her onto the wagon seat and then traipsing into the general store for her things. He carried her basket over his arm and placed it in the wagon bed behind the seat. "Mr. Metcalf said he took this from your credit. You still have some left, apparently."

"I think Max paid him a substantial sum on my account before he left town. I never seem to owe any money to the man."

"You bring in eggs pretty regularly, don't you?"

She cast him a scathing glance. "You don't buy this many provisions with the profit from a few dozen eggs, Brace."

"Metcalf said he could use some apples. You got extra?"

"You should know. You picked them." A pang of guilt touched her to the quick as she remembered his long hours in the orchard one Sunday, carrying bushel baskets of fruit into the root cellar for her. And then he'd lugged another bushel to town for Mr. Metcalf to sell in the store.

"I'll take a look when we get to your place." He climbed atop the wagon seat and lifted the reins. The team stirred into motion and Brace turned them in the middle of the road, heading for the farmhouse. "You haven't baked any pies at your place lately, have you?" he asked hopefully.

"I will on Friday if you want to come by," she promised. "Apple."

"Is there any other kind?" He slanted a grin in her direction as he slapped the reins on the broad backs of her team. But his eyes held a trace of worry, and Faith was prompted to reassure him.

"I'm all right, Brace. Truly, I am. I'm in the midst of making some decisions, and as soon as I know what I'll be doing, I'll let you know my next move."

"Well," he said, dragging out the single syllable. "If you're half as smart as I think you are, that move will be boarding a train and heading east."

Chapter Fourteen

"My wife tells me we're about to lose our neighbor." Nicholas sat down at the table, directing his attention to Faith. Lin and Katie carried serving dishes from the kitchen into the seldom used dining room, and Faith felt their interested looks aimed in her direction as she fumbled for an answer.

Apparently unaware of their interest in the conversation he'd instigated with his neighbor, he eyed Faith in good humor. "You might know you aren't allowed to have secrets around here, ma'am. Lin couldn't wait to tell me why we were using the dining room tonight. It seems there's a celebration at hand."

Discomfort rose within her, and Faith felt the crimson rush of blood stinging her cheeks. "You'd think this was the first time a woman ever announced the coming of a child," she said, attempting a light tone and failing miserably.

"Who have you announced it to?" he asked mildly, lifting a dark eyebrow in her direction.

"Not Max, if that's what you're asking," Faith told him bluntly.

Nicholas leaned back in his chair. "Why not?"

Faith thought his gaze hardened, his mouth growing taut as he awaited her reply.

"I won't force his hand that way," she said after a moment.

"You're not giving him a chance to make any sort of move."

Lin walked behind Nicholas and placed her hand on his shoulder. His own lifted to cover it, and as Faith watched, he applied pressure, as if to reassure his wife in some way.

"I think we need to eat," Lin said quietly, sending a small smile in Faith's direction. "I'm sure this discussion isn't helping our guest's digestion."

Nicholas bowed his head. "I'm sorry. I've been rude, Faith."

"No," she said quickly. "Just being a man and looking at this from a male viewpoint." It was a dig she could not resist. He and Max were like two peas in a pod—arrogant and smug in their own magnificence.

"Male viewpoint?" His words foretold his disagreement. "From a father's eyes, perhaps." He looked up at Lin. "Sorry, sweetheart, but this needs to be brought out. I don't think Faith has considered Max's rights in this issue. The man is going to have a child, or at least his wife is, and he's totally unaware of it." His jaw moved and his gaze flashed with a dangerous light. "If Faith were my wife, I'd feel betrayed that she thought so little of me, not allowing me to be aware of the most wonderful news a man can hear."

Brace stood in the doorway, his eyes fastened on Faith, and she felt his gaze warm her. "I think we need to give the lady the benefit of the doubt," he drawled. "She's working things out. Leaving everything she's accomplished in her life over the past years is a big decision to make.

She's gonna have to make up her mind where her future lies, I think.''

Nicholas slanted a look at the lawman. ''Poaching, Sheriff?''

Brace stiffened. ''Not so's you could notice, my friend. Faith is important to me, just as she is to you and Lin. If staying here is her choice, then we need to back her up.''

Nicholas shook his head. ''I can't go along with that one. Max has certain rights in this. I'll guarantee you one thing. If he knew the circumstances, he'd be on his way to Texas.''

Faith stood abruptly, her chair falling to the floor behind her. ''Well, I'll be *damned* if I'll sit here and be discussed as if I didn't have a brain in my head. This is my life, my child and my decision to make.'' She turned to face her host.

''Nicholas, you've been a good friend to me, but you don't know josh about my life before I arrived in Texas. I'm not carrying tales about Max, but let me tell you one thing. Before I tell him about this baby, I'll need to know that I'm number one on his list. Ahead of his business, for one thing, and *definitely* in first place when it comes to the women in his life.''

He grinned. ''Well, I know a little about men, and I can tell you right now that Max McDowell is head over heels in love with his wife. I don't need to know anything about your problems in the past. But I'd lay odds that one look at you right now, and he wouldn't be wasting any time convincing you that you're the most important thing in the world to him.''

''Me?'' she asked. ''Or the fact that I'm carrying his child?''

''They kinda go hand in hand, don't you think?''

''No.'' It was firm and final, a single word that spoke

her mind. And then she gave in to the urge to elaborate. ''The baby is important, but I have to come first. I existed in a beautiful house in Boston with a husband who treated me like a china doll. If he can't see that I'm a woman, aside from a wife bearing his child, then I don't want him and he doesn't deserve me.''

''Hear! Hear!'' Lin's voice was quiet but Faith appreciated her support. And then her friend circled the table, bent to lift Faith's chair from the floor and coaxed her with a hug and soft whispers. ''Sit down and eat, please, Faith. Katie will be hurt if you don't praise her efforts.''

Feeling a bit foolish for venting her anger at Nicholas, Faith nodded. ''I'm hungry. Even Nicholas's disapproval can't make me lose my appetite tonight.'' She cast him a final look of challenge and settled in her chair.

''Don't stay mad at me, will you?'' he asked in a low murmur. ''I don't want to be in Lin's bad graces.''

Faith managed a small smile. ''You might as well know that even without your influence, I'm planning on returning to Max. I've been thinking about it for the past month, and I've dithered back and forth long enough. I've yet to decide just how to go about telling him about the baby.''

''You're going back?'' Lin asked, catching the gist of Faith's speech. ''You've already decided? And here I've been so careful not to try to persuade you.''

Nicholas was silent, but Faith felt his approval in the slanting glance he offered. He reached to lift the lid on a serving dish, caught a scent of the pot roast it held and sighed. ''Ah, Katie, you never fail to delight me.''

The housekeeper slid into a chair across the table from Faith and shot Nicholas a wry look. ''You make my life worthwhile, sir,'' she said with a touch of acerbic wit.

''Can we pray first and talk about stuff later?'' Amanda spoke up distinctly, her small face decorated by a frown of obvious displeasure. "Suppertime is for eating food, and Katie always says we should eat while it's hot."

Faith smothered a laugh as the child registered her disdain of the grown-ups and their verbal dispute. "I agree, Amanda," she said lightly. "It would be a shame to ruin Katie's pot roast."

Nicholas smiled, his benevolence toward the little girl apparent, and then bowed his head as he spoke simple words of blessing.

"Well," he said to Faith a moment later, serving a portion of meat to Amanda's plate, "if you wait much longer, you won't have to make any announcement when you get to Boston. I think Max will be able to figure out the lay of the land all by himself."

"I'm not..." Faith looked down at herself, then blushed furiously. "I don't think it's apparent yet."

"What are you talking about, Auntie Faith?" Amanda asked as she held out her plate for a serving of potatoes.

"Nothing you need to worry about, sweet," Lin said hastily, rolling her eyes at Faith as she pacified the child with an elaborate procedure, making a volcano out of her mashed potatoes and filling the center of it with gravy.

Brace had seated himself next to Amanda and now he looked across the table and spoke quietly to Faith. "When do you plan on leaving?"

"Probably within the next two weeks," she said, splitting a biscuit and buttering it lavishly. "I only need to get rid of the chickens, find a home for Wolf and make arrangements to ship my mare."

"You'll take Goldie with you?" Nicholas asked.

Faith glared at him. "Did you think I'd leave her here for you? I'm sure there are livery stables enough in Boston to give me a choice as to where I'll put her. If I have to I'll pay for her keep until Max figures something else out."

''I'll be happy to take the dog off your hands,'' Lin said. ''He's good-natured, and Amanda's cat needs a challenge.''

Katie spoke up abruptly. ''If you're giving away chickens, I'll be first in line.'' She looked at Nicholas. ''Can you see to having a place for them within the next little while?''

His nod was quick, and then he spoke quietly in an aside to Faith. ''Will you move back in with him?''

''No.'' It was pure and simple, Faith had decided. If Max wanted her back, he'd have to come to terms with her. And the major stipulation would involve his mother's absence from their household.

''Are you going to let him know you're on the way?'' Brace asked. ''And I guess my next question is do you need someone to travel with you?''

Faith shook her head. ''I got here alone. I can go back by myself.''

It turned out not to be quite as simple as she'd thought. Shipping the mare was a major accomplishment. Goldie was not accustomed to being held captive in a dark, rumbling railroad car and she was unhappy with the whole thing. From her first tentative steps up the ramp into the car to the jolting of the floor beneath her as the train set off from the station, she rolled her eyes and whinnied shrilly.

Only the fact that Faith stood at her head, holding tightly to the halter and speaking in a low, quiet voice seemed to convince the horse that all would be well. Faith reluctantly left her when the train rolled into Dallas, and took her seat in a Pullman car. She would travel in greater luxury this time, she'd decided. Taking funds from the bank, she'd purchased a berth for sleeping, and ate her meals in the dining car.

Arrangements for her money to be transferred to a bank

in Boston after her arrival were made, and the manager of Benning's small bank wished her well as she tucked a small bankroll into her reticule upon leaving his establishment.

She'd packed only the clothing Max had bought for her, leaving behind her old dresses and the flour sack nightgown that was fit only for dust rags. Feeling luxurious in her wool cloak, she spread it around her, glorying in its elegance. Then, as the swiftly moving rail car warmed up from the press of passengers, she removed the wrap and folded it neatly.

That she was nervous was an understatement, she thought, envisioning her forthcoming meeting with Max. He would be surprised, she was certain. He probably wouldn't be too forthcoming, waiting to see how the wind blew. Max had been thwarted in his desire to haul her home with him. He'd likely make her eat a small portion of crow before he made her welcome.

But then, you never knew about Max. He'd changed in the months spent in Texas. Perhaps he'd be more approachable, more willing to bend.

Boston might have made him revert to the starchy businessman she'd married. He'd been somewhat of a stuffed shirt in the old days, she remembered. The man who had departed from Benning in August bore little resemblance to the husband she'd left more than three long years ago. And at the thought of his tall, masculine figure, she felt a warming within, like a fire that had been banked for the night and only required a bit of kindling to set it glowing afresh come morning.

She closed her eyes and he was there in her memories. Dark hair rumpled a bit in the morning before he had a chance to tame it into order. Hands that could control a stubborn horse or persuade an ornery woman to his purpose. He was everything she'd ever wanted in a man, and the flare of desire that rose up in her surprised her with its intensity.

Pregnancy probably had something to do with it, she thought. Lin said Nicholas had enjoyed her response to him all during the time she carried Jonathan. Faith would take care to hold her emotions at bay.

Now, she decided, was the time to rehearse the words that would apprise Max of her intentions, set the stage for their future. *I've come back.* No, that was too abrupt and simple. Maybe she should give him notice that she would not move back in the house with him. *I thought I'd take a hotel room while we sort out our differences.*

She smiled as she imagined Max's face should she spout those words. He'd react like a bull with a red flag. Maybe just a simple phrase—*You're going to be a father.* That would certainly seal her fate. Max would have her tucked away in cotton batting before she could change her mind.

Boston was chilly when she arrived, with a fine mist falling from the sky, and Faith rued the lack of an umbrella. No matter. Her cloak boasted a generous hood, and she pulled it up over her hair as she paced the length of the train platform toward the car where her mare waited.

A gentleman from the same livery stable where Max kept his mount met the train and walked beside her, pacing himself to her shorter stride. "We'll take good care of your lady, Mrs. McDowell," he said, his eyes admiring as he bent to peer beneath the folds of her hood.

Accepting the money she handed him, he approached the mare, whose disposition had not improved upon departing the car. And then she caught Faith's scent and whickered, tossing her head as her mistress reached for her halter. In moments, Faith had calmed the animal and she walked beside the livery owner as he led Goldie to where his own horse waited.

''Can I get you a carriage?'' he asked, frowning as if he hesitated leaving her on the busy street.

''No, I can take care of it. I'll need to make arrangements to have my baggage stored here until I send for it.'' Somehow the idea of showing up in Max's business office surrounded by a small trunk and her bundles didn't appeal to her. She spoke to an officious gentleman at the information desk and filled out papers for stowing her belongings, then stepped back out into the busy street outside the railway station.

Max's office building was tall—five stories—with his own suite on the top floor. She'd stood at the wide windows more than once, looking out on the bustling city, across to the waterfront where ships were docked, disgorging their contents in what seemed to be a never-ending stream.

Now she looked up at the building facade and drew in a deep breath. He might be in conference, up there in that luxurious office where an opulent carpet lay before his desk. Perhaps he would make her stand before him and state her case. She shook her head. No, more likely he would stand and greet her nicely, his Boston persona firmly back in place.

The elevator carried her upward and she noted the unfamiliar feel of weightlessness as it rose. Her stomach was already churning, and she swallowed desperately, lest she embarrass herself.

The dignified man who served as Max's secretary stood guard outside the wide door that led to the offices of Max and his brother. Her brother-in-law, Howard, was a cheerful man, given to kindliness, and as Faith approached the secretary, she decided it would have been easier to speak to that friendly face today than to confront Max on his home ground.

''Yes?'' The secretary—Jerome Waters, according to the

name plate on his desk—looked up at Faith and smiled politely. His was a new face, and Faith obligingly asked to see Maxwell McDowell, please.

"Have you an appointment?" he asked, and at the simple, negative movement of her head, he drew in his mouth and glanced down at the ledger before him. "I fear Mr. McDowell is quite busy this afternoon. Can I suggest you come back another time?"

Faith shook her head again. Her throat had dried up somehow, and the words she strove to speak failed her.

The secretary looked indignant. "Ma'am, surely you understand that Mr. McDowell is a very busy man." And then they were both stunned as one of the wide doors opened and Max himself stood on the threshold.

"I need to see my brother, Jerome. Round him up for me, would—" His voice broke off and his face froze; for a moment the frown he wore seemed to have taken up permanent residence on those carved features.

"Faith." It was an exhalation of breath, a single syllable spoken on a gush of air. And then he moved rapidly, crossing to where she stood, his hands grasping her shoulders as if he couldn't decide whether to clasp her to himself or shake the living daylights out of her. His fingers eased their hold and he glanced at his secretary, then back down at her sober countenance.

"Come inside," he said quietly, and then to his secretary, "I don't want to be disturbed, Jerome."

"Shall I find your brother?" the man asked, his eyes wide with curiosity.

"No." There was no mistaking the firmness of his reply as Max ushered her rapidly through the doorway and then closed the door behind them. "This way," he said, leading her to another door, one she knew led to his private office. Another room held Howard's desk, but for Max, nothing would do but the corner room, which had been his father's before his death. Now it belonged to the eldest son, and perhaps someday it would belong to the child she carried, Faith thought.

For the first time, she allocated the babe within her a gender, and thought of the tiny life she sheltered in the depths of her body as another human being. The fact brought a rush of heat to her face, as if she'd been overwhelmed by an open oven door on a hot summer day, and she faltered, reaching to touch the back of an overstuffed chair to balance herself, lest she fall.

"Faith? Are you all right?" Max asked, turning her to face him. "How did you get here? When did you arrive? Why have you come without letting me know? I would have met your train."

He was floundering, completely flummoxed by her arrival, she decided, and his surprise gave her an edge. And then he was silent and stepped back to lean indolently against the edge of the desk.

"Or are you here to tie up matters between us?" he asked. She thought there was a trace of fear in the dark depths of his gaze. But surely not. Max was fearless. A warrior, Lin had called him.

"Tie up matters?" She repeated his words and shook her head. Her voice hadn't improved any, she noticed, and perhaps he did, too, for he stood upright suddenly, turned and reached for a pitcher of water on a table. Pouring out a good measure into a glass, he kept his eyes on her, as if he thought she might vanish if he should avert his gaze.

"Drink this," he said. "You look as if you're about to faint." And then as she swallowed obediently, he searched her face. "You seem different. I can't put my finger on it, but there's something about you..."

She handed him back the glass and motioned to the chair. "May I sit down, please?"

"Yes. Yes, of course," he said, taking her arm. And then, in a rapid move that took her breath, he groaned and swept her against himself.

"Faith—I can't believe you're here." His words were spoken against her hair as he swept her hood back and buried his face in the coronet of braids she wore on top of her head. He inhaled deeply as if he savored her scent, and she closed her eyes.

It was all right. He was happy to see her.

"Here. Sit down, sweetheart. You must be tired from traveling." His hand on her arm, he eased her to the chair and then stood before her. "Are you hungry?"

"No, I ate lunch on the train. I'm fine, Max."

He backed to the desk and leaned against it again, his hip resting on the edge. "I don't know what to say. I was making arrangement to come back to Texas next week. I told Howard he was going to be on his own until the end of the year. I didn't know how long it would take to persuade you to change your mind, but I'd determined to bring you home with me, no matter what I had to do to accomplish it."

"Well," she said lightly, "I've saved you the trouble."

His eyes searched her face and he seemed to be searching for words. Crossing his arms across his chest, he asked the question she'd expected. "Why have you come back, Faith? What made you change your mind and return to me?"

The answer was simple, and it rolled from her tongue with ease. She'd thought of this moment, and knew she must make this final concession to him, knew that she owed him this much. "I was the one who left, Max. I had to be the one to return of my own volition. I didn't want you to talk me into anything. It had to be my own action, and I knew the time was now.''

She spread her hands wide and offered him a glimpse of the ring she wore. ''It was time to admit my cowardice at leaving, time to accept the blame for my wrongdoing when I walked away. It was time to make things right between us.''

''You weren't the one at fault,'' he began, but she lifted a hand to halt his words.

''We can talk about all of that later on.'' And then she spoke the words she'd decided would tilt his world. ''I'm going to check into a hotel this afternoon.''

''Like hell.'' Bold and chilling, the words reverberated in her ears. ''My wife will not be staying in a hotel, Faith.''

She stood quickly, alarmed, yet somehow pleased at the intensity of his denial. ''I won't stay in your family home, Max.'' She was gratified at the even tenor of her voice.

He eyed her briefly, and she thought a smile touched one side of his mouth as he replied, his words quiet and too acquiescent to be believed. ''All right.'' He nodded. ''That suits me.'' His jaw was firm, his eyes dark and searching as he scanned her and abruptly changed the subject. ''Have you lost weight?'' he asked sharply. ''Your cheekbones look hollow. You didn't need to get any thinner.''

''Me? Thin?'' She laughed mockingly, wondering at the incongruity of his query as it applied to her rapidly changing body. There was a definite thickening at her waistline, and her breasts were larger, more sensitive to the touch. And at that thought, she felt the flame of embarrassment touch her cheeks once more.

''Here,'' he said, moving toward her. ''Let me take your cloak. You must be warm in it.''

''No.'' She clutched it closer. ''I mean, I won't be here

that long. I just wanted to let you know I'm in the city and I thought we could—''

''Faith.'' He spoke her name again in that same firm, no-nonsense tone. ''Stop chattering and give me that cloak.'' His hands rested on her shoulders and then slipped to where the braided closures held it against her breasts. The backs of his fingers brushed against the fullness there as he slipped open the fastenings, and before she could halt his actions, he'd allowed the cloak to fall from her shoulders.

''There, now,'' he said, apparently satisfied to have his way, tossing the garment aside across another chair.

She tried to laugh, but the sound was broken and he looked at her keenly, his gaze narrowing. ''Are you about to cry?'' And if she did, what would he do? she wondered. And then it seemed his question was irrelevant, for tears trickled down her cheeks, and she found out exactly what his response was.

His hands slid behind her and she was enveloped in his arms, his mouth claiming hers in a single swooping gesture. He was warm, solid and strong, and seemed to have grown taller—which was foolishness, she thought. Max had quit growing almost twenty years ago. But her head fit nicely into the hollow near his collarbone and he tilted it at just the right angle, holding her in place for the leisurely exploration he began.

His lips and teeth tasted her mouth, delved into the small spot beneath her ear he was wont to nuzzle in times past, and then made a path across her throat, his hand grasping her hair, levering her head back to give him access to the tender skin he sought. Pins fells from the coronet she'd fashioned early this morning, scattering on the lush carpet beneath their feet, and she felt his fingers work at the braid, untangling the three strands with a practiced touch.

"Max—we're in your office," she said, breathless from the series of kisses that devoured her lips, barely allowing her to breathe, let alone voice a protest. And then she was beyond caring about all else but the heated dampness of Max's mouth as it wove its magic on her flesh.

He lowered her to a leather couch that stood against one wall, coming down over her, pressing his big body against hers as if he cared little for the layers of fabric separating them. His hips jerked once in a spasm she recognized, and she lifted hers to meet his thrust. His hands touched her breasts and she felt them as tentacles of fire against the tender, swollen flesh.

She ached for his possession, yearned for his body to claim her, rose with him in silent search of the closeness they craved. His hand was on her leg, beneath her skirts, his fingers pressing her thigh, and she heard a moan escape her lips.

A rap on the door and the voice of her brother-in-law brought her back to herself. As the knob turned, she heard Max utter an oath that stunned her. "Get out," he said loudly. "Go away, Howard."

"Max? What's going on? Jerome said a woman came up on the elevator and you dragged her into your office." The door opened as the words were spoken, and with a great flurry of skirts as Faith sat up on the sofa, accompanied by a loud thud as Max hit the floor beside her feet.

Howard entered the room. His eyes widened, his mouth snapped shut as he gave Faith a quick once-over, his dark eyes not missing a trick. "Well, it seems Jerome was right," he said brightly. "You certainly are a woman. Hello there, Faith. Good to see you again."

"Howard." It was all she could manage, what with brushing at her skirt and gathering her hair up in one hand.

He leaned back against the door. "I'm glad you showed

up, my dear,'' Howard said, gleefully observing his brother's disgruntled features. ''I had a vision of Max carrying you on board the train over his shoulder. That was how you described your intentions, wasn't it, brother of mine?''

''Get the hell out of here, Howard. If you value your life, take your miserable self out that door and close it behind you.'' Max was furious and Faith was hard put not to laugh aloud at his frustration.

''All right,'' Howard said obligingly. He waved his fingers at Faith. ''See you later, sister dear.'' And then he was gone, pulling the door shut behind him, only to open it again, sticking his head in long enough to offer a few words of advice to his older brother. ''Try locking it the next time.''

Max growled. There was no other word to describe the angry sound, and Faith thought of the dog she'd left behind in Texas. The sound was similar to Wolf's warning when a stranger came by, and he was set on defending his territory from intruders.

''This isn't the time or the place for this,'' Max snarled, crossing to the door and setting the lock in place. ''But I don't want to be interrupted again.''

He turned and shot her a look of apology. ''I was wrong to treat you so,'' he said. ''I lost my head.''

''Yes, I noticed,'' she said quietly, her fingers busy at forming a chignon with the mess he'd made of her hair. ''Would you mind picking up my pins for me so I can put myself back together?''

''Yes, of course,'' he said, going down on one knee to pick up several of the heavy bone pins. He handed them to her and watched as she slid them into the arrangement she'd fashioned. If Howard hadn't intruded... She couldn't imagine what might have happened.

Foolish woman. She knew exactly what would have happened, and probably for the first time in the history of this room.

"Now, let's do some talking," Max said. He looked down at her, his eyes focusing on the swell of her breasts, outlined nicely as she lifted her hands to pin her hair in place. A strange, edgy look shuttered his eyes and he grasped her hand, tugging her to her feet. "Let me look at you," he said roughly.

"Whatever for?" she asked, inhaling as she attempted to hold her breath a bit, easing the strain on her waistband. She'd already taken out the seams of her dress, and again it was tight, fitting her like a glove.

"Faith?" He stepped to her side, ran the flat of his palm down the slope of her breast and across her belly.

She slapped it aside. "Max! Stop that. What do you think you're doing?"

"I'm looking at you," he told her. And then he lifted his head and she was stunned by the appraising glint in his eyes. "Are you going to have a child? Are you pregnant, Faith?"

She could only nod.

Chapter Fifteen

"Why didn't you write and tell me?" he asked. "All I heard from you was that you were *fine.*" He clenched his hands into fists, harnessing the tension that her admission had brought into play. And then he voiced his greatest fear.

"What if you'd decided not to come back? Would you have waited until spring, or whenever the baby was born, to tell me about my impending fatherhood?" That Faith could have kept such an enormous secret from him was a bitter pill to swallow. He'd thought he'd made great strides in their relationship during those long weeks in Texas. But it seemed all for naught, for she apparently still dealt with the issue of her faith in him.

Staking a claim seemed to be his only goal for now, he decided, and with a smooth movement he set about establishing a foothold in her immediate future. He lifted her cloak and wrapped it carefully around her, whether wary of having the eyes of others on her during their jaunt through the building, or because her sudden trembling lent itself to the need of warmth, he wasn't certain. For now, it seemed imperative that he remove her from the office, gather her belongings from wherever she had them stashed, and then settle her in his home.

His arm circled her waist and he examined her face, aware that tearstains had left their mark on her pale skin. "Do you want to wash first?" he asked. "Do you need to freshen up before we leave?"

She shook her head. And then posed the query he'd anticipated next. "Where are you taking me, Max?" Her voice took on a firm note as she spoke aloud the vow she'd taken earlier. "I meant what I said about not living in your mother's house."

"The deed to that house is in *my* name," he reminded her. "But you're right. Essentially it is her home, and I'm not about to displace her from the spot she's familiar with." He opened the door and they walked past the entry hall and into his secretary's office.

"I'll be gone for the rest of the day," he told Jerome. "And for your further information, this is my wife. I am available to her no matter where I am or what I'm involved in."

"Yes, sir," the secretary said quickly, his eyes scanning Faith and his mouth offering a polite smile. "I'll let Mr. Howard know that you've gone for the day, shall I?"

Max's mouth twitched. "I think he's probably already figured that out for himself," he said dryly. And then he ushered her down the hallway to where the elevator waited. In moments they were in front of the building and a passing carriage stopped at Max's uplifted hand.

"Don't you use your own conveyance?" she asked as he helped her up the step and into the cushioned seat.

"It's easier to hire a cab," he said, giving an address to the driver. And then he turned to her. "Where are your cases?"

"At the railway station," she told him. "I didn't want to appear, bag and baggage, on your doorstep."

''Why not? It would have given me a better picture of your intentions.''

''I didn't have any solid intentions when I arrived,'' she told him quietly. ''I didn't know what my reception would be.''

''You knew I wanted you here, Faith. There shouldn't have been any doubt in your mind as to your welcome.''

She looked up at him, and he was lost in the blue of her eyes, his hands brushing back her hood to allow him access to the abundance of golden curls and waves she'd managed to tame. Her left hand lifted to touch his face, and her fingers traced the fine lines at the outer edges of his eyes.

''You haven't been sleeping well,'' she said, her own eyes filling a fresh rush of tears. ''Are you working too hard?''

He shook his head, careful not to dislodge her fingertips. And then he took her other hand in his and pressed his lips to the center of her palm. ''I've missed you terribly, Faith. My bed is wide and lonely without you. My heart has ached from the loss of your company with me.''

Her tears fell unimpeded as he spoke and he caught a glimpse of anguish in the depths of her gaze. ''I love you,'' she said, the words trembling on her lips. ''I wouldn't have made you wait until springtime to hear about our child, Max. I just didn't want to tell you in a letter. I felt it was news better delivered firsthand.''

''Thank you,'' he murmured, his gaze feasting on the rare beauty of the woman before him. ''I love you, too, Faith. Never as much as I do now, although I was certain I knew what the word meant, all those long years ago when I allowed you to slip away from me.''

She bent her head, resting her brow against his shirtfront, her sigh deep, as if she had indeed come home.

The house was set off the road, surrounded by white

board fences, and boasted a fresh coat of paint. White, trimmed with dark green shutters, it stood two stories high, with a porch that wrapped along the west side. Comfortable wicker furniture sat on the wide veranda and a swing hung at the far end.

The cabbie turned up the drive and looked back over his shoulder. ''This the place?'' he asked jovially. ''You visiting here?''

''No,'' Max said firmly. ''This is home.'' Possessive pride filled him as he surveyed the property he'd purchased with just this moment in mind.

''It's your house?'' Faith asked, her eyes wide with wonder.

''No,'' he said gently. ''It's *our* home.''

She shivered, as if anticipation held her in its grip, peering from the side of the carriage to where the gleaming fences enclosed a sea of grass, a horse grazing in its midst. ''That's your gelding, Max.''

''He's lonesome for company, sweetheart,'' Max told her. ''We'll need to send for your mare, won't we? I'll bet he'll spend the whole winter and spring wooing her.''

''Well, that's another thing,'' she said. ''I brought Goldie with me. I wired ahead and had her put in the livery stable where you used to keep your horse.''

Max laughed aloud, relief making him giddy. ''You really did intend to stay, didn't you?'' The fact that Faith had indeed arrived ''bag and baggage,'' with the most cherished possession she owned, was brought home to him in a rush.

''I would have fought for you tooth and nail if necessary,'' she told him bluntly. ''I never intended to cry defeat. Whatever it took, I was willing to take a stand for a life here with you.''

With a flourish, the carriage drew up before the front door, and Max lifted Faith from the step to the ground. The bill he slipped into the cabbie's hand brought effusive thanks from the man, along with an offer to return whenever Max should need his services again.

"If you wouldn't mind, I'd like you to go to the train station and pick up Mrs. McDowell's bags for me," Max told the fellow. He held out his hand, and when Faith drew the claim tag from her reticule, he leaned forward to deliver the slip of paper to the cabbie.

"Yes, sir," the man said, eyeing the large bill Max offered him. "I'll be back within the hour." With a snap of his reins, he drove off, circling a raised flower bed in front of the house and returning toward town.

Before they had climbed the first wide step toward the veranda, a woman swung the front door open and stood waiting, her dark dress and white apron marking her as the housekeeper.

Max escorted Faith across the porch, smiling at the waiting servant as she stepped aside to allow them entrance. "Mrs. Belmont, this is my wife, Faith."

The housekeeper's smile was welcoming as she took the measure of her new mistress, and Faith offered a slender hand in greeting. "Are you taking good care of my husband?" she asked, and then looked up at him. "I fear he didn't know I was arriving today. I hope I haven't caused any problems."

"Ma'am, the mister has had your room ready almost since the first day we moved into this house. Between him and my husband, they hauled furniture back and forth and hung those pretty curtains in no time."

"You put together a room for me? My room?" Her look was uncertain as she hesitated in the center of the wide entryway.

"It's a sitting room, sweetheart," he said. "James and I did whatever Mrs. Belmont told us to. It opens off our bedroom,'' Max said quickly, easing her mind. "I thought you might like a quiet spot to read or write letters or just relax.''

''*Our* bedroom?'' she asked, lifting her brow, as if she recalled the separate rooms they had had in the city house.

''I discovered I like having you close at hand,'' he murmured, bending to speak quietly in her ear.

With his hand at her elbow, they followed the housekeeper up the open, curving staircase to the second floor and down the wide corridor toward the back of the house. The suite of rooms Max showed Faith extended across the southern end of the house, each one large and well furnished. He escorted her into the sitting area, a luxurious haven with white wicker furniture and plump cushions filling a window seat.

''Oh, Max,'' she whispered, halting in the doorway to take in the soft, welcoming scene before her. Wallpaper of palest yellow scattered with faint traceries of green leaves covered the walls, and the cove ceiling was white, with a decorative border depicting white flowers with yellow centers in delicate nosegays, a subdued array of wildflowers that delighted the eye.

''It's beautiful,'' she said, turning to him. With a subtle gesture he dismissed Mrs. Belmont, and she left unobtrusively.

''Come and see the bedroom,'' he invited, holding out his hand. Faith took it, her face eager as she crossed into the huge room he'd prepared with her in mind. It was masculine in design, due to the use of his furniture from the house in town, but he'd had the decorator add small bits of frippery that would please Faith. He closed and locked the door behind them, and watched as Faith inspected the room he'd prepared for their pleasure.

A smaller chest of drawers against the wall was of the same dark wood as his own furnishings, but built on more delicate lines. A glass-topped dressing table sat between two windows, its skirt billowing in the cool breeze from the open panes. Dainty flowers that matched the border in her sitting room were embroidered on the fabric, and it resembled a bridal veil, layers of material offering a feminine touch.

A bouquet of yellow roses sat at the bedside, and Faith buried her nose in the fragrant mass of blooms. "How did you know to have these here today?" she asked.

"I've kept fresh flowers here on a regular basis," he said quietly. "I always hoped one day you would walk through that door, and I wanted it to be ready for you."

She blinked and swallowed, biting at her lower lip, then averted her gaze, as though she were uneasy here in this bedroom where the wide bed seemed to beckon them. "We have so much to talk about," she said. "Nicholas and Lin send their regards, and Brace wanted me to tell you—"

"Later," Max said, one hand lifting to silence the words that rolled from her lips. "That can all come later, Faith. Right now I need to see you."

"See me?" She looked puzzled, and he approached her slowly, lifting his hands to remove her cloak again, placing it across a chaise that stood near the dressing table. And then his hands were on her, unbuttoning her dress, sliding it from her shoulders and arms to fall to the floor. Silently, he removed her clothing, intent on touching the flawless skin beneath the layers of cotton and fine lawn.

Her undergarments were the ones he'd purchased in the general store in Benning, and he smiled into her eyes as he recalled the day they'd fussed over his buying new clothing for her. Now they fell heedlessly to the floor as he knelt at her feet to slide stockings and garters from her slender legs. Her hand rested on his shoulder for balance as she lifted her feet for the removal of the last stitch of clothing she'd donned on the train this morning.

And then he touched her with the sort of reverence he'd only felt heretofore within the walls of the church they'd attended during the years of their time together. As if he gazed upon a miracle, he looked carefully at her body, seeking the changes wrought during the past months.

He touched her breasts, noting the new fullness, the darkening of the crests, which tightened even as he watched his fingertips press against the firm flesh. She'd lost the narrowness of waist he remembered, her body expanding to accommodate the babe she carried, and he was stricken by a wave of yearning as he viewed the voluptuous curves that pronounced her a woman in the process of bearing a child.

His palms ached to explore her rounding figure, the affirmation of her pregnancy, and he gently touched her belly, as if greeting the child she offered into his keeping.

"When?" he asked.

"The first time you loved me in the farmhouse," she told him. "I knew then."

"You didn't say," he murmured, noting the intake of breath she could not conceal as his hands brushed against the golden curls at the apex of her thighs.

"It would have sounded foolish to speak of it, when there was no way to be certain," she said quietly. "I almost told you when you left, but I knew you'd make me go with you if I did, and I wasn't ready to leave. I wanted you to have time to settle things with your mother first, and get caught up on business."

"I'd have hauled you off with me, no matter how hard you protested," he said sternly. "My mother is not my top priority, Faith. Far from it."

"How does she feel about all this?" she asked, waving

her hand around the room. "Is she angry that you moved from the family home?"

"She got over it," he said shortly. "I fear we had some noisy discussions after we left Benning. I settled things with her before we arrived back in Boston."

"How angry with me is she?" Faith's words were hesitant and Max felt a pang of sorrow that she should be fearful of his mother's scorn.

"She knows that she will not have a place in my life if she doesn't treat you as she should. In fact, she admitted she had more respect for you, once she was able to get a clear picture of just what you accomplished after you left me."

Faith looked deeply into his eyes and her smile was radiant. "I want to get along with your mother, but you're the only person I have to please, Max." She looked down to where his hands lingered, and whispered, "That's what I'd like to do right now."

He felt his heart jolt within his breast as he heard her words of invitation. Rising, he swept her from her feet and placed her in the center of the wide bed, then crossed to the window to lower the sash, lest she become chilled from the breeze. With deft movements he stripped off his own clothing at a rapid pace, then approached her.

"I'm more than willing to oblige you, sweetheart," he said gruffly, the evidence of his desire apparent.

She held out her arms in open invitation, and he covered her softness with the full length of his body. Her legs opened, allowing him access there where he'd dreamed of being during the past three months, and his sigh was deep as he settled against her.

"I'm heavy," he murmured, his mouth at her breast, his lips drawing the swollen crest into his possession.

"No," she said, denying his fear. "I want you right

where you are. I've craved having your weight on me, the feel of your long legs against mine, your hands on my breasts and your mouth against my skin."

She was eager for his loving, her skin warmed by the flush of desire, yet he knew a moment's hesitation as he lifted his head to look into her eyes. "Is it all right? Safe for me to love you?" he asked.

"Lin said it would be fine until I'm too big for you to get close enough to—" She halted abruptly, a pink flush brightening her cheeks. "I shouldn't have told you that," she said. "You'll think I discussed this with her."

"I suspect you needed someone to talk with," he said. "And who better than a woman besotted with her own husband? Nicholas told me once that he's a lucky man. I understood exactly what he meant by that statement."

Max bent to touch the tip of her breast with his tongue, then suckled it, glorying in the responsive rise of her hips against him. He was trembling as his hands slid beneath her, lifting her to his manhood. "Take me," he whispered, begging her indulgence as he pressed for admission into that secret haven where he'd found the greatest joy of his life. "I don't think I can wait," he said gravely, easing into the damp folds that enveloped him. And then he held himself still, waiting until her flesh accommodated his pulsing arousal.

"I need you, Faith...like a thirsty man needs water," he growled fiercely, and indeed, he was filled with a desire for her that superceded any yearning he'd ever known. She drew him close, her arms strong as she accepted him into her depths, bending her knees to enclose him, opening to the pressure of his manhood and, on an indrawn breath, granted him the gift of her body.

"Max." It was a whisper, a sound of delight, a trembling sigh that told of longing and desire held in abeyance, and he was swept up in arms that enclosed him, warmth that invited him to sate himself in the depths of her body.

Caught up in the rhythm he could not control, he felt the spill of his seed, there at the mouth of her womb, where already his son or daughter formed just beyond the fragile barrier he touched. "Did I hurt you? The baby?" he asked quickly, fearful of doing damage with the impetuous force of their mating.

"No, we're both fine," she whispered, her hands cradling his head, her fingers lost in the fine dark hair.

"I'm sorry," he said, lifting up to peer into her face. "I haven't been that thoughtless since I was eighteen years old."

"Oh? You didn't come to me a virgin?" she asked, her eyes sparkling with hidden laughter as her palms cradled his face.

"I was twenty-eight years old when I married you, sweetheart. I hate to speak of it, but I'd taken several women out and around the town, and found none of them were what I was looking for in a bride. When I saw you, hiding in a corner at your uncle's house that day at Christmastime, I knew before I spoke to you that you were the woman I'd been waiting for."

"You did?" she asked, her eyes wide with discovery. "I never felt...exactly...needed," she told him, as if she searched for a word to describe the memory of those early years. "I knew you liked the way I looked and you enjoyed my bed, but other than that, I felt like a vase on the mantel that you glanced at once in a while and admired from your exalted position as head of the house."

"I didn't know how to tell you, or show you, how I felt about you, Faith. I don't suppose I realized the depths of my feelings until you were gone. In fact, it wasn't until I arrived in Texas that I discovered that love was the driving force behind my need for you.'' He bent and kissed her with tenderness, hoping to express with his body what he'd failed to reveal in words during that long-ago time.

Her mouth opened to his, an invitation to possess. He accepted her silent plea with a groan, turning to his side and drawing her with him, the better to caress her at his leisure, the easier to bring her the fulfillment he'd denied her with his swift taking.

It was dark outside the windows, and moonlight shed a path across the pale carpet when they awoke, and Faith felt a pang of embarrassment as she thought of the housekeeper and the supper she had likely kept warm for their benefit.

''Max?'' she whispered, and felt the brush of his fingers against her breast. She was spooned against him, and he sighed, his breath ruffling her hair.

''I suppose you're hungry,'' he muttered, his voice husky with the unaccustomed nap they'd enjoyed.

''Now that you mention it,'' she said, turning in his embrace to face him, ''do you suppose there's something in the kitchen we can eat?''

''I suspect the warming oven has two plates filled with food, and if it's cold, we'll fix something ourselves,'' he told her. ''There's something we need to discuss. We'll put together a meal and then talk.''

''My aunt and uncle are coming?'' Faith heard the shock in her voice, and felt a twinge of resentment that Max had arranged for this meeting to take place without her knowledge. They sat across the table from each other, feasting on overcooked chicken and potatoes liberally covered with gravy that had turned thick in the oven.

''I've been in touch with them since I came back East,'' he told her. ''I sent for your brother, too.'' He gnawed at the chicken leg he held as if it resembled ambrosia instead of a leftover that had been more palatable hours ago.

"Tim?" She was stunned. "I haven't seen him in more than six years, since our wedding, in fact."

"And why was that?" Max asked quietly. "Have you any idea how badly he wanted to come here, to see his sister?"

"No, I don't suppose I do. After our wedding, my aunt Grace and uncle Clive seemed to vanish from my life. They were glad to be rid of me, I think. It was purely duty that compelled them to take Tim and me into their home when my parents died. I was a strange little duck, pretty enough, but terribly shy, and Tim was determined to get into hot water on a regular basis."

"He went to New York to university," Max told her. "And then began work in the stock market there. He's quite successful, I understand. I located him and invited him here for a weekend, the actual time to be at my discretion. And then I began to think about your aunt and uncle and the house you lived in during your younger years, and I decided that they had had an influence on you that had harmed you enormously."

"They were decent to me, even though I don't think they were overjoyed to take on two children." Her words were quietly defensive, as if she willed herself to forget the barren, lonely days and nights of her high school years. The parents she'd loved so deeply had gone from her life, replaced by a pair of reluctant, impersonal guardians.

"Decent? Were they?" Max asked doubtfully. "As I recall, they seemed relieved to be rid of you, and the more I thought about our problems during the long nights I spent without you, the more I wondered how many of your small insecurities could be laid at their feet." He leaned across the table and touched her cheek with his index finger. "You were so certain that you had nothing to offer me, and I wearied of trying to bolster your confidence. More's the pity.''

She buttered a slice of bread and nibbled on the crust. ''I was a mess,'' she admitted, thinking of her unhappiness during those long-ago days. ''But I don't see that having my family here to visit will be of benefit to either of us now.''

''I want them to see you as you are in this house, Faith. A vital, glowing woman with confidence in herself. They might enjoy your company, and at least I'll have the satisfaction of making them see what you've become—in spite of their neglect. I contacted them and suggested a visit, at a date to be decided upon. I'll send them a note and offer an invitation for next weekend. Will that suit you?''

She nodded, aware of Max's maneuvering for her benefit. And her eyes filled once more with gratitude as she recognized the wisdom of his perception of her early girlhood trials and tribulations. And then he caught her attention, grasping her hand.

''As to your brother, he's a bit embarrassed that he lost touch with you, and he's champing at the bit to renew old ties with his sister.'' Max leaned back and grinned indolently. ''I've already told him I may be able to offer him a better position than the one he's currently holding in New York. That sort of put the icing on the cake, so to speak, so far as he's concerned.''

''You mean, have him move back to Boston?'' Her words were eager, and Max's eyes lit with pleasure as he realized her delight in his manipulations on her behalf.

''If it pleases him and suits you.'' His eyes begged for her approval. ''My aim in life is to fill your days and nights with joy, Faith. If that involves mending ties with your brother, and making you realize that your unhappiness was not self-induced during our years of marriage, I'll be content. I want you to recognize that others lent a hand in the crumbling of the image you saw in the mirror each day.''

''You've been a busy man,'' she managed to whisper, aware that once more tears were sliding down her cheeks. ''I'm leaking all the time these days,'' she said, smiling through a misty haze. ''Lin says it's a major symptom of being in the family way. My feelings are close to the surface and I seem to have the need to shed tears on a regular basis.''

She wiped her mouth with the napkin and sighed, replete with the food they'd shared. It had been a strange meal, this first supper in their new home. Probably not the fanciest of surroundings, she thought, looking around the kitchen. But it had been wonderful, comforting and filled with a communication between them that had brought peace to her heart.

Max leaned over the table, took the napkin from her and, with a clean corner, brushed away the dampness from her cheek. His smile was gentle as he dropped a kiss on her brow. ''So long as these waterworks aren't caused by something I've done to upset you, I'll happily contribute our supply of dinner napkins to the cause,'' he murmured.

''And now,'' he suggested, rising and lifting her from her chair to hold her close to his side, ''do you think we could go back to bed?''

''How will you get to work in the morning?'' she murmured, her head pressed against his shoulder as they climbed the stairs, side by side.

''I'll have James drive me in, and then catch a cab home. That way you'll have the carriage if you want to go out.''

They walked to the back of the house and entered their room, pausing on the threshold to view the bed. It was stripped of the quilt, the top sheet was tangled in a heap on the carpet and the pillows were tossed across the mattress in abandon.

''I'll have to sort it out before we can occupy it for the night,'' Faith said. She pulled the belt of her dressing gown tightly around her waist and picked up the sheet from the carpet, shaking the wrinkles from it, then spread it across the bed.

''No sense in being too fussy,'' Max told her. ''I have a notion it won't look much better by the time we go to sleep.''

She lifted her chin and sent him a sharp look. ''I suppose you think you need to catch up on lost time.''

He smiled, and she was lost in the dark beauty of his heavy-lidded gaze and wavy rumpled hair. The man was incorrigible and she was truly smitten with him. Tomorrow she would arrange for the delivery of her mare, and check out the barn with a foaling area in mind. Her thoughts swirled as she plumped the pillows and then pulled back the sheet in preparation to crawling beneath the fine linen fabric.

''Take off the robe,'' Max said quietly. ''You don't need it, sweet.''

''I don't?'' She shrugged, sitting on the edge of the mattress. ''How will I ever manage to stay warm?''

''Give me five minutes,'' he bargained, ''and I'll show you.'' His own dressing gown hit the floor and he slid between the layers of bedding, reaching for her with a passion she recognized and welcomed. ''Make that two minutes,'' he murmured, his mouth warm, his hands firm against her lush curves.

''No rush,'' she said with a satisfied smile. ''I can afford to be patient. I'm planning on keeping you busy for the rest of our lives.''

Epilogue

Spring arrived with a flourish in Boston. Flowering fruit trees lined the white board fences along the winding drive, and in the pasture a golden mare cropped placidly at the lush grass. Her sides were bulging with the new life she carried and she moved slowly, as if conserving her strength for the coming birth of her foal.

The woman who watched from a vantage point just to the west of the house made a soft sound with her tongue against the roof of her mouth, and the mare lifted her head, her ears flicking forward. With ambling steps she neared the fence and accepted the bit of carrot the woman held out to her, a dainty procedure that occurred daily right after breakfast in the big house was completed.

"How does she look?" Max asked, striding through the grass to enclose Faith with his arms, his hands settling on the curve of her belly.

"About as graceful as I do," Faith retorted, laughing to soften the truth of her words. "I remember wondering how Lin was ever going to get rid of the load she carried before Jonathan was born. Now I'm feeling doubtful about my own ability."

"The doctor says you'll do well," Max reminded her,

his hands cupping the weight of their child, easing her heavy burden. He lowered his head to brush his lips against her hair, then turned her around with gentle strength, loving the feel of his child between them. As the babe protested the close quarters inflicted on him by his father, he concentrated on the small movements of what Faith had promised him would be a son, smiling as a fist or knee poked at him.

''Surely you can't get much larger,'' he said, looking down at the bulk of his child. ''I'll begin to worry if you don't take to your bed soon.''

''It's been just a week short of nine months,'' she reminded him. ''I'm going to finish hemming diapers today, and then I'll be ready.''

''You could have bought them ready made from Mrs. Belmont's sister. She does it for a living,'' he said, amused at Faith's attempts to conserve his enormous resources.

''She already made most of the baby's gowns and blankets,'' Faith said. ''I may sit on the porch when the sun touches it in the afternoon. It's getting warmer by the day.''

''Be careful not to take a chill,'' he told her, and then turned her away from the horse, which had dropped her head to graze. They walked to the house, where Max kissed Faith long and lovingly, as James Belmont looked the other way. ''I'll be home early,'' Max whispered. ''Will you be all right?''

She nodded, feeling somewhat akin to the mare, complacent and wrapped up in the marvelous process of containing a new life within her womb. The carriage was waiting for Max by the door, and he climbed in and lifted a hand to wave.

Faith watched it roll down the drive, then turned and went into the house. She went through the day wrapped in a haze of contentment, and fell asleep in the midst of hemming diapers. Sitting in a rocking chair near the window, her head resting against the high back, she dozed fitfully, awakening as the east wind began to blow up a sudden squall. The rain fell in hard, driving sheets, and when a particularly loud crash of thunder startled her, she jolted upright in the chair, her sewing falling to the floor.

"Mrs. Belmont?" she called, and was met with silence. Faith rose and felt a twinge that began in her back and cascaded around to gather with a thrumming beat beneath her bulging belly. Her palms slid to support the weight of it and it grew taut with unbelievable tension beneath her hands. Her breath caught at the sensation of dampness between her legs, bringing a frown to her brow.

"Max?" She called his name with a sense of panic. Surely he was due home. The sky was dark with lowering clouds, and lightning flashed amid them. Wind blew, rattling the shutters and the air inside the house was suddenly chill.

The front door slammed open and heavy footsteps approached the parlor door. "Faith? Why isn't there a lamp lit? Are you in here?" Max stood in the gloom of the unlit foyer, dripping water onto the tiled floor.

"Yes, I'm here," she said, and then cleared her throat, aware that her voice was thick with apprehension. "I think I'm going to have the baby. Max, I'm frightened. I called for Mrs. Belmont and she didn't answer. Something's very wrong."

"Where could she be?" he asked, his voice rising sharply as he shed his heavy topcoat and tossed his hat onto a chair.

"I don't know. I was sleeping and just awoke." Warmth flooded her garments and with a gush of fluid, she felt the helpless sensation of losing the waters in which her child had been cushioned against harm for the past nine months.

"Oh, dear." It was a soft admission of helplessness, and Max sped to her side.

"What is it, sweetheart? What's happened?"

"I'm a mess, Max. I've just managed to ruin the carpet, I fear."

"Mrs. Belmont." His voice rose in a roar, and the woman came flying from the back of the house.

"What's wrong, sir? I just stepped out onto the back porch for a minute to bring in a bucket of rainwater for Miss Faith to wash her hair tomorrow. What's happened?" Her experienced eye took in Faith's circumstances, and with a cluck of her tongue and a sage nod of her head, she took charge of the situation.

"You'd better tell James to go for the doctor," she said judiciously. "I'll just take this dear child upstairs and get her ready for the big event."

And so she did. Max did as he was told, as did James. It was no time until the doctor arrived, climbing the stairs to the second floor, where he set the situation to rights in short order. His chuckle relieved Max's mind as a black bag was deposited on a chair and hot water was delivered to the bedroom, by the vigilant housekeeper.

Faith's labor was progressing at a rapid pace and the doctor kept an eye on her as he scrubbed his hands and arms in her china bowl, rinsing well as Max stood helplessly beside the bed. Waving his damp hands in the air to dry them a bit, the physician approached the bed, and nodded with satisfaction as he beheld the woman there, her straining body poised to deliver her child.

"You aren't going to make me miss my supper, are you, ma'am?" he asked with a grin. "I told you some women were built to have babies, and you're one of them.

"Everything's under control, Max," he said, offering a bit of comfort to the anxious man who seemed to be having second thoughts about the process of becoming a father. And then Faith cried out, caught up in the urgency of labor that would not be halted by the absence of a physician's guidance.

Even as he bent to assist her, she strained, squeezing Max's hands and clinging to his strength as the tiny form of their child came into view. "I don't know why you called me out on such a nasty afternoon," the doctor said. "You've got this down pat, ma'am."

Lifting the infant boy in his hands, he rubbed the tiny back with vigor, then wiped the residue of childbirth from his mouth and nose with a clean cloth. In less than an instant the silence was broken as tiny lungs filled with air and released it in a resounding cry.

"I knew it would be a boy," Faith whispered, her gaze caught by the dark hair on the round head. And then the doctor tipped him into full view and her claim proved to be true as the obviously masculine form was held aloft for her inspection.

"Thank you for my son," Max said, his voice choked with emotion as Faith reached to touch his face. He bent to kiss her and then Mrs. Belmont was there at the foot of the bed, holding a blanket to receive the plump form as the doctor cut the cord that had joined mother and child during the past months.

The housekeeper wrapped the babe securely and turned, placing him in Max's arms, her smile dazzling as she pronounced the new arrival a dandy young man.

Settling on the edge of the bed, Max bent to press his lips against Faith's forehead. "Thank you, sweetheart," he whispered, and then placed the squirming, squalling infant in his mother's arms.

"I appreciate your speedy work, ma'am," the doctor said, tending to details and then briefly giving instructions to Mrs. Belmont for Faith's care. "You're in top form for a city woman," he said bluntly. "You've got a strong, healthy wife," he told Max. "And a beautiful son."

"She's tough," Max said with pride. "You ought to see her shoot a rifle and ride a horse. She's been riding every day up until a couple of weeks ago."

"But I'll probably have to wait for a couple of months before I get back on Goldie," Faith murmured. "We have a foal to deliver first."

"*You'll* deliver the foal?" the doctor asked, his gaze fastened on Faith's smiling face. And then he turned to Max. "A woman of many talents," he said. "You're a fortunate man."

"She's a woman worth her weight in gold, and then some," Max said, his fingers lacing through the curls that tangled damply against Faith's shoulders and fanned against her pillow. "Tested and refined by adversity," he murmured in her ear. "Pure gold."

"She's a rare breed, I'd say. Where'd you find your wife, anyway?" the doctor asked, rolling down his sleeves.

"In Texas," Max said softly. "She's pure, unadulterated Texas gold."

* * * * *

0306/04a

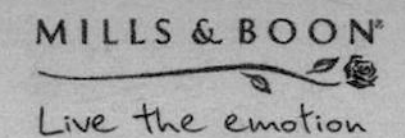

Historical romance™

A PROMISE TO RETURN

by Gail Whitiker

Nicholas Grey, Viscount Longworth, fell in love with Lavinia Duplesse on the day she married another. Now she is a widow, and their love has a second chance. But Nicholas is sent to France on a dangerous assignment. Badly wounded, he eventually returns. Is happiness about to be snatched away from them again? Because Nicholas has no memory of the woman he loves…

THE GOLDEN LORD

by Miranda Jarrett

Miss Jenny Dell knows how to act the lady to perfection – though nothing could be further from the truth! And it's a lady Brant Claremont, Duke of Strachen, sees when he comes upon Jenny injured on his estate. Hiding a shameful secret of his own, Brant has shut himself away from Society. Could caring for this mysterious girl force him to realise how lonely he has become?

REGENCY

On sale 7th April 2006

Available at WHSmith, Tesco, ASDA, Borders, Eason, Sainsbury's and most bookshops

www.millsandboon.co.uk